PLANET EDEN

CREATION SERVES. LIFE ENDURES.

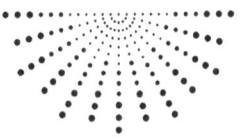

F.R. WILSON

Planet Eden

F.R. WILSON

PLANET EDEN

Published by

Detroit Ink Publishing

Detroit MI USA

Cover Photo Credit: Reto Stocki

Publisher's Note:

This is a work of fiction. All events and characters in this story are solely the product of the author's imagination. Any similarities between any characters and situations presented in this book to any individuals, living or dead, or actual situations are purely coincidental.

ISBN: 978-0-9995739-7-6

Printed in the United States of America

ALSO BY F.R. WILSON

Cast A Long Shadow

Hearts of Fire

PART I
THE PRIMAE

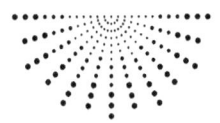

CHAPTER ONE

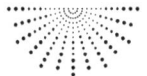

*B*efore the elevator doors could close, Eleanor shouted. "You're late. Spencer wants to see you ASAP."

Eleanor is more like your little sister who gives detailed reports of your actions to your parents rather than the office receptionist. "He's got company, looks official." She said with an accusation in her tone.

"On my way," I waved as I passed by her desk. I knocked on the door and entered a solemn scene; I saw Spencer, my editor, and two serious-faced thirty-something's dressed in standard government black suits leaning toward each other in a conspiratorial huddle.

"Good," said Spencer looking up. "Close the door and have a seat Chris." There was a guilty thickness in the air as though I was entering the principal's office. Spencer's blank expression confirmed my feelings.

"Christopher Chapel, this is Detective Albert West with the local PD and Special Agent Timothy Shanks with Homeland Security." Both men rose from their chairs, shook my hand, pressed business cards into my hands and reseated themselves without saying a word. I nodded a cautionary acknowledgement.

Spencer stepped from behind his desk. "I'll give you some privacy.

Take as much time as you need." He left without giving me another a glance.

My reporter instincts began evaluating the men and the situation. Something was off. I couldn't find a reason for my being here.

West was pudgy with cynicisms etched on his suburban frat boy face. He held his hand as if he was holding a cigarette and chewed impatiently at the inside of his cheek. *"An ex-smoker,"* I thought. His flat top haircut and pinched expression screamed ex-military. Shanks was tall and lean. His regulation haircut, sensible shoes and bland tie stamped him as a career bureaucrat. He sat relaxed and detached, but straight backed as if he was in church. An aura of placidity surrounded him. They both looked as if they didn't have one thing in common. An odd couple, if ever there was one.

A silent uncomfortable few seconds passed. "Mr. Chapel; Chris. May I call you Chris?" West finally asked, never looking at me when he talked.

"Sure," I said. "What's this all about? Homeland Security?" I asked, pointing at Shanks.

Ignoring my question, he continued. "Do you know Walter Vaughn?"

"Yes," I nodded. "Of course, you already know this, or you wouldn't be here. Walt and I are old friends."

"When was the last time you saw him or spoke to him?"

"I haven't seen or spoken to Walt in about three weeks or so. What is this all about? Is this a clearance check or something? Is he alright? Is he in some kind of trouble?"

"Where were you yesterday at about seven pm?" West asked in his nasal voice, still ignoring my questions.

"I was here at the job."

"Were you alone?"

"No," I snapped. "I was working with Sarah. Wait a minute. What's the...."

"No, Chris this is not a clearance check. I'm sorry about the questions, but we had to ask. We've already talked to Sarah. We just had to hear it from you," Shanks said, jumping in. His voice was a smooth baritone and he spoke in a practiced measure.

"I'm sorry to tell you this" his voice followed his head and bowed an octave. "Mr. Vaughn is deceased. His body was found yesterday evening."

I gripped the arm rest of the chair and closed my eyes. I wanted to scream, "No, you lie!" but all I could manage was stunned silence. I stared straight ahead. My heart pounded in my ears. I wanted to vomit.

"As an investigative reporter, we know he often tackled some difficult assignments, possibly his death is tied to what he was working on. Do you have any idea what that might be?" Shanks continued.

I forced the breath out I was holding. "No, I don't. Like I said, I haven't seen Walt, lately. But, he did keep a journal. Anything he was working on would be there," I offered, finally finding my voice. It took all I had to maintain my control.

"Describe this journal?" West ordered. They both flipped out notebooks and produced pens.

I cleared the lump growing in my throat, closed my eyes and pictured the book. "It's small, pocket sized, a three-ringed binder, made of leather. Its' black and has his initials embossed in gold in the bottom right hand corner, *WHV*, Walter Henry Vaughn." I said the name slowly. I knew this information because I gave the journal to him for his thirtieth birthday.

"How did he... die?"

I saw the reluctance on their faces as they looked at each other. Shanks was the braver one. "He was decapitated."

My hands became a fist. I stood baring my back to them, burying my fist deep in my pockets.

"That is the main reason I'm here. We know that Mr. Vaughn went to the Middle East about two weeks ago. Since decapitation is the preferred method of execution for Islamist terrorists, we are speculating about a possible connection. If there is a connection between what happen to Mr. Vaughn and his trip to the Middle East, that may mean there is a terrorist cell or at least sympathizers in the area.

Depending on what he was working on, what he did and who he saw in the Middle East, there may be national security implications. With the large Arab community, here in the Metro Detroit area it makes the possibility of infiltrators very possible."

"Walt didn't work on that kind of stuff. I don't know what he was working on, but I'm sure it had nothing to do with terrorists. He hated that kind of stuff. Walt just didn't do stories like that." My agitation was seeping into my voice.

"Walt was big on notes and lists and on staying organized. He wrote an entry in that journal every night. It's his own cryptic shorthand, but whatever he was working on is there. You'll see he had no connection to terrorists." I moved to the window, hiding my clouding eyes. "Have you talked to Caroline?" I asked.

"Caroline Walker, the editor at the *Detroit Free Press*? She's in the dark as well. He was due to give her an update this week on his work, but he didn't have a chance to do that." Shanks answered.

"What are you working on?" West asked.

"Me?" I asked turning to face them surprised at the question. "Prison reform. Didn't Sarah tell you? There's no connection here."

West nodded. "Oh yeah, right. Well this is just a preliminary inquiry. We'll be in touch later after more facts are known. We appreciate your cooperation and please get in touch with either of us if anything comes to you or you come across any information that might aid in the investigation."

"Uh huh." I mumbled. I don't remember them leaving

In the elevator, Shanks said, "West, there's no way this Chapel is a real suspect. Considering his solid alibi and their relationship, I would say he's free and clear. I think that we should use him to do some of the leg work for us."

"I noticed you were already pretty much giving away the ranch. Is that the way they do it in Homeland Security? Tell everything you know and let the suspects work their own case?"

Shanks snickered. "Give me a break. With a completion rate of nineteen percent, you guys need all the help you can get. Maybe you should enact that policy as standard procedure. It might give your police department some credibility."

West gave him a look meant to shatter glass. Shanks smiled. "Okay then, like I said, he's no suspect and he's an investigative reporter so let's let him investigate." He raised his brows, "Use the resource, as it were."

"What is it you have in mind exactly?" West asked looking up at the floor numbers rather than acquiesce to Shanks.

"Let him do some digging around. We'll feed him some tidbits and let him shovel through the manure. Let him carry the load. We've got other things to keep us busy. If he finds something we just step in and take the credit."

West nodded a reluctant assent.

I sat in Spencer's office numb. I had been holding their business cards the whole time and now they were tiny balls of sweaty paper. When Spencer returned, he suggested I take the rest of the day off. I took his offer and left the building.

I didn't go to my car. I just started walking. Despite the coolness of the September air I walked with my jacket open. I flipped up the collar against the chill and buried my hands in my pockets. Images of Walter were racing through my mind. I felt like I had to view them all right now or my mind would lose them from the overload.

"He's gone. You've lost him." I hadn't lost him. I had thrown him away. We weren't a couple anymore because of me. He loved me. Despite my doubts and insecurities, he really loved me. I loved him too, but I wouldn't let us be a couple. I just kept messing it up. Always keeping thing at an arm's length. I didn't know how to let it be. Walt wanted commitment, marriage, and children. I wanted…I didn't know what I wanted. I was afraid of being treated as different, as damaged goods, as a freak. I wanted to be like everybody else. He wanted us to

live openly without any shame or incrimination. But I was a coward. I couldn't live with the stares and whispers. I was gay, but the crap you have to put up with made keeping it to yourself easier. Being Black has its own set of issues. But, fighting the world on two fronts, black and gay; I wasn't up to that struggle, especially the way people are so passionate about both. I lived in Michigan and my family lived in Georgia partly because I had to get away from that very kind of thing. They never did understand. They never would. I decided it's better to be forgotten than to be rejected. So, I left.

I insisted that our relationship remain between us, as private as possible. I would say, "It's not that I'm ashamed or anything like that. It's just that our careers and our social standings would suffer if people knew." I knew that was a lie and so did he, but he wouldn't argue. That was why we worked at competing papers. If we worked at the same place it would be too easy for people to get ideas. Actually, it was really my fears and insecurities that were the obstacles.

Walt was accepting and comfortable with himself. "Who cares what people think or say about us? We've got each other and that's enough for me. I wish it was for you." He'd say with those damn hurt-filled brown eyes.

The night our relationship broke, a group of fellow reporters from both papers, the *Detroit News* and the *Detroit Free Press*, had gotten together after work at a club downtown. We were celebrating the winning of a prestigious award by one of our own. The pink-haired copy girl said in passing, "You two make a great looking couple."

"What do you mean by that," I snapped, ending the evening on a sour note. That night, at the apartment we shared, I went bonkers. I ranted about being labeled and stigmatized. Walt just listened and took it all in. He never fought back. That was his way. Nothing makes me madder than someone who won't fight when you want to. I started sleeping on the couch. A week later I said, "We should take some time apart."

A week later he moved out. He would call me a couple of times a week; "I just called to say 'h" and let you know I love you. When you're ready I'm here." For the last three weeks or so, I'd let his calls go to voice mail and then delete them without listening. I think I treated him that way just because he would let me get away with it. I never worried because I always knew he would be there, no matter what. We'd had other separations. They would last a couple of months and then we'd get back together. All would be forgiven until the next time. Now that wouldn't happen. I was such a damn idiot.

Hours later, I got to "our" apartment. Even though it was "my" apartment first and he had moved in with me, I still considered it our apartment. I had to get the super to let me in. My car, my keys, my phone and everything else were back at the paper. It didn't seem to matter. When I walked in Walt was everywhere. I never realized it, but he never really moved out. Everything from the furniture we picked out together, to his plants, to his ugly lava lamp were there. The keepsakes we had collected from our travels seemed to be there just to taunt me. Everything was pregnant with memories of him. I stood in the hall looking at our wall of pictures; what we called our "Hall of Memories."

I showered and brushed my teeth. A hazy image of Walt smiling stood behind me. I could see him in the foggy mirror. I felt his arms close around my waist and his warm kiss on the nape of my neck. I don't know how the mirror broke. I just heard the shards of glass crunching under my feet as I left the room. Pulling the comforter over my head I tried to hide myself from his memory and forget the world existed at all.

When I finally drifted off to sleep, I dreamt about our great vacations. Walt and I had traveled the world together. We visited India, China, Australia, Africa, South America, and all over Europe. Our pact was that we would travel through six of the continents and leave Antarctica for everybody else. Neither one of us was that fond of the cold. We always had such a great time. Walt was naturally interested in other people and places. I was envious of how easy he was with people no matter who, where, or what they were. He'd always said, "I'm half black and half white so I'm a little bit of everybody." I have never known anyone so easy about life, so at peace with himself. The fact that he liked who he was, made it easy for him to like others and for them to like him. That was one of the reasons I loved him. They knew he really cared and accepted who they were. That's why people liked him so much.

I on the other hand was stand-offish and brooding. I always felt judged and marginalized. He was the bridge, my safety line. When I'd retreated to my usual corner, he'd always pull me back to the center.

My night took a bad turn. I started dreaming that I was surrounded by darkness and all I could hear was Walt calling me. "CC where are you? I need you." I tried to get to him, but I couldn't find him. "Hold on baby. I'm coming." I shouted. I woke up sweating, panting, and reaching for him. The rest of my night was spent sitting with my arms wrapped around my legs rocking and staring at shadows on the wall.

When the alarm went off at six o'clock, I decided I had to go see Margaret. I got dressed, took a cab to the office, and picked up my things. For the longest time I sat in front of her well-manicured suburban house. I didn't know what I could say to a woman who had taken me in as a son and was now faced with the loss of her real son, her only child.

Margaret was a force. She was the kind of dynamo who ran the block club, the PTA, and the family reunion all at once. All the while planning a wedding and cooking Thanksgiving dinner. Everybody goes to her if they want answers. When she spoke, you listened and believed. Her bobbed blonde hair, short substantial frame and steady, soothing voice stood in contrast to the respect she commanded. Margaret talked with authority and would broker no opposition. In addition to her formidable skills, her heart was gentle and large enough for two bodies. Walt called her, "The General." He'd joke "Patton would stop by to get lessons in leadership from her."

When she opened the door, we stared at each other for a few seconds before falling into each other's arms in a waterfall of tears. I had not realized that I hadn't shown any real emotions. I hadn't cried one tear since I got the news. When I was told that Walt was dead, my whole being had gone into lock down. I was mad and sad and in disbelief, but I hadn't really allowed it to sink in. I just hadn't really felt anything but shock. My mind had gone into standby mode and my heart had stopped cold. It wasn't until I saw Margaret's blood-shot blue eyes that I felt the torrent break through. I let it flow. My heart felt like it was being physically being ripped from my chest. I cried until I thought the tears would wash my eye balls away. I cried for Walt. I cried for Margaret. And I think I cried most of all for myself. We stood there. A sobbing mess, for five or ten minutes before Margaret pulled me in and closed the door.

"I'm sorry," I kept saying. "I'm so sorry."

"What are you sorry for, Chris? You didn't do this."

"I wasn't there for him. I…I failed him."

Wiping her own eyes and handing me a tissue for mine, she said, "Chris, I know how Walter felt about you. Walter was very open with me and I'm very grateful for that. You have nothing to blame yourself about. When Walter first came out to me I was horrible to him. I rejected him and said some hateful things. I cringe when I think how small-minded and small-hearted I was."

I nodded in acknowledgement. Walter had told me what a hard time she had coming to terms with who he was. "It took almost two years," she said, "before I came to my senses. Gradually I came to realize that whatever or whoever my son was, I loved him. And with love comes acceptance. Thank God, his father was a sensible man. He loved and tolerated us both. Carl was a remarkable person. I wish you had known him. That man could love a bullet headed for his heart. If he hadn't been there I might have lost my boy years ago."

She held my hands and spoke in a soft whisper. "My son loved you and that makes me love you even more, for the happiness you gave him. When he brought you into our family you became my son too. I know you two had problems. But, who doesn't?"

She squeezed my hand. "Chris, take it from a weary old woman who has lost many people that she loved; life is hard, but love is so much harder. If you two had more time I'm sure things would have worked out. We both know what a loving human being he was and you, my child, are just as loving. Even if you don't realize it sometimes. Let's not let regrets and misery take our wonderful memories of him away."

I laid my head on her chest like a new born child. "I'm supposed to be comforting you not the other way around," I whimpered.

"Honey, this is comfort. To see and to know he was loved like this. That someone he cared so much for cared for him just as much. Yes, this makes things easier. Besides," she said managing a smile. "I still have you. Don't I? Come on let go get some coffee." Holding my hand like I was two-year-old, she led me into the kitchen.

"The FBI and Homeland Security came by yesterday." Margaret said over the noise of clanking dishes. "They searched his room. I told them the room held only childhood things, but they searched anyway. They kept asking about a book, a journal."

"Yeah, Shanks and West," I said as she shook her head in agreement. "I told them yesterday that Walt kept a journal. They seem to think that maybe what happened to him had something to do with what he was working on."

She stopped and stared glassy eyed into space. "Why did they have to...?" Margaret put her hand up to her throat.

"I don't know," I said interrupting her before she said it. "That's why they wondered if it was terrorism."

Taking a breath and composing herself, she said, "Walter wrote about corruption, graft and crooked politicians, not terrorism."

"I know. I told them as much. This whole thing makes no sense. When they questioned me yesterday, I could tell they didn't know anything. This terrorist thing just doesn't fit. I think I need to find out what this is all about."

"I don't think that's a good idea to go messing around in this. Don't make me lose another son. Let the authorities handle it," she said giving me her *this is an order* stare.

"I can't just sit back and do nothing. I'll just ask a few questions and shake a few branches to see what falls from the trees. I won't shake too hard. I promise."

Margaret held my hand and gave me a worried smile. After cake, coffee and some more comforting we went to make arrangements for the funeral. I left that night promising to return the next day.

"Bad business when we lose one of our own like this," Spencer said. "Do you have any idea what he was working on that would cause someone to go to this kind of extreme?"

"Not a clue. This wasn't Walt's style. There is the possibility this had nothing to do with his work." Spencer nodded. The idea made me uncomfortable.

"There was a time when a journalist was respected, but now we're just so much fodder." He circled his office as if he was pacing off the measurement for new carpet. Spencer habitually tugged up sagging pants that were pressed down by his overhanging belly. He was a stout intense man with an unruly crop of gray and brown hair, squinting brown eyes, small hairy ears, and a mouth that seem to move before the words came out. We used to joke that talking to Spencer was like watching one of those old Japanese movies where the words and the movements of the mouth never matched.

"Spencer, I'd like a few days, maybe a week or two off. I need to do some things and Walt's mother could use the company. Sarah can take over the prison reform piece. My notes are up to date. The story is almost ready, only one interview left to do. I'm sure Sarah can finish it alone."

"It's alright with me. Look, I know that you're going after Walter's story. Just be careful and keep me informed on your progress. You're a natural newsman, Chris, and getting to be a damn good one to boot; just remember: don't let your personal involvements get in the way. You may find out things that you won't like. Remember the story is the story and that means the whole story, the good and the bad."

The funeral was a blur. Margaret handled the day with her usual competence and composure. I was a zombie. I didn't care to see anyone except Charlotte. She was our closest and dearest friend. She and Walt had been high school sweethearts and then best friends. When he came out, he told her first and it had only deepened their relationship. Charlotte was the one who introduced us. She and I once lived in the same building down the hall from each other. I met Walt when we helped her move. Right away she saw something between us and encouraged us all the way.

Charlotte came in, put her arms around me and whispered in my ear. "I'm so sorry CC. How are you holding up?"

"Okay, I guess." I said trying not to burst into tears.

"It's hard to imagine him gone. I can't believe anyone would want to harm him. Walt was such a thoughtful and gentle man."

Margaret walked up behind us and put her hand on Charlotte's shoulder. "I was beginning to wonder where you were."

"I just got back in town this morning about five. The job, you know. Mom finally got in touch with me yesterday morning. I tried to call both of you." She looked at us with a furrowed brow. "Nobody would answer the damn phone. I nearly went crazy trying to get back here. Luckily I was able to bully myself onto a flight." She gave a half smile.

"Have you been taking good care of The General?" she asked, staring me down. "You know you have to use a firm hand with her. She thinks she's the whole damn army and can win the war all by herself."

"No," I admitted. "I've been derelict in my duties. I'm afraid she's been taking care of me." Charlotte gave her a frown.

"I'll take care of both of you," Margaret said pulling us into an embrace. "Enough of all this foolishness. We have business to take care of." She grabbed our hands and led her troops into the service.

I hung around until everything was over and ended up spending the night in Walt's old room. It was comforting. I felt close to him. I looked around the room at his things as if seeing them could piece him back together. The wall of photographs, his high school and college graduation pictures. Pictures of Carl, Margaret, Charlotte and me. His baseball signed by Hank Aaron, a trio of skate boards, another ugly lava lamp, and a poster of his hero, "Mr. Spock". He was such a *Star Trek* geek. Being near his things made me feel like I was near him.

I stared at his college picture, dissecting every pixel in the print. Walt was a handsome guy, but he never acted like he knew it. He had big curious brown eyes and thick eyelashes that looked like centipedes. He still wore that same close cropped curly hair even after all these years. I could smell the herbal shampoo he used to wash it. His lopsided smile looked like he had painted it on in the dark. And that one dimple that made his puffy cheek look like it had been punctured by a pin prick.

"I miss you," I whispered. "I'm sorry. I wasn't strong enough."

I heard Margaret weeping during the night. There was no reason to disturb her and add my tears to hers. Hers were the tears of a mother for her only child. I had little comfort and no remedy for them, so I let them wash me to sleep. I could only swear to the darkness that I would get whoever did this.

CHAPTER TWO

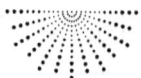

Over potato pancakes with raspberry syrup, sunny-side-up eggs, sausage patties, and lots of hot coffee; Walt's favorite breakfast, I told Margaret, "I'll go and make arrangements to have his things packed up and moved out."

"I'll get you the keys. I appreciate you doing this. I have to admit I haven't the heart for doing it myself. Not right now."

"Never mind about the keys. I have a set."

"Of course you do," she stopped and smiled. "Of course, you do."

I stood in front of the apartment door holding the keys, afraid to go in as if I would find him there waiting for me. I opened the door to a disaster. The room had been ransacked. Book shelves were overturned, and the books were ripped apart. The sofa and chair had been shredded as if an animal had been clawing at them. Every room and every item had been destroyed. I went to the manager and brought him up to see the destruction.

"I haven't let anybody but the police in here," he said. I told him I would make arrangements to have the place cleaned up and anything salvageable packed up and removed. I headed home with the intention of confronting West and Shanks about this. When I pulled in front of my building, they were parked outside waiting on me. I jumped out of the car, slammed the door and charged at them.

"What's the big idea of trashing Walt's place like that? What the hell do you think you were doing?"

"We didn't trash anything. We searched it, yes, but I assure you. We didn't trash anything," West retaliated.

"I was just there and it's a junk heap. The manager said that you were the only ones who have been there. How do you explain that?"

"It seems we are not the only ones searching for something, I would say," Shanks suggested.

I stopped cold. The thought had not occurred to me. "But, he said, "no one else has been there."

"Just because he didn't see them doesn't mean they didn't get in," he added.

"It seems there may be more to this than we thought," West said. "We came to ask you a couple more questions, but I think we should sit down and have a more detailed talk."

"There's nothing more I can tell you. I didn't know what Walt was up to and I don't know where his journal is. I have no idea what any of this is about."

"Well it seems that you and Mr. Vaughn were closer than you let on. Why did you tell us you were just *good friends*?" he asked using air quotes. "It would seem to me that *friends*," He emphasized the word friend again. "*friends* as close as you two were and who shared the same profession, as well, would know more about what each other were up to than you let on?" West raised his brows to drive home his point.

"My relationships and the closeness of them is none of your damn business. I don't like what you're implying, as far as what we were *up to...*" My turn for air quotes.

"The answer is nothing. I've told you all we were *up to...*" again, with the air quotes. "If you have anything more to say to me I think maybe, you can talk to my lawyer." I started to walk away.

"Mr. Chapel; Chris," I heard Shanks' voice. "We aren't trying to pry into things that aren't any of our business and won't help the case. It's just that there's nothing here and we're lost at sea without a compass. Something's going on and we're just trying to find out what. Maybe not in the subtlest way," he gave West an 'are you stupid look.'

I turned and looked at Shanks, ignoring West. "I want to find out who did this as much as anyone. I have not held anything back. I just don't appreciate being brow-beaten and treated like a suspect. This good cop, bad cop thing you two have got going has out lived its usefulness and is just irritating."

"Alright," he said with his hands up in surrender. "Just one question, then. Did Mr. Vaughn ever mention, 'The Primae?'"

"'The Primae?' I never heard of it. Walt definitely never mentioned that name to me. What is it?"

"We don't know, but it came up in a data sweep that also brought up Walter Vaughn's name." West said, rejoining the conversation.

"A data sweep huh. You guys are really reaching." My reporter instincts kicked in. "Any terrorist connection? Is it a business, a cult, or maybe a family name?" I got two shrugs of the shoulders.

Shanks looked at West and they exchanged a nod. "Chris," Shanks said, moving in uncomfortably close. "We know that you took some time off from work and we figured you're going after this mystery."

I tensed. *"Were they following me?"* But, held back to see what he had to say.

"I should tell you to stay out and let the professionals handle it, but to be truthful, we haven't a clue and time may be important So, let's make a deal to cooperate with each other. We'll keep you in the know if you'll do the same for us. For reasons we don't understand, this thing has some powerful people antsy. I don't mean to sound insensitive, but the death of one journalist is not earth-shattering news. There must be something big behind it. We know that you may have contacts and methods that may produce some results we can't or at least haven't gotten to yet. Because of your relationship with Mr. Vaughn, something may be significant to you that we'd just bypass. Keep us apprised of what you're doing and what you find out and we'll do the same. No matter how insignificant you may think it is.

Don't hold out on us. This is definitely dangerous business. We can't keep you safe if you're not honest with us."

He looked at West who was staring me down like a Doberman waiting for me to break and run. "Okay, is it a deal?"

I looked from West to Shanks and reluctantly nodded. "It's a deal."

"What's your first move?" asked West.

I smiled. "Find that journal."

CHAPTER THREE

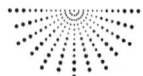

*I*t wasn't until I actually sat down and started focusing in on the journal that I realized how difficult it would be to find. How could we know if it still existed? Why would he hide it? If he didn't, the question was, what happened to it? If he hid it, the questions were where and why? Did he suspect someone was after it? Did the people or person who killed him take it or was it just lost? Did they destroy it? Did he destroy it? I thought about the apartment. Who trashed the place? Did they find it? If they had, there would be no reason to rip the apartment to shreds looking for it. No, I had to believe the journal still existed, unless they found it when they searched his apartment. I had to find out. A quick call to Margaret, complete with a warning to be extra careful of strangers, a hot shower, and I was done for the day.

The next morning, I decided to visit some of Walt's haunts. Maybe one of them would provide me with a clue. I hoped to find something that would make a connection and lead to the journal. I went to our favorite spot on Belle Isle, Sunset Point, the corner of the island that overlooks the downtown Detroit skyline. I went to our favorite fishing spot, a pier down by the Ambassador Bridge. I then went to the Main Library on Woodward across the street from Wayne State

University. Walt used to spend hours there researching and writing; he said it made him feel smarter being around all that accumulated knowledge.

"What a great place to hide a book, among other books. But, what a nightmare to pick out just one," I thought. My next stop was across the street at the museum, the Detroit Institute of Art, to the Antiquity Section. Walt had a jones for history and old relics.

When I stopped for lunch I realized that this was getting me nowhere. I hadn't found a clue. Nowhere I had been was bringing me any closer to the journal. Then it hit me. What was I doing? I wasn't looking for the journal, I was looking for Walt. I was trying to be with him. Going to his favorite places was keeping him close to me. Spending time in places he loved was spending time with him. The loss swept over me harder than ever. I nearly passed out from the revelation. It took all that I was to keep going. All I wanted to do was crawl into a hole and cry.

After an hour of moping, I called Shanks. He wasn't available, so I had to talk to West.

"Have you found something?" he asked me.

"No. I just called because I don't know where Walt's body was found. You never told me."

"We searched that area thoroughly. There's nothing there."

"Where?" I asked, irritated.

"On Belle Isle. Southwest corner of the island …"

"Sunset Point, where the park overlooks downtown?"

"Yeah, that's right."

"I've been there too. Okay, I've got nothing to share right now, but I'll keep in touch." I hung up before he could reply.

I called The General to check in on her and then called Charlotte and made plans for dinner.

CHAPTER FOUR

*C*harlotte Anderton is Mother Teresa, Indiana Jones, and Frank Lloyd Wright all rolled into one. She's an architect who travels around the world building medical facilities for the poor. Charlotte is always in some place no one has ever heard of doing her humanitarian thing. She's the kind of girl you'd want to know but would be afraid to marry. Her "girl next door" good looks kept a line of fellows following her, but she just sends them packing.

Charlotte always said, "I've got plenty of time for men and babies. Right now, I've got a mission. I want to make my mark while I still have the energy and freedom to do so. Besides, I'll be even hotter when I've lived and marinated a bit more."

"Okay CC, tell me the truth. How are you doing? Are you really alright?"

"Yes, Charlotte. The idle times and especially the nights are a little rough, but basically I'm dealing."

"I know you, CC. I'd bet you're carrying around more guilt than I've got fat on my thighs."

"Wow. That would be a heavy load indeed."

"Hey, you better watch it. I'm a woman with a knife within reach and I'm not afraid to use it." We broke out into a laugh.

"That felt good. I don't remember the last time I really laughed. It's so good to be with you."

Charlotte reached over and put her hand on mine. "I know, baby. I miss him too. We'll get through this. It'll be alright. I promise." She took in a deep breath.

"There were never two people I've known who loved each other more than you two did. All people had to do was see you two together and they knew."

My lip quivered. "I gave him such a hard time sometimes." I confessed to my plate.

"CC, Walt understood. He used to tell me how it broke his heart the way you used to beat yourself up. But, you know Walt. He was the kind of guy who would just sit there and let you do it your way. He'd let you beat the hell out of yourself. Not say a word, or move a finger, but when you finally got over yourself, he'd be there, with open arms."

"I know. It used to royally piss me off, but I loved him for it." After a great dinner and good conversation, we had a drink to end the evening. I hadn't felt so at ease in days.

"I've got to leave for Bamako, Mali day after tomorrow. I've got a ton of things that need taking care of tomorrow. But, I want you to come over to see me tomorrow evening. Around six-ish?"

"I'll try not to be fashionably late."

CHAPTER FIVE

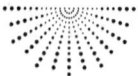

*T*he next day I went to see Caroline and I talked to some of
the others at the *Free Press*. They couldn't provide me with
anything helpful. "What about his things?" Caroline asked. "Will you
take them to his mother? You were closer to him than anyone else."
She trailed off and looked away as if she knew she was going somewhere she wasn't supposed to.

I cleared out his desk and packed up his things. All the while I felt
like I was doing something wrong, as if I was erasing his memory like
he had never mattered. Just sweep him away and call next. I left, box
in hand, without saying goodbye.

I thought about calling Shanks and West but decided not to. There
was nothing to tell them and if they had something for me they would
have called.

At half past six I rang Charlotte's doorbell. "Come on in, hot stuff.
I've got the highballs already cooking."

"You cooking? I hope I've got some *Pepto* at home."

"I'll have you know that there are some things I can cook." Taking
on a haughty tone. "I can boil a mean pot of water, my fried eggs are
legendary, and as for my highballs, well let's just say, your taste buds
will thank you."

She added in a rushed tone, "I hope you did eat before you came. All I've got in the fridge is some "been there way to long" Chinese take-out and stale crackers. We could go out and get something if you like."

"Are you kidding? Do you think I would come to your house and actually eat something? I love you Charlotte, but I'm not suicidal."

"I'm going to pretend there's a compliment in there somewhere or else I'd have to seek retribution." Her left brow arched like the back of a black cat.

We laughed, talked and drank for hours. "I've got something for you. When I got home the other day and picked up my mail at the post office, there was something in it for you."

"Who would send me something here?" Suddenly I couldn't breathe.

"It's from Walt, isn't it?" She nodded, reached under her chair cushion and handed me a manila envelope. I held the envelope as if I was checking for a heartbeat. There was no doubt in my mind the journal was inside.

"There was a letter in it giving me instruction to make sure you got this. It was eerie to read. It read like he knew he wouldn't be here. I hope he didn't know this would happen." There was fright in her voice. We shared an awkward moment. Charlotte broke the tension with one of her classical references.

"I don't know what this is all about. It's so very James Bondish."

"That would make you a Bond girl." I joked, trying to avoid thinking that Walt knew he was in danger.

She primped. "Beautiful, intelligent and sizzling hot, perfect casting. If I say so myself. So, who are you, Q?"

"No, not Q. I'm not that clever. More like a male version of Money Penny with an attitude problem." I started to open it but thought better of it. "I'll open this later, okay."

She just nodded and smiled. When the evening was over, and I was standing at the door saying my goodbyes, my phone rang.

"Where are you? Are you alright?"

"Who is this?"

"It's West."

"I'm fine. What's going on? Have you found something?"

"You need to get to your place right now. And be careful. Keep your eyes open." He snapped.

"What's wrong?"

"Just get here, man."

"Okay, okay I'm on my way. I'll be there in fifteen minutes."

"Everything alright?" Charlotte asked.

"I don't know. I've got to go. Love you and be careful with those bed pans."

"Don't worry about me." She laughed. "I never get personal with strange bed pans. You take care of yourself. I'll call you soon as I get near some modern technology."

"And thanks," I said waving the envelope at her. When I got to the car something told me to hide the envelope. I wanted to read what was inside before I let Shanks and West in on it. I went to the trunk, pulled back the carpet, and pushed the envelope under the spare tire. West and Shank were parked in front of my building when I arrived.

"What's so urgent? Have you learned something?" I asked.

"A call came in from your building manager. There was a report of a disturbance and when we came to investigate, well you better see." Shanks said. We rode up to my floor while I explained I was at a friend's house for drinks. The door to my apartment was cordoned off with crime tape. West pushed the door open to a reproduction of the scene at Walt's' apartment.

"What the hell…? Who did this?"

"We had your name and address tagged. When the call came in an alarm went out and we hot-footed over here. When we saw this mess, we didn't know if we'd find you in there. Since there was no sign of you, we had to consider that you might have been kidnapped or taken away and killed. I called and well..." West finished by pointing at the mess before us.

"Chris," Shanks asked. "Have you found the journal?"

"No, no I haven't," I answered, keeping my expression as neutral as possible. I wasn't technically lying. Even though I was sure it was in the envelope, I hadn't seen it. So, it was only my belief that it was in the envelope. It was like my grandfather used to say when my grandmother would catch him not telling the whole truth, "I was just painting the barn with bullshit to fool the flies."

"Somebody must think you have it. Maybe you're being followed. Have you noticed anyone or anything strange?" I shook my head no as I walked around in shock.

"I don't know what's in it, but somebody really wants that thing," West said, scratching his head. "Look, we want you to come down to the station with us. I don't want to put you in protective custody, but until we can get a handle on this thing I don't think it's a good idea for you to be alone and unprotected. At least that will give us some time to arrange guard duty."

"Okay." I mumbled as I sheepishly followed them to their car. *"Walt, what in the hell were you involved in?"*

We never noticed the cold black eyes and sneering smile that watched and followed us to the station.

CHAPTER SIX

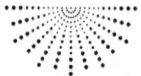

"Where's Kelp?" asked Hayden Ward.

"Still on assignment," replied Willis.

"This journal, do we have any idea what exactly is in it? Could there be anything that could compromise our operation or are we chasing ghost?"

"We do not know for certain, sir. The reporter Mr. Vaughn may have some connection with the Ceteri. He did meet with Fawaiya in Dubai. What he learned or what exactly transpired between them we do not know. We can only speculate that Fawaiya told him everything. As you know, before we could extract any information from him Kelp happened. Kelp did as Kelp does."

"Yes, what Kelp does so well. In this case, too well and too soon. What about Fawaiya?"

"He has gone underground as far as we know, but the search continues. It has not been very easy to locate him. Once you mix with the populace, finding one particular person can be very difficult."

"I suppose that will have to do for now. The minute Kelp arrives I want to be informed, even if we are in session. Let me know when the others arrive so we may get this meeting under way." Willis bowed and left the room.

Ward swiveled his chair around to face the wall of windows. He looked down from his office on the top floor of the Haverstal Building in downtown Detroit. The sight of scurrying people angered him. To him they were huge bugs, despoiling everything. Just insignificant things believing their pitiful little lives mattered. The thought made his revulsion grow ever deeper. "The sooner we rid ourselves of you the better."

Hayden Ward was CEO and Chairman of the Board of Global Oil Inc., the largest energy company in the world. GO Inc. controlled vast quantities of oil reserves on all seven continents, dozens of refineries, scores of off shore oil rigs, fields with billions of kilos of natural gas, and the most profitable operations of fracking ever. Hayden Ward arrived on the scene six years ago. He appeared out of nowhere and bought major stock in the company, when it was then the eighth largest energy company. Hayden joined the board, and within three years he was chairman. Within another year he had increased his ownership to over half and had become CEO as well. He aggressively took the company to new heights and unbelievable profitability. Hayden crushed anyone or anything that got in his way. The stock-holders were ecstatic. The board was elated. The politicians, at least those that he supported, were pleased and obedient. The regulators, environmentalists, and other energy companies feared, despised, and hated him. It was known that to cross Hayden Ward was not only a bad career move, but it could be a deadly one as well.

If looks were any indication you would think Ward was the favored Ivy League boy, all grown up. He was 45 years old, tall, with a cleft chin, an athletic build with a prominent Roman nose, pronounced cheek bones, a crop of well coiffured blond hair, and a movie star's smile. His cold steel blue eyes had the intensity of a cobra's stare. When he spoke, there was no inflection or emotion to his voice, only a hollow sense of foreboding, as if every word were a warning.

There was a knock on the door; Willis opened it. "They're assembled, sir."

"Fine, I'll be right there." Willis nodded and retreated. Hayden put on his suit jacket, took a look in the full-length mirror making sure everything was immaculate, nodded his approval at his own reflection, and headed for the meeting.

When he arrived at the conference room, Willis was waiting. He opened the door and followed him in. Hayden descended into the chair at the head of the oval table like a king reposing on a throne. Willis took his place, standing to the left behind Hayden, waiting for a call to serve.

To Hayden's right sat Calvin Stone, CEO and Chairman of the Board of Castleland Industries. A middle-aged man with a receding hairline, a waistline that spoke of over indulgence, and a hard angular face meant to intimidate, his audible breath sounded like a blacksmith's bellow.

Castleland Industries is the largest purveyor of coal in the world. They own 65 percent of coal production in the United States and have a hidden share in another 17 percent. Castleland has holdings in all coal production in the world, as well as major interests in landfills, sewage removal and treatment, and toxic waste storage and removal, including nuclear.

To Hayden's left, perched like a lap dog waiting on table scraps, sat the Reverend William Milborne. An accomplished speaker and prolific writer who has the ear of an impressive list of world leaders, Milborne has been an advisor to four sitting United States Presidents and scores of movers and shakers. His mark is on almost all major events for the last 20 years. Thinning slicked back salt and pepper hair, a clean-shaven face, and weary gray eyes gave him a kindly grandfather look. He is pastor of a mega-church, The True Light Church of Deliverance; boasting a congregation of over 55,000 active members and a mailing list in the millions. "Brother Milborne," as he is known, is a popular televangelist. He is the spokesman for the Super Pac titled "Americans for Morality," an outspoken ultra-conservative group heavily into conservative legislation all around the world. He boasted weekly on his television show that he is a cultural warrior, sanctioned, armed, and ready for battle.

At the opposite end of the table sat Douglas Henry Handover, posed as if he were sitting for a portrait. He is the consummate celebrity, famous by proxy. He is renowned for being rich and famous. Douglas is the sole owner of the Hanover fortune acquired at the tender age of 16. His father, mother, and two sisters were murdered by unknown assailants while he was away at boarding school. Handover is a Rhodes Scholar with PhDs in Art History and Philosophy. He delights in igniting social controversies, then sitting back to watch the combatants slug it out. His curly black hair, perfect alabaster teeth, iridescent brown eyes, and gym-toned body make him one of the most eligible bachelors in the world. His lack of modesty, lack of humility, and aggressive arrogance also make him one of the most disliked. But, in popular culture, money wins out.

"Gentlemen," Hayden said, silencing the whispers. "May we get to the business at hand? I believe you have had time to review the reports before you. All pertinent information and projections are there. All the data has been correlated and updated with predictions and cost analysis included. Are there any questions?"

He looked at each in turn and continued. "Good, down to new business. I propose a gradual reduction in the price of crude oil by 20 percent and coal by 15 percent to encourage consumption. Naturally there will be opposition from the Russian Federation and by OPEC. We can placate the Russians with political and financial support for their expansion into Eastern Europe. As for OPEC, any support they can garner for the containment of their revolutionary minded citizenry will go a long way. I also think that perhaps the encouragement of another western military adventure to that part of the world will take the combatants mind off of the ruling families and give them a new villain, or should I say, remind them of an old one."

"What about China? Their economy has leveled off and so has their coal consumption. Their oil usage has increased due to the increased sale of automobiles, but electric cars are on the rise. If we lose that huge population to renewables it will set us back substantially" added Stone.

"You are quite right, Calvin. If you look at, I do believe it is page sixteen. Yes, page sixteen. We have anticipated the Chinese's lower coal requirements and have offset that by increasing hard industries and in turn more consumption in not only the African nations, but also Bangladesh and Pakistan. Moving manufacturing production to these areas will more than offset any loses of usage in China. Besides, if the Chinese feel they are falling behind they will ramp things up and return to the tried and true in an attempt to maintain their dominance. After all, the world's population demands cheap goods and there is definitely enough of the poor to produce them. Not to mention their governments will overlook environmental regulations to stay competitive."

"What about South America? That part of the world has been uncomfortably quiet for some time," asked Milborne.

"At last report they had reduced consumption by another three percent taking them to about a sixteen percent decrease in the last twenty years. At present about 45 percent of the energy needs of the continent are met by renewables. The combination of sugar cane, wind farms, and solar energy has had some impact, but it's negligible. With the shifts in the climate and wind patterns, their sugar cane crops are down thirty-seven percentage points and their wind farms are barely producing two thirds of the expected yield. The stats for solar are unchanged and expected to remain flat. With the alterations in the climate, their usefulness and effectiveness are minuscule."

Hayden continued. "Do not be deceived, by no means is anyone on a path to eliminating fossil fuel usage. No country on the planet is. Even the so called "First-world" countries like the USA, Europe, etc., are highly dependent on fossil fuels and continue to be. There are those that are attempting programs, with only minor successes. Remember gentlemen, our goal is to make sure that we reach a tipping point that cannot be recovered from before that happens. We have the very powerful ally of economic interests on our side. This will always cause nations to go with the cheaper, reliable, tried and true methods, ergo fossil fuels. With the unprecedented disruptions in the weather patterns, increasing volcanic and earthquake activities we have engaged two new useful allies; uncertainty and fear. The irrational behavior that this increased loss of control can and will produce is a boom to our objectives. We simply have to use them effectively and our success is guaranteed."

"I agree," chimed in Milborne. "As long as we control the patents on the most promising forms of renewables, continue our influence on regulations, and press the need for increased economic growth. I see no obstacles we cannot surmount."

"There is a two percent temperature increase that is expected to rise to as much as six and a half by the end of the century. CO_2 levels have more than doubled since the onset of the Industrial Revolution. Ocean acidity is on target to reach critical mass in under thirty years. Regulation is virtually none existent. The tipping point is at hand," trumpeted Hayden.

"I don't see anything in this report about a recovery plan. What preparations are being made to aid in the repair of the planet after the infestation has been removed?" Stone asked.

"That is being considered and carefully planned. You will soon have a detailed agenda outlining all proposed activities," answered Hayden.

"This is all very impressive, Hayden, in its subtlety," Hanover chimed in. "I know you believe in the long game. But there are more direct and faster ways of getting this done. You pride yourself on your great strategic mind, but is there a plan B, perhaps?" asked Douglas his voice dripping with sarcasm. "Or maybe even a faster plan C? We have been actively pursuing your stratagem for some time now. I don't mean to be the voice of dissent, but in this race, we are not the hare, we have become the tortoise."

"But, did not the tortoise prevail in the end?" Hayden asked shifting his eyes, but not his head to Handover.

"That my dear Hayden, was a fairy tale and a very implausible one at that. This is a bit more consequential."

"Are you questioning my leadership, Douglas?"

"With the slow pace of your progress and this business with the reporter, perhaps a fresh perspective is needed. After all, we all have a major stake in this operation."

"What happened with the reporter was a bit too much enthusiasm from Kelp."

"Kelp is your pet. Is it not? Which makes you responsible."

"Kelp will be dealt with and contained. You need not worry about that. As for the reporter, no information was lost, no levees were breached. I admit we are not sprinting toward our objective, but considerable progress is none the less being made. You as well as everyone else know that we must operate under certain restraints. I assure you this plan is solid." Hayden said, the hollowness of his voice resonating even clearer than usual.

"My sources do not share your optimism about this business. It appears that Kelp's actions have put us at risk of exposure. That is something we cannot tolerate. Anonymity is one of our greatest assets. It must be maintained," said Douglas.

Hayden raised his brows. "Your sources? I see. It does please me that you are showing such intimate devotion to the cause. But, let me reiterate that things are in hand."

"I do hope so, my dear Hayden. Patience, unlike time, does have its limits and I do believe we are reaching ours."

Hayden smiled tilting his head. "Is that a threat or perhaps a warning, Hanover?"

Leaning over the table and staring directly into Hayden's eyes, Hanover said, "Threat? Why I would never think of such a thing. Just a kindly reminder from a friend, a comrade in arms." He ended with a deceitful grin.

A tap at the door caused Willis to move. He stepped out and spoke to a young man in mumbled whispers. He returned, leaned down to Hayden. "Kelp is here," and resumed his station.

"If there are any other concerns gentlemen, Willis will be happy to assist you." He rose and left the room.

"We have been dismissed gentlemen. Our leader," Douglas said the words as if they had soured in his mouth. "...has other matters of greater import than us. I for one am growing weary of these calls to arms just to be lectured to and dismissed out of hand."

"Perhaps there is some validity to your point, Hanover." Brother Milborne said. "We'll have to review our options and then…"

"Remember who we are dealing with and what's at stake," warned Stone.

"There can be no harm in looking at all the options. There may be alterations that can be made that could hurry things along. That can only be good for the project, right?" Brother Milborne asked.

"Yes, alterations. You go ahead with your analysis. I for one have had enough talk. Perhaps a little proactive action is in order." Douglas huffed as he left the room.

"We can't afford dissension when we are so close," said Stone as he and Brother Milborne followed Hanover.

"I do believe that dissension in our ranks maybe the least of our problems moving forward." offered Brother Milborne.

Hayden entered his office, sat behind his desk, began shuffling papers, and without looking up said, "step forward." A figure emerged from a dark corner of the room and stood before the desk.

Kelp moved as swiftly and silently as a jungle cat, like a shadow lost in the blackness of night. Because he was outfitted in total black from head to toe, if you did not know Kelp was there you would think this mirage was just a trick of the light, a refraction of dusk in the spectrum. The only discernible parts were strings of oily coarse hair hanging down the back from underneath the hat. A face shrouded by the brim of a low-slung hat and gloved hands, it was difficult to tell where Kelp began and the shadow ended; he seemed to be a phantom of darkness.

"Your rash actions," Hayden began looking down as if reading the words. "…have cost me valuable effort and time. As well, because of the sloppy manner in which you executed things I have had to answer for things that have put my standing in question. This is unacceptable. If I cannot depend on you then I have no need of you. Is this understood?"

"Yes," Kelp's voice was an echo.

"Have you found the journal?"

"No."

"What are your realistic possibilities of recovering it?"

"I cannot say. I have searched the apartments of both reporters and it was not there. This reporter, Chapel, is hunting for it now. I believe he may be my best possibility. When and if he finds it, I will retrieve it from him."

"Take no new actions other than to follow him unless he finds it. If so, retrieve it from him. Draw as little attention as possible to your activities. I do not need a line of cadavers raising more suspicions and leading back to me. Where is this reporter now?"

"I followed him to the police station. That is where I left him."

"I see. There is nothing we can do to discourage the authorities' involvement without raising more suspicions. Make sure you do nothing to promote or increase their interest in this matter. You must learn to contain your propensities for violence until they are truly needed. Do you understand?"

"Yes."

"What of Fawaiya?"

"Eliminated. I also had to remove two others with him. I left the building in flames. There will be no remains."

"What has become of his work, his writings?"

"All that I could not retrieve went up in the fire."

"At least that door is closed." Hayden finally looked up from his desk. "This will be your only warning. You are dismissed." Kelp silently exited the office without making a sound.

CHAPTER SEVEN

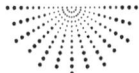

$\mathcal{I}$ awoke the next morning with a stiff back and the taste of stale fear in my mouth. A night of sleeping and sitting up on a hard wood bench was not forgiving. Drinking over cooked coffee didn't help, either. Shanks, who had spent the night at the station as well, guided me into an interrogation room where West, who had gone home to sleep in his own bed, was waiting. He was irritatingly fresh.

The square room had one window on the door and it was covered with a blind. It also was the only way in or out. Inside was a steel rectangle table and four cushion-less hard wooden chairs. My ass ached just looking at them.

"Good morning," sang West.

"That's a matter of opinion," I groaned.

"You're alive and the sun is shining. What more could you ask for?"

"Knock it off West!" Shanks yelled. "Let's get down to business so I can go get some of that home comfort that you soaked up last night."

"Some people just aren't morning people, I guess," West laughed and took a seat at the far end of the table.

"Chris, in about an hour your guard detail will be ready, and you can go home and cleanup." Shanks said. "There will be someone

parked outside your building 24/7. He will be a duly appointed officer, so he will be armed and will use deadly force if necessary. If you
are leaving, inform the officer ahead of time, so he can be ready to
accompany you. He'll be in regular contact with us. That way we will
be aware of your whereabouts. This only works if you cooperate. Do
you understand?"

"Yes, I've got it."

"I'm sorry to say, resources are limited, so only one officer will be
assigned to you at a time."

"After a night of thinking about this, I'm not sure this is a good
idea." I offered "I'm not exactly helpless. I think I can take care of
myself."

"Famous last words," groaned West, shaking his head.

Shanks looked at me and I could see in his eyes the fatigue I felt.
"Look Chris, you remember our mentioning that Walter Vaughn went
to the Middle East." I nodded yes. " We have good intel that he met
with a man, a sort of Muslim spiritualist name Fawaiya in Dubai.
Because Dubai is more or less the Switzerland of the Middle East, we
assumed it was a matter of financing for terrorists. But Fawaiya has no
links to terrorists, as a matter of fact they avoid him. He's considered a
heretic. Regular Muslims, if there is such a thing, avoid this guy. Only
the most hardcore go near him. It's a wonder the purists haven't done
this guy in. He has some very radical teaching about the end times and
such. Anyway, after he met with Mr. Vaughn, he and his disciples went
underground. Fawaiya and two of his disciples were found dead a
couple of days ago. They were decapitated and partially burned.
Somebody is very good with a sword. Just by happenstance, when the
building collapsed it upended the leg of a nearby water tower that fell
over on the fire and put it out. If that piece of awkward good luck
hadn't come our way we would not have known what happened to
them, and this odd piece of the puzzle would have been lost."

"What the hell was Walt meeting with a spiritualist for? He wasn't
even religious. And to go all the way to Dubai to do it? This is crazy." I
said. "What about the Primae? Anything on that?"

"*Nada*," said West. "Hey, you do realize that we have been the ones doing all the giving. When do you think we could expect something coming from you?"

"It's just me. I don't have the resources of the federal government and Detroit's finest at my beckon call. I'm trying. Hopefully something will come up soon." I thought for a moment "How about this? I provide proof that the journal at least still exist?"

"Just how are you going to do that without actually finding the journal?" asked West smugly crossing his arms over his chest.

"Well, it was my apartment that was trashed. If I didn't have an apartment for them to search we would never have known they're still looking for it, which means they don't have it." I smiled and left the room to wait on my ride. I think I heard West mumble something about a "smart ass." That made me smile.

The sight of the mess in my apartment made me even more tired than I was. The mattress was shredded, and there was no way I could sleep on what was left. Whoever did this has some serious anger issues. I turned the sofa upright and laid down. I was asleep in seconds. When I awoke late that afternoon, I looked out the window to check on my babysitter. He was parked directly across the street. My car was parked three spaces behind him. I figured I'd wait until dark and go down with the pretext of getting something out of the trunk. I'd put the journal in my gym bag and return to the apartment with no one the wiser. After I had time to read and study it, I would turn it over to Shanks and

West. They'd be mad I had held out on them, but that couldn't be avoided. In the meantime, I had a lot of cleaning to do.

At about dusk, I walked out of the front door of the building and the officer got out of the squad car and approached me. "Going some-where?" he asked.

I looked at his badge for a name. "Officer Foster, I have to get my bag out of the trunk. You know, work stuff." He nodded and returned to his car. Foster stood at the car door watching me without getting in. I opened the trunk, fumbled with the carpet, got the journal, slipped it in my gym bag, threw the strap over my shoulder, closed the trunk, and started back toward the building.

I turned to wave my triumphed goodbye to my babysitter as I reached the curb. Looking his way, I saw something strange. A shape, a figure or something appeared on top of the police car. The next moment, Foster's head hit the ground. Before I could tell my feet to move, a car squeaked to a stop beside me. The door flew open and someone shouted, "Get in." I just looked at the shadow or whatever it was coming my way.

"Get in or stand there and die." Without thinking, I jumped in. The car sped off with me falling in and the door hanging open. Someone laid across me reaching for the open door screaming, "Go, go," as we raced down the street. I twisted to look out the back window and the shadow was chasing us. We were speeding down the street away from it and it was gaining on us. The door slammed shut and we finally began to outpace it.

I was panting and hugging my bag. "What just happened?" I asked, my mind still reeling. "What was that?"

"What just happened? We just saved your life." Her voice was crisp with a tinge of a laugh in the background. "What was that? That was Kelp."

I looked into the excited gray eyes of a young woman. She had a ponytail of chestnut-colored hair, a small button nose, full smiling lips, and an expression that said both fear and pleasure like someone who just got off a roller coaster.

"Who are you?" I asked coming to myself. "...and him?" referring to the driver. "We've got to go back. Foster. We've got to help Foster." Remembering after I had said it that I saw his head hit the ground, no longer attached to his body.

"I'm afraid Mr. Foster is beyond our help, Chris," said the driver, looking at me through the rearview mirror with resolute eyes.

"How do you know my name? Stop the car. Stop right now and let me out."

"After what you just saw back there do you really want me to stop the car? Because if you do I'll turn around and take you back.

Your choice." His voice was solid like he spoke from a position of authority. He had the air of someone who was used to being in charge. But, the casualness of his windblown black hair and the calmness of soft brown eyes made him seem like a regular guy. I didn't answer. "Okay then. My name is Ben and she's Kate. We were coming to hopefully have a talk with you when...well when things started happening."

"Yeah," said Kate. "When Kelp started happening."

"What's a Kelp?" I asked.

"That is a very good question, and one that I'm afraid I would have trouble explaining. At least in a way you would understand. Kelp is a *Perdidi Unum*."

"A what?"

"A lost one. Let's just say that Kelp is bad news, very bad news. We got away only because Kelp didn't know we were there. Had Kelp known, we may all have ended up like Foster. The *Perdidi Unum* are fearless, highly skilled, and ruthless." Ben said.

"Alright," I said. "You saved me. Thank you. Thank you, very much. Now would you please drop me off at the nearest police station?"

"You never asked what we were coming to see you about." Ben said.

I clutched my bag tight against me. "I think I have a good idea."

Kate laughed. "You've got it all wrong. We don't want Walter's journal."

"No, we don't," said Ben. "As a matter of fact, what's in there is what he mainly learned from us. That is us and Fawaiya. I'll tell you what. We'll go someplace safe. You read the journal and then we'll talk."

"What makes you think I have the journal?"

"Well you either have the journal in that gym bag you're hugging so tightly or else you have an unusually close relationship with your jock strap," Ben said with a laugh. Kate added a chuckle of her own.

"Don't mind him. We know because we saw you stick it in the trunk the other night when you left the blondes house".

"You've been following me?"

"Yeah, trying to find the best time to approach you. But, when your place was trashed, and the police whisked you away, we had to wait until you returned," said Ben.

"So, you two knew Walt?"

"Yes, we did," Said Kate. "I'm sorry about him. He was a good guy."

"Did...did Kelp?" I stuttered.

Ben pressed his lips together and nodded as I met his eyes through the mirror. "Let's not talk anymore until you've read the journal. Much of this you won't understand until then."

We drove in silence until we reached a large warehouse complex on the far northwest side of the city. Kate got out and moments later a steel garage door opened, and Ben drove in.

"You can go into the office over there and have some privacy," Ben said.

"Am I your prisoner?"

"No, you are not," he insisted. "Look, please read the journal and if you want to leave you can just walk out that door and forget you ever met us. Okay?"

I shook my head in a reluctant yes and went into the office. I opened the gym bag and removed the manila envelope. My hand slid over it, squeezing and clutching it as if I could read the contents by touch. I opened the seal and found a letter with the journal. Those words that looked like they were about to fall off the page were definitely from Walt's hand, full of his mixed lettering. Walt was inconsistent with his lettering. A word would start out with capital letters and end in small one or vice versa. Or the writing would start out as cursive and end with printed letters. "I write the way I think. Some word are more important than others. Some come faster than others. When I change my thoughts, my writing changes." My eyes grew cloudy and heavy as the voice, his voice, in my head read his words.

CC,

If you are reading this letter things have gone upside down and I am either being held captive or worse. I'm sorry to hand this off to you, but there is no one else I trust or believe in as much as I do you. What I am about to tell you is fantastic, unbelievable and frightening, but true. It took me a while to really wrap my head around it myself, but it's all incredibly real. If I can't finish this, I can think of no one better to take over than you. Read the journal. Find the Ceteri. Trust them. They will help. But before you get to that, there are some things I need to say to you.

First and foremost; now and forever; I love you. I don't think you ever truly understood how much or truly believed it in your heart, because deep down you don't think you deserve to be loved. You are so wrong. For someone so smart you can really be a dumbass about some things. I love you baby, and always have. From the day we stood on opposite ends of Charlottes' sofa and stared at each other I wanted you. I knew at that moment I would always be yours. I know you have your demons and as much as I would like to slay them for you, I know that I cannot. So, I've waited patiently hoping you would see what I see and learn to accept and love yourself so you could love me. I know you care, but I also know that until you really accept and love yourself you can never truly love anyone else.

These weeks away from you have been the worst hell. I have been tempted to come to you and kick your stubborn ass, hoping in the process I could kick some sense into you. I wanted to shake you, "we are wasting precious time!" Now I'm afraid we may never have another chance. I want to thank you for the years of friendship and the great times we've had. Even though we were never all that we should have been or could have been, what we did have was good, really, really good.

I Will Love You Always,

Walt

PS - Take care of the General. She loves you too.

I felt the whole world fall away. It was as if everything ceased to be real. I had never felt so alone or so vulnerable before. He was really gone and never coming back. My heart felt like someone was pounding on it with a sledgehammer. He was right. I had been wasting precious time and now our time had passed. I don't know how long I sat and cried. But I wept until my shirt was soaked and my eyes burned. No one ever disturbed me. I finally exhausted my tears. Finally, with swollen red eyes, I read the journal.

Emerging from the office, I angrily faced Ben, Kate and two others who I hadn't seen before. "I don't know what you did to Walt to make him write this, but there is no way in hell I buy any of this!"

"I know," said Ben holding up his palms as if to push back the fury I was hurling at him. "There's a lot to take in, but I assure you that it is all true. Walt stumbled on to it and it cost him his life."

"Angels, Nephilims, a shadow war, a conspiracy to eliminate mankind? Come on," I said. "This is crazy. Walt wasn't into this kind of stuff. He didn't even believe in God. None of this can be real. I won't believe it."

"It may sound strange, but it's deadly serious. You've read his journal, haven't you?" asked Kate. "Don't you trust Walter? What he wrote? Don't you think he was skeptical too? But, he was convinced. He found out that all of this is real. Very real. He understood the struggle we are all in."

"Who is we?" I asked. "In this thing," I held up the journal. "He mainly talks about some prophesy, his meeting with Fawaiya, and some corrupt businessmen. I guess you're supposed to be the 'others' he talked about?" My chest was heaving and pounding with indignation.

"Yes, we are. We are the others. The Ceteri," Ben said proudly. "Calm down, Chris, and we'll tell you the whole story."

"No. I'm getting the hell out of here. You people are crazy or something. What are you really? Some kind of doomsday cult, religious fanatics, or something worse?" I headed for the door.

"Before you go, don't you want to know why Walt died? Can you really walk away and be satisfied not knowing what someone you loved died for?" His words stopped me cold. I turned around to face him. I wanted to keep walking, but the chance to know why Walt died ate through my anger like an acid. I didn't understand why I had to lose him. I had to know. I needed to know. "

"Alright you Bastard, Talk!"

CHAPTER EIGHT

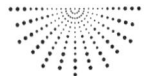

"There is not just one, but two wars going on. The first is a war for this world, for this planet. Before humans existed, earth was a true paradise. The whole planet was a paradise. It was a lush jewel, a near perfect physical manifestation of heaven. It was literally heaven on earth. You could say it was not the "Garden of Eden", but the "Planet of Eden." This was the birthplace of the beings you call Angels. On this "Planet of Eden," Angels existed and ruled supreme as the near perfect physical beings on the near perfect physical plane.

"I won't try to explain the theological aspects of things, but let's us say that humankind was created as an afterthought; as a companion of sorts. As time passed, the number of humans grew. As the numbers grew so did their minds. Humankind evolved and was no longer satisfied with the status of being just a companion, a pet, a 'less than.' They wanted their own life, their own destiny. Humankind became dominant as a species. In God's eye, humanity found recognition and favor. The Earth was ceded to humankind as a home.

"There were those who did not and still do not agree with or like this. This decision has caused a great rift to form in the ranks of the Angelic classes. Even though most accept the state of things, some are determined to remove what they call the blight on the land; the infestation of humanity. They want their Eden and their status back. Because of the dispensation granted you by God, there is nothing that they could do directly to reclaim the earth for themselves. But, they can aid you in your downfall by promoting things that will cause you to eliminate yourselves. Throughout the centuries there has been an Angelic hand pushing and prodding you into wars, genocides, pandemics, promoting self-destructive behavior of all kinds; anything that would bring the species to an end. Many times in human history their efforts have almost succeeded. Several times you have come to the brink, but you somehow managed to come to your senses and pull yourselves back from the edge. The Primae..."

My eyes grew wide at the mention of the name.

"Yes," said Ben, nodding in acknowledgement. "I see you have heard the name. That is why Walt went to Dubai. Fawaiya found the scrolls containing writings and prophesies of the Primaes and their efforts. He insisted on seeing it for himself. We tried to stop him, but he was nothing if not persistent and through."

"Fawaiya is dead." I said.

"I'm not surprised." He said. "Kelp no doubt."

"The authorities asked me if I ever heard the name Primae before; if Walter ever mentioned it. Who are they and what do they have to do with this? The journal wasn't totally clear. It mentioned them, but not by name. He does not go in exact details. Beside the journal is about his story. It's more about what he personally was feeling and thinking."

"The Primae, the First Ones, are the architects of your downfall," offered Kate.

"Why do you keep saying our fate, your downfall? You sound like you're not involved in this."

"I'm getting to that. One thing at a time. I don't want to give you too much without some background. I want you to totally understand everything, Okay?" Ben said. "Their latest and maybe best plan has been global warming; climate change."

"Climate change? What could this have to do with climate change?"

"The Primae control almost all the world's energy production. All the fossil fuel. They have been promoting the expanded usage of oil, coal, increasing deforestation, nuclear, you name it. While all the time stifling alternative sources and blocking regulation. They are behind almost all the campaigns of the climate deniers. They fund scientists and institutions to debunk and cloud the issue. Billions of dollars are poured into anything that will counter conservation efforts; all to accelerate the onset of climate change. If they can get the planet to the point of total climate instability, climate collapse, no matter what you do at that point it will be too late to counter the effects. It will eventually make the planet uninhabitable, killing off your species, and they can reclaim this Planet of Eden for themselves."

"But that would take years, decades, even centuries. That makes no sense; the place would be uninhabitable for them as well."

"You don't seem to understand who you're dealing with." Kate added. "These are almost immortal creatures. All they have to do is put things into motion. Get things to that point of assured success and they can sit back and wait. This is a long game. They have time. It's the human race that doesn't have the time."

"But, climate change is ..."

"Is real," said Ben. "The ice caps are almost all gone, massive hurricanes, supersonic tornadoes, severe hemispheric-wide blizzards, tsunamis that are a hundred feet high; everything is stronger and more frequent. Predicting the weather is more like a throw of the dice than ever. Earthquakes are happening in places that never saw them before. The tectonic plates are beginning to shift erratically. If you don't believe me, check the number of volcanic eruptions that have already happened this year. Their number is growing exponentially. Sea levels are rising, animal extinctions are happening at an unprecedented rate, extreme droughts, continent-wide forest fires, desert expansion, ozone depletion, and on and on. Not to mention the increases in human illnesses like asthma, autism, diabetes, and various cancers. Practically every year there is the threat of some new disease. You are killing yourselves and the planet; turning your home into a cesspool and dumping ground. One thing plays off the other and makes everything worse," Ben paused and massaged his brow.

"You have to understand that there is a balance and humankind has upset that balance. The effects of industry and population on the planet have reached a point where you are using the planet's resources much faster than they can be replenished or repaired. You're producing harmful waste and byproducts that contaminate and destroy other resources. You upset the natural function of the biosphere. You're overwhelming the planet's ability to regulate itself. The Primae are hurrying you to the point where the planet will be so depleted and toxic that it can no longer sustain Human life; ergo the end of the Human Race."

"If they destroy the earth, then they won't have it either," I said, pleading more than stating.

"They're counting on the belief that you can't really kill the planet. You can only disrupt its natural state causing it damage, yes, but not irreparable damage. Once it has expelled its infection..." he targeted me with a finger.

"That infection is you. They're betting the earth will survive and overtime it will recover and be better than ever. They're probably right. The Earth is a living, breathing entity infested with the sickness of humanity. They just plan on curing it by making it sicker. Taking it to the brink of death until it starves off the infection. Like you starve off an illness with a fever."

"Who are these Primae?"

"Leaders of industry and society. The council, so to speak, right now are Hayden Ward, Calvin Stone, Reverend William Milborne and Douglas Handover."

"Whoa," I said. "Those are big names, some powerful men. You're trying to tell me that those men are Angels?"

"No, these are not the men you think you know. They have been taken over by First Ones." Ben said.

"What, they're possessed?"

"Something like that, but not exactly," Kate said, moving close to me. "Purebloods like the Primae have the ability to transfer, to relocate their consciousness. They exist in a state of near pure energy which allows them to be in and out of this world; in a level of existence that we can't relate to. First Ones have the ability to project their essence into another body and to assume that identity. When a person is taken over by a First One, the essence of the First One is so powerful that it literally burns the original inhabitant out. The men you knew before are gone. They will never return. When the First Ones leave there is nothing left but a vacant shell. Unless you are a First One yourself or at least have something in common with them, you would never be able to tell the difference."

"You mean to tell me that there are aliens living among us?"

There was a collected laugh among the group. "The First Ones aren't aliens. Remember they were here first that's why they are called," he used air quotes. "...First Ones."

The foolishness of my statement caused me to blush and I quickly changed the subject to alleviate my embarrassment. "How do you know for sure they are these First Ones you keep talking about?"

"We're sure they're the ones," smiled Kate. "We have someone on the inside. That's how we stay up on what they're doing. It's how we got some of the documentation and proof that we have."

I asked tentatively. "Are you First Ones? Are you Angels?"

Ben laughed. "No, we are the Ceteri. You know Kate. This is Jacob and Horus." He pointed to the two others. "Just myself and a hand full of others. We are the children of First Ones and humans."

I took a step back. "Wait a minute. You're Nephilims? Part Angel?"

"Yes, we are." He stood a little taller. "Half-breeds, in the good sense of the words."

"This is getting crazier by the minute..." I said. "Then why would you want to stop the Primae? They're your people, aren't they? Wouldn't their objectives be yours too?"

A palpable tension filled the air. "The Primae are purist, fundamentalist. They consider you vermin and us abominations. After they deal with you, their attentions will turn to shaving us off their backs. That's the second war I was talking about. So, you see we have a personal interest in stopping them. Not just because what they are doing is wrong," Ben stamped his foot. "But, this is our world too. We either deal with them now or deal with them later."

"I don't mean to sound sacrilegious or anything, but why doesn't God just step in and put an end to this?"

"It doesn't work that way, Chris. God doesn't just sit around watching us like a babysitter waiting to chastise disobedient children. Besides, there is such a thing as free will. You have to understand Angels aren't divine like God. They're really just another species of creature. I'll admit they think better of themselves, but they are mortal. Advanced and highly evolved, but mortal. The rules apply to them as well as every other being."

"Okay, let's say you're right and I buy into this. And I'm not saying I totally believe this, but how are you going to stop immortal beings?"

"Like I said before they aren't immortal. They live a very long time and have enhanced physical abilities, at least compared to ordinary humans, like being stronger, healing faster, being able to influence and effect the minds of others. Things like that, but they do die. They can be killed. Secondly, one of drawbacks of First Ones inhabiting human bodies is those very abilities are hampered, reduced. It takes a lot of their energy to keep from burning up their temporary homes, most of their energy is occupied with that. Which in turn makes us more of a match for them. Because of that, we're close to being on the same level. Once they're locked in a body it's not so easy to get out. It takes time and effort."

"We have talents and skills of our own, thanks to our own unique parentage. We may look ordinary, but I assure you we are quite capable." He emphasized his point by lifting a muscled arm in the air.

"Besides..." he flashed a sword I hadn't noticed. The thin rapier was melded so close to his side it looked like a stripe on his pants. "... like I said, even Angels can die."

I looked around and everyone had their hand on blades and were nodding their heads in agreement.

"This is where Walt came in. He was going to write the story and expose the corruption, the bribes, and the illegal activities. That would put a wrench into some of their activities and stop most of the destructive happenings that are going on. Revealing their duplicitous actions would deal with the human half of the equation while we dealt with the second half of the equation, removing the First Ones. If things worked as planned the whole structure could collapse. Then people would be able to step in and work on salvaging the planet."

I don't know why, but I erupted. "You got Walt involved in this madness and got him killed! You damn bastards!"

Everyone tensed. Kate leapt to meet me face to face. "You wait a minute. Walt was a good man. We cared about him. Nobody here would ever have hurt him. Besides, he's the one who hunted us down. He wanted to do this. We told him that it could be life or death, but he thought it was the right thing to do. Walter believed in something other than himself. He cared about others. He believed in what we are doing. Just because you don't believe in or care about anything else, don't blame us."

"But, he's dead and..." The words died on my lips.

"And," Kate continued more softly, "...we're sorry about that. But, he chose this. It could have been anyone of us. We would all lay down our lives for this. He will never be forgotten for what he tried to do for us, for everyone. I assure you he will be avenged." Everyone nodded in agreement.

Ben stepped forward. "Chris, if you want to avenge him help us stop the Primae. I'm asking that you take over where Walter left off. You have his journal. We have his notes and all the documents you need in the office. Everything is on the computer and there are paper copies as well. What we've collected fills in all the holes. Please, look them over and let us know what you think and what you decide. There's no pressure. If you don't want to get involved any deeper, you can just walk away. No strings, no hard feelings."

I stood undecided for several minutes. My desire to get justice for Walt was fighting with my sense of apprehension. I didn't trust these people, but I couldn't just walk away. Walt deserved better. He wanted me to do this. He asked me to do this. I couldn't say no. No one said a word. I silently nodded my ascent, turned and walked into the office.

CHAPTER NINE

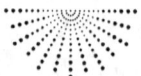

*K*elp entered the office and stood before Hayden's desk. Hayden rose and walked to face Kelp.

"I said to acquire the journal and not to create any more incidents. It seems that you are unable to control your tendencies and follow simple instructions." His voice was serene and expressionless. Hayden pivoted and brought his hand up delivering a backhand slap that sent Kelp sailing across the room into the corner. Pale pink blood trickled from the corner of Kelp's mouth.

"If things were not at such a delicate point I would end you," Hayden said calmly as if asking you to pass the butter. He never looked at the prone figure. Only the crimson pallor of his eyes betrayed his anger.

"Bring Chapel and the journal to me. Alive and undamaged. I will deal with this personally." Hayden returned to his desk and resumed his reading, never looking up or acknowledging Kelp as the figure rose silently and left the room.

A rap at the door and Willis stuck his head into the room. "Mr. Hanover is here sir. Shall I show him in?"

"Yes," grimaced Hayden, betraying his dissatisfaction at Hanover's' appearance. Douglas Hanover sauntered into the room. "What can I do for you Hanover? I am very busy."

"Aren't we all, my dear Hayden?" He walked about the room examining items and frowning his disapproval. "I won't take up much of your precious time. I just came to inform you that I have the happy fortune of acquiring the launch codes to several Russian ICBMs with active multiple nuclear warheads. They are armed and at my disposal. Unbeknownst to the Russian government, of course. As I suggested the other day, there are more immediate ways to facilitate our objectives," A sarcastic grin painted his face.

Hayden fixed his eyes on him with a stare of exasperation. "Nuclear war? We have discussed this before Hanover. Nuclear war can have unpredictable consequences. The use of nuclear weapons would do more harm to the planet than would be desirable. The obvious contamination alone would be counterproductive. The damage would be unacceptable. Recovery times would be greatly increased, which would be an anathema to what we are trying to do. There is always the possibility we could cause problems the planet would never fully recover from."

"Yes, yes. I've heard all those spurious arguments before, complete conjecture," Hanover waved off the comments. "Let me say that there are those of us who have reached a point of exhaustion. This subtle game you are playing has worn away our patience and we require some real progress. Results, Hayden, without these prolonged delays. At the rate we are going I will burn through three or four more of these flimsy shells."

"Hanover, I tire of your theatrics. I am sure they keep your society amused, but your antics hold no sway in my office. You have been given your assignments and are expected to carry them out without delay or alteration. I suggest that you forget your codes and return to your duties. Now if you will excuse me. I have much to prepare for." He lowered his head and returned to his pile of paper.

"Bravo Hayden," Hanover faked applauses. "Always the cool, the calm, the impenetrable commander in chief. So sure and unflappable." He ruffled his shoulder as if shaking off a shiver.

"As for my codes, they will remain safely with me. I will try to keep them away from itchy trigger fingers. Let us hope that your plans come to a conclusion before that happens." He moved to the door but turned to face Hayden.

"Oh yes, I called an emergency meeting for tomorrow so we can collectively reevaluate our options." Hanover stared sternly at Hayden emphasizing the words. "Have a pleasant day" he smiled his usually half smirk and opened the door. Willis nearly fell into the room.

"Listening at keyholes, Willis? Such a tacky habit," Hanover laughed and left the room.

Hayden and Willis shared an uncomfortable exchange.

CHAPTER TEN

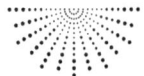

A knock on the door brought me out of my concentration. "Come in."

Kate entered with a tray. "I thought that you might be a little hungry by now. We didn't have much available. I hope a sandwich and a coke are alright."

"Thanks. I sometimes forget about eating or sleeping. When you get involved in a story you can lose all sense of time."

"Yeah, Walter used to do that too. He would stay in here for hours, pouring over documents and making notes. The only time he left this room, sometimes for days, was to call you."

I didn't look at her.

"Are you going to write the story?"

"Yes," I said sharper than I meant to.

"Thank you," she sighed. "I think Walter would want that." Kate made a sound as if to speak, stopped, and finally said, "Can I ask you a question?"

"Go ahead."

"Why didn't you answer Walters' calls? I know he called you over and over."

"I don't think that's any of your business. I don't want to talk about my relationship with Walt."

"I'm sorry. I don't mean to pry or offend you it's just that he used to talk about you sometimes. After talking about you he would get really sad and bury himself into his work. His pain was so obvious. I learned to care about him. He became a friend. I just wanted to understand."

"Look I don't mean to be rude, but I need to get through these papers so I'll be prepared to write this tomorrow."

"Okay, sorry." She faked a smile and left.

I didn't want Kate to see my clouding eyes or the guilt I was carrying. How could I make her understand what I didn't understand myself? How could I explain the regret I had for not taking Walt's calls? The shame I felt for not being there. What could I say about the loathing I felt for not being there when he needed me. How could I explain denying the best thing that ever happen to me?

CHAPTER ELEVEN

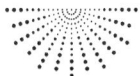

*B*en snatched the door open. His voice was loud and intense. "We've got to move our time table up. Things have changed. We need to act tomorrow."

"What's happened?" I asked.

"The Primae are meeting tomorrow. Something big seems to be in the works. There may to be dissension in their ranks and we need to move before things get beyond our abilities to act. Now is the time to strike, while they're off balance."

"I need to make a couple of phone calls. People are looking for me."

"I think you'll be safer if nobody knows where you are. We can't risk any breaches. The Primae have a long reach. They have influence in places you'd never expect them to be. And don't forget, Kelp is looking for you."

"So are the authorities. After all, one of their officers lost his head remember? I'll call my editor and let him handle the authorities. I also need to call Walt's mother and make sure she's alright."

"Alright, in fifteen. We've got communications that even the NSA can't track. It will allow you to make contact and keep your location a secret. But, we need to move soon; there is a lot that has to be done."

When I emerged from the office again, everyone was standing around the van in a circle holding hands. "What's going on?"

"A little reflection. Time to pray." Ben said as if my asking was ridiculous. On the opposite sides of me Kate and Jacob each held out a hand. Everyone locked their gaze on me. Unsure of what to do I stood like a child on the corner crossing the street alone for the first time faced with a flood of speeding car.

"It's an act of acceptance. What you believe is personal between you and your conscious." Kate whispered. "You above all should be able to understand that."

I hesitantly cupped their hands in my sweaty palms as Ben began. "We come together with humility and gratitude..." Kate gave my hand a reassuring squeeze. I thought how Walt must have dealt with this. Neither he nor I were religious, but this situation, these people, changed everything. They had accepted him and me and made no judgement. How could I do any differently? My world, the world was changing quickly and in so many ways I wasn't sure if I had what it took to survive it. Opening myself to new things was never easy. Walt would leap head first into the cold water where I was the one who waited for the water to get warm. My zone of comfort was getting smaller with each new scary prospect appearing all around me. The groups collective "Amen" brought me out of my fog.

Ben, Kate, Horus and I left the warehouse in a windowless van and headed northeast on the freeway, further away from Detroit. Ben and Horus sat up front. Kate and I sat in the back. "So, you're really a Nephilim?" I asked.

"Yes."

"Exactly how does that work? I mean, I've read the Bible. Most of it anyway. Aren't Angels supposed to have wings? And aren't you guys supposed to be giants? I mean all that, Sons of God and Daughters of Man, stuff." Not waiting for an answer, I asked. "Who are your parents?"

"Are you always in reporter mode?" I hunched my shoulders. "Okay, the *Readers Digest* abridged version." Kate smiled.

"Birds have wings, not Angels. The giant thing is just like the wing thing. It's not to be taken literally. As for my father, he was an ordinary and very kind Human named Henry. My mother, Jessie was an Angel who fell in love with him. He didn't know what she was until they came for her. Although Angels live among humans, they aren't supposed to consort with them. It seems they have some kind of code of conduct and some council that arbitrates these things. An Angelic morality police, I guess you could call them. Anyway, they came to take her away, for the sin of fraternization; the sin of falling in love."

Kate sighed and shook her head. "My father tried to fight them off. They killed him and took my mother away with them. I was in the yard in the doghouse with Hector, my beagle. I saw the whole thing. I watched my father die while my mother begged them for mercy. All I could do was hug my dog and cry. They never even acknowledged me. They dragged her away and eventually came back, rounded me up, and shipped me away. I was put in an orphanage and stayed there until Ben and the others found me. I've been part of the Ceteri ever since."

By the time her story was over her expression was a blank as a starless sky.

"I'm sorry."

"Thanks, but it was a long time ago. I learned a long time ago to deal with it."

With a sideways glance I asked. "How long?"

She snickered. "Didn't your editor ever tell you it's not gentlemanly to ask a lady her age, Mr. Newsman?" she said with an "I know what you're up to" grin.

Feeling a bit embarrassed and transparent, I was glad the van came to a stop.

"You two keep a watch. I'll take him in. We'll be back soon." Come on, Chapel." Ben led me to the door of a small stone building. We descended two flights of stairs and went through a couple more doors before we came to a dead end. He pressed some points on the stone wall and a passage opened up. Inside were computers, routers, monitoring screens and all kinds of high tech gadgetry.

"What is this place?" I asked.

"It's a power hub for this area. It's out of the way and perfect for us. We added a little communication lab of our own. Tapping into the energy supply gives us all the juice we need to run our equipment and use their tower. Our signal bounces off a couple of satellites and a half dozen such locations around the world. As long as we don't maintain a fixed signal for an extended period of time we remain untraceable. Just sit here and dial your numbers. Don't tell anyone where you are or who you're with. The less you say the better."

I nodded my ascent and called the paper. "Spencer, its Chris."

"Chris, are you alright? Where are you, son?"

"Yeah, I'm fine. I'm safe. I'm hiding out. There's somebody out there trying to kill me."

"The authorities want to talk to you. They don't look very favorably on one of their officers having his head lobbed off."

"I was there. The killer was trying to get to me. I barely escaped. I need you to call Shanks and West and let them know I'm okay. Tell them I'll get in touch with them soon and explain everything."

"Have you found the journal yet?"

"Yes, I have it and what's in it will blow the roof off of some important penthouses. I have names, dates and corroborating documents. This is big Spencer. Walt had them dead to rights. I'm going to write the story and I need to know that you'll print it."

"Bring in what you have. All of it and we'll go over it together. We'll get legal to take a look at it and go from there."

"No, Spencer. There's a timetable in play. We've got to move on this right away."

"Look Chris, come in. How long do you think you can avoid being found out? Kelp will find you and then its game over."

I paused and looked at the phone, unsure of what I'd heard. "I've got to go Spencer. I'll get back in touch." I hung up ending the communication and looked at Ben.

"He mentioned Kelp. I never told him about that. I never said that name. How does he know about Kelp?"

Ben shook his head. "I'm not surprised. I told you the Primae have a long reach. Somehow they've gotten to your Spencer."

"He knows I have the journal."

"That can't be helped now. We just have to move forward."

I called the "General" and made her agree to go out of town for a couple of weeks. Ben made a few calls and updated his people. We got into the van and headed back to the warehouse.

CHAPTER TWELVE

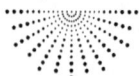

*F*or the next 10 hours I read, I wrote, and I worried. Walt kept very good records and wrote very through notes. He had assembled all the links in the chain. The names, dates, times, connections, amounts; it was there. Once I had the finer details the Ceteri had gathered, the story virtually wrote itself. All I had to do was assemble the pieces into the frightening picture it painted. The scale of this thing was truly global. The money trail alone was enormous and very dirty. I felt soiled just writing it. The Primae had bought, bribed, and coerced hundreds, if not, tens of thousands of politicians, government officials, regulators, and suppliers, anyone who could be compromised. The corruption reached everywhere from the White House, to the United Nations, to board rooms, and even to the mail rooms of every major corporation on the planet. The names on the list were a veritable *who's who* of every money bag who had wielded power in the last fifty years.

It even stretched down to the guy who pumped gas at the local station and the tanker drivers who hauled the fuel. Every country and every government was implicated. Every accusation was backed up with solid irrefutable evidence. This story would have made Walt

Henry Vaughn a household name and the darling of the journalism world. It would also have made him a lot of powerful enemies.

The problem was how to get the story out. Spencer was compromised. I didn't know how deep he was in, but I could no longer count on him for support. He had become the enemy. If I couldn't trust him who could I trust? The thought struck me. *Did Walt start to believe I was the enemy? When I didn't answer his calls, what did he think? Did he think I had betrayed him and started to work for the Primae?*

The idea made me sick. It made me angry, too. "No," I said aloud. He knew me better than that. If he thought he couldn't trust me he never would have sent his journal to me. He believed in me. I wouldn't let that trust down. A new sense of purpose started to wash over me. I had to do this not only because it was right. I had to do this for Walt. I had to live up to his belief in me. I was not going to let him down again. I realized I had to do this for me as well. It was time I took a stand for something, no excuses, no rationalizations.

"I need to get to an internet café," I told Ben.

"Why?"

"Since you have limited service here I don't trust that your connection can handle the job and besides if we do it here it can be traced. At a café it won't matter because we'll be in and out. We know that Spencer has been compromised, so we can't use him. We can't be sure that anyone can be trusted. If I get to an outside internet terminal I can post this thing. Put it on a delay. That will allow it to be posted when we want it to be. Once it's on the web, it will go global and no one can suppress it. I'll post the article and send copies of the files along with the documentation to every major news bureau in the world. The Primae maybe powerful, but they can't stop everybody in the whole world at once."

"That's a good plan," Kate said.

"I know where there's a café that's open 24/7," Horus said.

"Jacob and I can't leave now. We have things we need to get ready for tomorrow," said Ben.

"Horus and I can take him," Kate suggested. "We'll be careful. We'll keep a low profile."

Horus, Kate, and I left the warehouse and drove a few miles to the Sky Writer Café. It was a dimly lit little coffee house with a dozen or so wooden tables and harp backed chairs. Each table was fitted with a plastic table cloth and a laptop on it. The only customers were a couple of teenagers chugging energy drinks and playing video games. There was a dark-haired woman in thick glasses with a monster stack of books towering around her, looking like she needed an energy drink. I took an empty table toward the back while Kate ordered coffee. Horus waited outside guarding the van and the door.

I got to work uploading the article and the files. I put the file on a twelve-hour delay to be sent to every address in my and Walt's contact lists. Then I included all the major newspapers, news publications, blogs, chat rooms, and watch groups in the world I could find an address for with instruction to pass it on. I looked up at Kate who had been silently watching me. Taking a sip of the overcooked coffee, I whispered, "For you Walt," and hit the send button.

"In twelve hours the whole world will know. There's no turning back now."

Kate nodded. "It's time we got back. We've been gone a while. Ben will be worried. He sometimes acts like an over protective mother hen."

"Don't knock it." I said. "Having somebody that cares is a..." I couldn't finish the sentence.

"I understand," she said as we walked out. "Where's Horus? Wait a minute. Something's not right." She pushed me behind her and reached to the back of her waist and pulled out a gun.

"Stay right here. Let me check this out." As she approached the van a shadow descended from atop the vehicle, knocking the gun from her hand and landing onto of her. Kate was pinned to the ground and Kelp raised the sword to strike.

"Kate! No!" I shouted. The sword stopped. Kelp looked down on her. In that moment Kate managed to kick Kelp from atop her and roll toward her gun. Kelp used the hilt of the sword and struck her on the back of the head. She sprawled out face down on the ground. Kelp rolled her over and stared at her.

I turned to run. I felt a hand-like a vise grip my shoulder. I was spun around, and everything went black.

When I awoke I was in a windowless room, sparsely furnished with a leather sofa, an oversized chair and a three-legged table. I rose and tried the door.

"Hello, hello is anybody there?" Moments later the door opened and a small, slim, sedate-looking man with soft unassuming features came in.

"Is there anything I can get for you, Mr. Chapel?" he asked in a servile voice just over a whisper.

"Yeah, you can get me the hell out of here."

"I'm sorry Mr. Chapel, but I cannot do that. What I can do is provide you with food, drink, or medical assistance if you need it."

"Who are you?"

"You may call me Willis."

"Well, Willis. I don't like this one bit. What do you want with me?"

"I am not at liberty to speak on that, but I'm sure your questions will be answered shortly. Please try to cooperate and things will go much better for you. Now if there is nothing I can get for you..."

I headed for the door. I threw it open and looked into the cold hard eyes of Kelp banishing a steel blade. I stepped back from the door.

"As you can see," Willis said. "We," he emphasized the word, "are not alone." He raised his eyebrows as if to say something I didn't understand. Willis left, closing the door on Kelp's menacing glare.

There was a mumbling of voices in the hall. The door opened, and Hayden Ward walked in.

"Mr. Chapel," he said as he took a seat in the chair. "Do you know who I am?" I nodded yes. "Then you are aware that I do not play games. Where is the journal and the documents?"

"I don't have them. I'm sure your associates have already searched me."

"You know where they are, and I will have them. I will not bore you with threats. I will apply to your intelligence to see that your position is untenable." He stared at me with unblinking serpentine eyes.

"Mr. Chapel, I am aware of your alliance with the Ceteri. It is unfortunate that you have chosen to align yourself with those reprobates. I suppose that they have contaminated you with their fantastic dramas. I will not try to reeducate you, nor to recruit you. I will state plainly and succinctly that what you are in possession of will be mine. I will not wait on it for an unlimited time. Consider your options. You will see you only have one."

"Like Walt's options? Did you offer the same health plan to him?"

He shot me a look of utter contempt that froze the blood in my veins. "What happened to Mr. Vaughn was unfortunate, but that is in the past. The present issue is your continued good health. Do not tax me Mr. Vaughn. You will not appreciate the results." He stood and left the room never looking back.

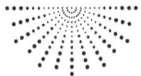

CHAPTER THIRTEEN

"*Y*ou sure you're alright?" Ben asked Kate as he pulled the van out of the parking lot.

"Yes, I'm fine. I'll just have a hefty lump on my head. I'm sorry, Ben."

"Don't apologize. We knew Kelp was out there. It had to be done. I'm just glad you're alright."

"Where's Horus and Chris?"

"I found Horus' body behind the building. He's in the back of the van." Kate turned and saw the blood-stained tarp covering her friend's body.

"No other signs of blood. Kelp must have taken Chris. That means that the Primae have him. Did he have a chance to set up the delivery?"

Kate nodded.

"Good," Ben said. "Chris doesn't know the location of our headquarters, so he can't give that away, but still he does know things they might be able to use." Ben cocked his head. "I doubt if even the Primae can bring down the whole internet."

"Kelp attacked us as we were leaving. Chris had already set it up on delay. It'll happen in about," she looked at her watch, " 10 hours." Kate paused and cleared the lump in her throat.

"Ben, why didn't Kelp kill me? I was down and there was no way I could stop the blow. Kelp hesitated. I looked straight into those soulless eyes and Kelp froze. What could have caused that?" Ben looked away shifting uncomfortably in his seat.

"What is it Ben? You know something, don't you?" Kate grabbed his arm causing the van to wobble across the center line. "Tell me. What is it?"

"I'm not sure."

"Yes, you are. You're always sure. Come on Ben. Don't hold out on me now. We've been through too much for you to do this to me. Now tell me."

"I hoped I'd never had to say this to you. But, I think Kelp is Jessie, your mother," he blurted out.

"My mother! No, that can't be possible? My mother is dead."

"I'm afraid it's true."

"How can you be sure?"

"I've been pretty close to Kelp and I'm sure." He looked straight ahead down the road. "Sometimes when they take someone they don't always execute them. At least not right away. Some are sentenced to punishment and imprisonment. Some are condemned to a special kind of hell. After a certain amount of time they are released to serve as bonded agents. I think that's why Kelp didn't kill you. She recognized you and didn't want to kill her own child."

"My mother," she said shaking her head. "I don't believe it. That creature cannot be my mother."

"You have to understand Kate, after you have been in that place you aren't you anymore. You are changed forever. You're no longer a First One. You're a thing stripped of all compassion and freewill. You're half a soul. They aren't first one anymore. They are not even male or female anymore. They're a base creature, a thing. Something closer to dead than alive. Something that's between worlds. That's why they look like phantoms. That place feeds off their souls, draining their very essence. They have no conscience, no feelings, no free will of their own, only a commitment to blind loyalty. How else do you think they could do the horrible things they do? Violence, pain, and death are all they understand. Being as they are, The First Ones can use them as tools to do the things their pure hands won't touch."

"How do you know this? How can you be sure?"

"My father told me. His best friend was like Kelp. He had to kill him. It was the greatest tragedy of his life." Ben hung his head. "To have to kill someone he considered a brother. It haunted him the rest of his life. He had no choice. It's the only way they can be released from their living nightmare." He added. "It was a mercy."

"That doesn't prove Kelp is my mother!"

"I've fought Kelp. I didn't want to believe what I was seeing, but after tonight, I'm sure it's Jessie. I'm sorry, honey. I know you don't want to hear this."

Kate leaned back into her seat and let the truth run from her eyes in a flood of tears. The look she saw when their eyes met she realized was cold, but there was something else there. A hint of recognition. Kate felt as if her heart had been stabbed with a shaft of ice. Her long dead mother, the woman she worshiped as a saint, was a mindless killing machine. No longer her mother, but her enemy. "A Perdidi Unum," she whispered. They rode to the warehouse in silence.

At the warehouse, Jacob and a half-dozen others were waiting. "Where's Horus and Chris?" asked Jacob, moving to Kate's side. Ben jerked his head toward the back of the van and said, "Kelp."

"I'll be happy to be the one to take that creature's head!" Jacob shouted.

Kate shot him a look, causing him to take a step back, then she stormed out of the room.

"What did I say?" Jacob asked.

"Just let her be. She'll be alright." Ben said, without explanation. "The Primae have Chris and we've got to get him back. I don't know how long he'll survive. We have a responsibility to him. But, we can't let the loss of any one individual stop what we have to do. We just have to keep moving forward. Everything is in play. In about nine hours the story will hit the web and the whole world will know. We have until then to do what we have to do. Check the supplies and the weapons. We move in four hours." Everyone broke ranks and got busy.

CHAPTER FOURTEEN

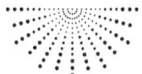

*H*ayden, followed by Willis, walked into a room rumbling from the frenzy Hanover had stirred up. Milborne was flushed and visibly shaken. While Stone's furrowed brows were tightly arched like an awning over his skeptical eyes, Hanover was triumphantly smiling at his work.

"Hayden, is this true?" asked Milborne.

"You will excuse me, but I was not privy to Hanover's performance, so I must be informed as to what it is you want conformation of."

"Why the string of dead bodies, the missing documents, the threats of exposure? Do I need to say more? You led us to believe that things were contained. That you had everything in hand. We had no idea of the length and breadth of the breaches that have occurred."

"William, I am sure that Hanover has exaggerated the point."

"Really," interrupted Hanover, and sitting erect in protest. "Is it true that documents, valuable incriminating documents that could compromise us, all are missing? Is it true that highly sensitive information has been made known to our enemies? Not to mention the cavalcade of bodies that have been left to provide a trail of evidence that may eventually implicate us all?" He swept his arm dramatically ending with his hand pointed at Willis. Who outwardly remained poised, but inside his heart raced like a stampeding stallion.

Hayden gave Hanover a look worthy of Medusa. Hanover merely smirked and leaned further onto the table. For the first time there was a creeping emotional inflection in Hayden's' voice.

"I will admit there have been some irregularities, but it has not altered our objectives nor interfered with their implementation."

"I beg to differ," Hanover said sternly. "It appears to me that things may be ever so gradually spiraling out of control. I propose a radical shift in tactic or the situation may totally fall off the rails."

"The nuclear option is out of the question, Hanover." Hayden growled through clenched teeth. A crimson flush painted his cheeks. "To abandon a plan that is so close to fruition would not only be foolish, it would be counterproductive and dangerous."

"Perhaps," interjected Stone, flapping his chubby cheeks as if he were chewing the words. "We should at least consider it. We should not limit our options. It's just not practical. After all Hanover has assured us that he has the means and..."

"This is pointless. We have discussed this and decided." Hayden insisted.

"You decided," corrected Hanover.

"To unanimous agreement, if I recall correctly," added Hayden, recovering his bluster.

"But Hayden, things have changed and I dare say have grown a bit concerning," pleaded Milborne. "Can't we at least reconsider the alternatives?"

"Very well," said an exasperated Hayden. "I will have refreshments provided and we can waste time rehashing old decisions," Hayden signaled to Willis, who acknowledged him with a bow and left the room.

"That's all we ask," responded Hanover, smiling and leaning back like a spider admiring the new web it had created.

CHAPTER FIFTEEN

*T*he door cracked opened and Willis slid in. He raised a silencing finger to his lips and whispered. "Mr. Chapel, I only have a moment. Your friends will be here soon. Stay alert." I looked at him with suspicious surprise. He nodded and slid back out the door.

Willis met Hayden in the hall outside the room of the meeting. "Come with me," said Hayden. They entered his office. Hayden seated himself. Willis stood before the large mahogany desk looking forward, never daring to allow their eyes to meet. "How long did you think that you could keep betraying me, Willis?" he asked casually.

"Sir?"

"Come now, man. Did you really think that you had not been detected? As long as your infractions were small and of no consequence I was willing to overlook your little acts of treason. After all our nature is not one of servitude. I could not reproach your acts of self-assertion. But, you have swayed too far from the path and your actions have become onerous, causing me bothersome complications. What do you have to say for yourself?"

Willis stood silently his only reaction was a bead of sweat that tickled down his back. Hayden nodded, and Kelp stepped from the shadows. With a lightening flash of steel Willis' head hit the ground. Hayden stood and left the room.

CHAPTER SIXTEEN

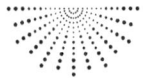

The Ceteri, alerted by Willis, ambushed the catering truck at the loading dock and confiscated the uniforms of the driver and assistants.

"What about Willis? It's about time we got him out of there and let him join us." said Kate.

"I think you're right. If things go well there won't be any need for him to remain here," agreed Ben.

They rode the service elevator up to the top floor and were met by a nervous young man who directed them to the conference room and then disappeared down a side stairwell. After the second elevator came up with the remainder of the group, they moved down the hall making sure the floor was empty except for the Primae. The group halted at another bank of elevators. Ben looked at his watch. "He should be here about now." Moments later, an elevator door opened, and a tall figure stepped out.

"Timothy, my brother," the two embraced.

Timothy Shanks swiped at Kate's nose. She smiled and hugged him. "Hi, Uncle Tim."

"How's my best girl?"

Kate opened her mouth to speak, looked at Ben, dropped her head and said, "We'll talk later."

"We're ready," said Ben. "We'll deal with the Primae. You find Chapel and get him out of here. We may need him later."

Timothy nodded and headed down the hall, his back pressed to the wall.

Outside of the conference room, Ben heard heated conversation. He looked back at his crew. "We'll go in first." He pointed to the three of them dressed as caterers. "When we're in and things begin to happen, that's your cue." Everyone nodded. He knocked and opened the door. Kate, Jacob and Ben entered pushing carts full of beverages and platters of food. The Ceteri members keep their heads lowered avoiding eye contact with the arguing Primae.

CHAPTER SEVENTEEN

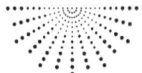

$\mathcal{T}$imothy approached a dimly lit hall and peered around the corner. Kelp was standing on guard. He drew his rapier and stepped openly in the hall. Kelp flickered, raised her blade and charged at him. Their blades met in the air with a loud clank. Exhibiting the speed of super human beings, they thrashed and parried casting steel on steel sparks into the dim light. Kelp drew first blood when she avoided a thrust by side stepping an arching swing and reacted with an upward slash that cut across Timothy's left arm. He shouted and retreated.

The commotion caused the Primae to look up. Hayden headed toward the door. Ben, Kate, and Jacob sprang into action producing blades and charging forward. The room erupted in chaos. Everyone rose, sending their chairs falling to the floor. The door burst open and the rest of the group streamed in sending Hayden back pedaling. Jacob sliced at Stone, who despite his healthy build moved with surprising fluidity. Ben managed to nick Milborne before Milborne retreated behind a chair he grabbed as a shield. Hanover crashed into the incoming crowd trying to make a way out of the door. They pushed him back and he planted his hand on the table and cartwheeled over it. He snatched the pole of a flag stand and brandished it as a weapon.

Hayden made it back to the table, reached under it and came up with a blade of his own. Kate joined Jacob and they descended on Stone cutting him several times before Kate delivered a decisive swipe that removed Stone's head. His large body swayed and teetered before falling to the floor with a thud. Ben sliced away at Milborne's chair. Joined by one of his second tier, they backed Milborne into a corner. Hayden ran forward pivoted and removed the head of one of the Ceteri and continued the swing to slash another across the chest, sending him to his knees. Hanover used his spear to impale one of the Ceteri who was rushing him and took his sword. With his chair now down to a couple of sticks, Milborne held them like daggers and charged screaming, "I'll kill you...you filthy..."

Ben went high, and his companion went low. They left Milborne in three pieces. Ben approached Hayden, followed by Kate. Hayden smiled and faced the two, taunting them with his blood-stained sword.

CHAPTER EIGHTEEN

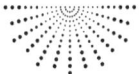

*K*elp, swinging for the kill, over-extended herself and received a nasty slash across her thigh. Kelp winced and stepped with a noticeable limp. Timothy faked a lunge and pivoted instead delivering another deep cut down her back. With pale pink blood covering her clothes, Kelp was more visible than ever. She growled and charged, swinging her blade side to side. Timothy dropped and rolling under her blade and delivering another slice across her other thigh with the effort. Kelp collapsed to her knees. The hat fell from Kelp's head and she looked up at Timothy with blood-red eyes of rage.

Timothy froze. A flash of recognition crossed his face. "Jess! Oh my God! Jess. Is that you?"

His shock made him drop his guard. Kelp took advantage. She lunged forward and stabbed him in the side.

"Jess. No!" he shouted falling back. "Don't make me do this! We can do something for you. Think about Kate!"

Kelp stood and leapt at him. Timothy turned on his right foot and brought the sword down on her neck as he spun around her. The blade sliced through her neck cleanly and swiftly. Her head dropped to the floor. Eyes of red flame burned up at him before blinking to a cold dead black. He knelt beside the blackened body and stared at the face he once knew as a friend. Rising on wobbly legs, and holding his bloody gut, he went to the door.

"Shanks," shouted a surprised and relieved Chris when the door flew open. "What are you doing here?"

"Saving your sorry ass. Now come on. I may need a little saving myself." Chris saw the bloody hand pressing into Shanks side and rushed to hold him up. Together they made their way to the elevators. The noise of fighting down the hall drew their attention.

"That's the others, isn't it? We've got to try to help the others?" Chris said.

"No sir. I'm all played out. Don't worry. They can handle it. No argument. Let's go," Timothy ordered.

"Why didn't you tell me that you were part of this?"

"Before you met the Ceteri it would have been useless information. After they made contact, things were moving too fast there was no chance."

"What about West, is he in on this too?"

"Hey, Mr. Reporter." he said looking down at his bloody hand. "Can we wait a while on the interview?"

"Sorry," We made our way down to a sedan and headed to the warehouse.

CHAPTER NINETEEN

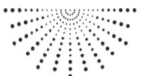

*J*acob and his companion advanced on Hanover, who hopped on the table and danced to the opposite end.

"Come on, you half-breeds," he said. Jacob approached causally. Hanover rushed in and met a slice across his arm causing him to scream out in pain and drop his sword. Hanover slid his finger along the blade and tasted the blood. He spit it out, "an inferior vintage."

Hanover slashed at Jacob, who bobbed on his toes, faked a left pivot and spun 180 degrees to the right swinging up the sword and slicing Hanover across the neck. Hanover stood in shock, his hand clasped to his neck. He gurgled out a curse and fell to the floor his head dangling by a small string of skin. "How would someone with taste like yours know?" Jacob said looking down at the body. He rushed over to aid his fallen companion.

Ben and Kate stood face to face with Hayden, swords at the ready. Hayden met them both stoke for stoke never yielding any ground. His speed and reflexes thwarted every attempt thrown at him.

"It's over Hayden," Ben said. "It is only a matter of time before we put an end to this."

"It is not over. I will never be over until you and your human stench has been eliminated."

"You're right," said Kate. "Not until there isn't a First One anywhere."

Ben swung wide, opening himself up to receive a powerful counter slash that took off his left arm at the elbow. He cried out in pain and fell back. Kate stepped in as Hayden took a moment to enjoy his handy work. She swung, slicing Hayden across the midsection causing a deep cut that almost disemboweled him. He staggered back, and Ben, energized by his anger and pain, swung his sword at eye level and cleaved Hayden's head in two. Blood and brains sprayed across the room. Hayden toppled over like a fallen tree. Ben collapsed to his knees, blood still gushing from his severed arm. Kate rushed to hold him up. She ripped up her smock and placed a tourniquet around his bleeding arm.

"Oh my God, Ben. You've lost so much blood." Her eyes were wide with fear and panic. "What can I do?"

"You've done enough. I'm not alright, but I'm not as bad off as I look. The tourniquet will do until we get back to the warehouse."

Jacob, supporting his injured comrade, hobbled over. "Can we get out of here?"

"Can you make it down without me?" Kate asked with a plea in her eyes. Ben gave her a worried stare. "I have to, Ben. You know I have to."

"Alright," he grunted standing on wobbly legs. "Don't be long. We're in pretty bad shape here. I'm going to have Jacob set the charges for fifteen minutes. This place is going up like the fourth of July. We can't leave any evidence we were here." She nodded, picked up her sword, and headed out.

"Kate," Jacob yelled after her.

"Let her go, Jacob. She has to do this." Ben said, leaning against the wall as he watched her run out the door.

Kate found Willis's body in Hayden's office and continued down the hall until she found Kelp's body. Unsteady and emotional, she knelt down to the blackened body. Searching desperately, she looked to find the mother she remembered. Unable to see the woman she once knew, Kate settled for the memory she had been holding in her heart since childhood. "I'll never forgot you." Her voice was hoarse and choked with emotions.

"I don't care who or what you have become, I remember you. I love you and missed you. I'm sorry I didn't find a way to save you. To bring you back to me." Shaken and tearful, Kate rose and ran down to join the others.

CHAPTER TWENTY

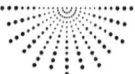

*T*he airwaves were frantic with the news of the explosion and fire at the penthouse offices of Global Oil. Helicopters with hoses and drop buckets were used to douse the blaze with gallons of water and fire retardant, but to little benefit. The blaze had a life of its own. It burned intensely for thirty-six hours, taking off the top eighteen floors and sending giant plumes of smoke in the sky. The building was so tall and the fire was so high up, there was little the fire department could do but monitor the burn and hope the fire suppression system would help with the lower floors. Pictures of the inferno dominated the news until they were eclipsed by the article going viral on the web.

The world erupted with outrage. There was blanket coverage all over the world. Reaction was quick, intense, and violent. The frenzy couldn't be suppressed. Spontaneous protests, rallies, demonstrations, and riots occurred all over the planet. Some officials were dragged screaming from their offices and hung in the streets. Others committed suicide, and some surrendered themselves to authorities, seeking protection. The people were crazed with anger. Most felt betrayed and duped; their desire for vengeance was insatiable.

Conspiracy theories of all kinds cropped up, everything from global crime syndicates, to governmental overreach, to new world imperialism, to alien invaders. No person or institution was free from suspicion. Those who tried to calm things down or were slow to judgement were labeled collaborators and were attacked where ever they were found.

The article and documentation caused governments and international corporations to run for cover, trying to invent plausible stories of denial. Alliances started falling like pebbles before an avalanche. Everyone began pointing fingers and making their own accusations of complicity, corruption, coercion, bribery, and graft. Allies turned on each other at a rate that over whelmed the world's justice systems. People were clamoring to be the first one to speak out and speak up, making deals that would save their lives and their fortunes.

The world's stock market collapsed, and commerce came to a virtual halt. Economic systems were in a free fall. Governmental bodies everywhere were declaring "States of Emergency" and "Martial Law," but with little or no authority, their efforts were in vain. They issued orders and decrees their armies and police forces refused to enforce. People, for once, having proof they couldn't trust their elected officials and their governmental bodies started to take personal responsibility and citizen control. A new sense of community was being born amid the chaos. Militias and citizen patrols, grassroots committees and NGOs popped up everywhere, taking possession of government buildings, corporate facilities, and public lands. Some cities burned like giant bon fires. Others maintained a controlled anarchy, with a citizenry living on a razor's edge. Cries of unity, solidarity, and the people first were heard on every street corner.

Slowly, cooler heads began to rise to positions of authority. The anger and frustration of the people began to turn to worry and despair. The populace was forced to take another look at the state of the world. The realization that mankind and the planet itself, were in dire straits caused a reorganization of priorities. New calls for responsible actions were taking over where before there were only the calls of more, faster, and bigger. Ideas and initiatives for progressive action, forward-thinking responses, and responsible behavior were taking hold and growing. People were frightened but determined to right the ship. People everywhere begged the scientific community to come up with a global survival plan.

The need to have someone to blame and punish caused an intense manhunt for Hayden Ward, Calvin Stone, Reverend William Milborne, Douglas Henry Hanover, and half a dozen others. Their effigies were burned in the streets, along with the logos and standards of most major corporations. Nothing alleviates guilt and shame like finding another to blame and punish. A multinational line had formed issuing criminal indictments and demanding extradition.

The name of Walter Henry Vaughn was becoming an honored household name. He was hailed as a global hero. People everywhere were praising him and offering awards and accolades along with their heartfelt thanks. Some people refused to believe that he was dead. They were convinced he was in hiding for his safety. Offers of sanctuary and protection were coming in from all corners trying to bring him to the spot light.

"It was considerate of you to put Walter's name on the article," Kate said. "He would be very proud of you."

"It was his story and his story to tell. I just wrote it. He deserves the credit for it and for so many other things. Besides, it's the least I could do for him; making sure his name and his sacrifice aren't forgotten."

"What are you going to do now?" she asked.

"I don't know. I can't go back to the newspaper. After finding out about Spencer I just wouldn't feel comfortable there anymore." I turned away from Kate.

"Walt was my anchor. Now that he's gone, I feel adrift. I don't know who I am or who I can trust anymore. I don't know where I belong. All I know is I'm not who I was. It seems everything has changed. I think I'll leave for a while. There're too many memories and too much to remind me of him."

"Yeah, memories," Kate swallowed a sigh.

"Maybe I'll join the rebuilding efforts. We have a world to save and make right. What about you? Now that the Primae is defeated what will you do?"

"All the Primae weren't defeated. The rest have just gone to regroup. This was just a setback for them. We'll have to stay on our guard. There are others out there like us, like me. We've got to find them and..." Kate smiled and changed the subject.

"I hope we've stopped things in enough time to reverse the effects. I know there will still be difficult times ahead, but hopefully we haven't gotten so close to the tipping point that our efforts were in vain. I'll be counting on you guys to pull us back from the edge."

I nodded in agreement. "The road back will be a difficult one with lots of potholes and pitfalls. But, it's a road we have to travel. I think we're up to it." We shared a worried smile. "I didn't tell the whole story. Do you think the world is ready to learn the truth about you? I mean about Angels, Nephilims, and all that?"

"I don't know. Maybe we shouldn't press our luck. With all that's already going on, I'm not sure the world could take it. And I'm not so sure we're ready to become the center of attention."

"I'm don't know, Kate. I think people can handle it. I'll admit it did freak me out a little at first. I got over it. I think everybody else would too. After all, differences aren't new. Maybe we've been under estimating ourselves for too long. It can be hard and scary to face the truth, but when you do, it's not so bad. You get the chance to learn just what you're made of. There's no reason we can't for once think more of ourselves than always just thinking about ourselves."

The End of Part I

PART II
THE CETERI

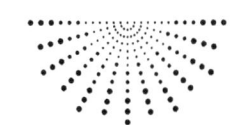

CHAPTER TWENTY-ONE

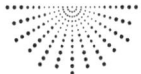

"*A*re you going to avoid me forever or are we going to eventually talk about this?"

"I'm sorry Uncle Tim," Kate mumbled like a child apologizing for not putting away her toys.

"I haven't been avoiding you on purpose. I've been really busy." Timothy raised his brow and gave her a sideways glance. Kate read the signs and relented.

"Okay, may be a little." She looked away. "I'm just not ready to talk about it right now. I'm still processing."

"Kate, I won't insult you by saying I know how you feel. I just want you to know, I knew Jessie a lot longer than you. She was a friend, a good friend. I loved her too." The memory snagged at the sides of his mouth, dragging it into a frown. He stroked her hair.

"You look a lot like her when she was your age," Tim cleared his throat. "Ah...I know you must have some pretty messed up feelings about me right now. Just know that I love you, kid. When you're ready to talk about this I will be here. Ready and willing..." Tim spread his arms wide, a pleading look in his eyes.

Kate hesitantly move in and hugged him. *"How am I ever going to make this right with her?"* Tim thought. *"How do I heal this?"*

"I love you too, Uncle Tim. I promise. We'll talk soon." The words left her lips, but never reached her eyes.

Tim kissed the top of her head. "Okay sweetie. No pressure." Stepping back, he looked her in the eyes and smiled. "See you at the meeting later?" Kate forced a smile and walked away.

CHAPTER TWENTY-TWO

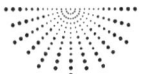

"We've got a lead on a couple of kids. I'd like to get on this as quickly as possible. There has been some disturbing news that the Primae have changed their tactics since our take down of Hayden and his bunch. We're moved from being a nuisance to a real threat."

Ben paused and looked at the group. "A more radical arm has taken over. They're no longer just relocating the young ones. They're eliminating them."

"You mean they're killing them, don't you?" Kate corrected him.

Ben pressed his lips together, embarrassed to say it. "I'm afraid so." He rubbed his stump of an arm and looked to Timothy for support.

Jacob leapt from his seat. "Those bastards. Coming after us is one thing. We can hit back, but to go after the kids is…"

"What are we going to do about it?" Kate interrupted her chest heaving with anger.

"We'll deal with the Primae later. The first order of business is getting to the kids before they do. There are two we're sure of. The first is Wanda. She's from Greece. Her father Claude had already warned his wife Kristina that someday the Primae might come for him. They tried to remain off the grid but were discovered and tracked down. He left her with instructions on how to get in touch with us. With the information she gave us we have been able to locate the girl. She's been adopted by a family in Texas. The adopted family have no idea about her origins. With the Primae's new policy she and her new family are in jeopardy. Since we know exactly where she is, she will be our first concern."

"Are they bypassing the orphanages these days?"

"When she was taken they weren't. But they are now, Josh. She was in play before everything changed. Wanda's less than a year old. The younger the child, the easier it is to get them adopted. She was snatched up immediately." He signed to his right. "You're up, Tim."

"We don't have the exact location of the second child," Timothy began. "But we do know that he's on the island of Puerto Rico. There's something a little screwy about this case. They speak English almost as much as Spanish in Puerto Rico. That goes against the Primae's past practices of putting the children in countries where they don't speak the language. It seems this would pose a problem. This child is eight years old and can tell someone what happened."

Timothy paused and ran his hand through his hair, resting his hand on the back of his head as if he was keeping the thoughts from seeping out his scalp. "I won't be going with the team after the girl. I'm heading to the island to pin down the boy's location. Ben will join me once the girl is safe. By the time he gets there I hope to have done the preliminary work and we can extricate the boy quickly."

"Any questions?" The room remained silent. Timothy held up a finger walked to the door and waved in a thin, weary-eyed man with dred locks. Exhaustion hung on his face like sweat. Timothy and his guest stood at the head of the table.

"This is Bernard Kaplan. His son is our lost boy." He turned to Kaplan. "Why don't you fill them in, Kap?" Kaplan wavered. "Go ahead, man. You're among friends here."

Kaplan scanned the faces at the table. He braced his self against the table, leaning forward and talked to its surface. His braids hung down like the branches of a weeping willow.

"Helen, my wife, was murdered..." His voice was heavy with

emotions. "I was away on business when they came for her. The police located me and told me she was dead." From behind the tangle of hair a tear struck the table.

"I braced myself and asked about my son, afraid he was dead as well, but there was no sign of him. He had disappeared." Anger began to mix with the sorrow. He raised his head and looked at the faces around the table. "I flew home and began searching for him. I searched everywhere. I begged the police and the government for more help. I even hired a private detective. I hoped for a ransom demand or something, but nothing ever came."

Kaplan looked away wiping his face with the back of his sleeve. "Then last week Timothy came to me and told me about all of this. I still don't know if I believe all this, but I'll be a part of anything, I'll do anything, or I'll go anywhere to get my son back."

Kaplan swallowed a sob. "He's all I have left." A whimper riding on a demand entered his voice. "Please help me." He collapsed into a chair, covered his face with his hands, and gave way to his sorrow.

Timothy rested his hand on his shoulder. "We'll get him back, Kap." Timothy turned to the others. "We had Kap speak so we could put a face on this thing. We want you to understand how urgent things have become. Not just for the kids, but for their parents as well. These are our people. They are us. The boy's name is Jairo. He may be living on the streets, lost in the population, or in some rural orphanage and no one believes his story. I'll have to cover all bases when I get there. Luckily Puerto Rico is a contained space. As long as he remains on the island, I'll eventually find him. Either way he's alone in a strange place and no doubt scared. Few of us can image how he must feel." Timothy looked to Kate.

"They left you in Poland didn't they Kate?" She nodded and turned away as if the memory wouldn't find her if it didn't see her face.

Try as she might, the pictures of huddled masses of ragged and unfed children flooded her mind. The feelings of cold and hunger clung to her memory like wet clothes. The two years of not knowing where she was and why nearly drove her crazy. Memories of angry strangers yelling at her in a language she could not understand, the beatings, the nights spent scared and crying, and curled up in a dirty corner, still haunted her dreams. Watching her father die and her mother being dragged away begging and screaming, and now dumped in a strange place was too much for her young mind to bear. Closing herself off and withdrawing into her own world saved her life and her sanity.

"Kate are you with us?" Ben asked returning to leading the meeting.

"Yeah, I'm here. I was just wondering when we're going to get started?"

"If you had been paying attention you would know that you aren't going. Your assignment is here to help Titus."

Kate jumped to her feet. "Ben, you can't leave me behind. I want to go. I need..."

Ben interrupted her. "The decisions have been made, Kate. Our team has been set." Kate started to speak.

"That's final. You are dismissed." Kate puffed up her cheeks like a chipmunk with a mouth full of berries and stomped from the room.

Timothy stood next to him. "If I were you. I'd stay away from the weapons rooms for a while."

"She'll be alright. She's just too close to this." He waved his hand. "She's too emotionally attached."

"I want to come along, Timothy." Kaplan said joining their side.

"Sorry, Kap. This will be too dangerous. I'll probably run into the Primae and things could get dicey. Besides I'll move faster alone."

"You can't stop me, Timothy. I'm going. He's my son."

"I agree with Timothy," said Ben. "You would be a liability. There is no way I can allow you to go. You'd help more staying out of the way."

"He's my son, damn it! You can't do this!"

"You're not going! This conversation is over!" Ben shouted.

"I guess I'm dismissed, too!" Kaplan shouted as he stormed out.

"Two for two. You're not a very popular guy today Ben."

"The price of leadership," Ben sighed, falling back into a chair, stroking his stump like a kitten.

CHAPTER TWENTY-THREE

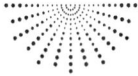

"*B*en, we need to talk."

"Is it your turn, Titus? Is everybody around here out to pick a fight with me today?"

"I don't know about everybody else, but you assigned me to look after things while you're gone. I'm just trying to give you a heads up before you leave."

Ben nodded. "I'm sorry, Titus. Things have me a little on edge."

"Uh huh," Titus replied. "Anyway, it's crazy out there, man. Here's the condensed version. First, we've been arranging your travel. We're going for speed rather than comfort. I found a sweet tricked out Charger. It's super charged with four on the floor and..."

"I got it Titus. It's fast."

"Oh yeah, okay." Titus responded, a bit dejected.

"Anyway, the borders are locked down tight. Scrutiny of travelers is tighter than spandex on a fat lady. Everybody is suspicious of everybody else and on their guard. Flying inside the country is more difficult than flying out. That's one reason for the car. We've arranged for Calvin Little in Corpus Christi to fly you to the island once you've rescued the girl. He runs a charter with a couple of corporate Cessnas™."

Titus held up his hand. "Before you ask, why Texas and not Florida, let me tell you. Florida is suffering from some pretty nasty flooding and most of the southern coastal areas are dealing with some treacherous winds and ocean surges. So, you're going by way of Texas. As for getting there, you can make it in about 20 hours. The only real problem will be gas. It may be scarce, so you'll have to keep an eye out for any opportunity to fill up. You have to be ready to move as soon as we get the transport in place. We're fighting the elements here. Oh yeah, keep a special eye out for road bandits. The stories are that they're raping and robbing everybody they can catch. As you would expect, people are taking advantage of this crisis."

"We'll be careful. Go ahead."

"Second, David's been going over our finances and things look okay so far but, the markets are in flux. I mean, seriously. It's like tracking an ant through tall grass trying to compute money these days. Luckily our reserves weren't in the public domain. Hopefully the monetary system will level off and stabilize soon or our dollars will be as dead as the presidents on them. The value of things changes from hour to hour. It's gotten real cutthroat out there. People are charging black market prices for the simplest of items. Thirty dollars for a loaf of bread, fifty dollars for a gallon of milk." He shook his head.

"I hope somebody gets a handle on things soon or we're going to see real war breaking out everywhere. Nothing makes people madder than being hungry."

Ben stared ahead, gripping the stub that was his left arm.

"Third, the Primae. That's a big question mark. They've all gone ghost. We can't find any of them anywhere. The ones we know of have dumped their shells and you know, returned to the "big where ever." We can't be positive how large their numbers were, but we're pretty sure there weren't many actually here. I have no doubt the hard-core ones will reappear, but we don't have any idea where or as who. Whenever they show up, they will be brand new and more determined than ever. That whipping we gave them has no doubt pissed them off. You'll have to be on your guard until you figure out who's who." He gave an embarrassed smile. "I guess you already knew that part, huh?" Ben slowly nodded. "Just trying to be thorough. As for anything else, it can wait until you get back."

"Nothing you want to yell at me about?"

Titus hunched his shoulders. "I could if you want. I heard about you and Kate and I figured I would give you a break. But if you insist..."

"No thanks. I appreciate you staying on top of things. Keep up the good work. You have the authority to do whatever you think is necessary. I've got other fires to put out."

"Go in with cake." Titus yelled at the retreating man. "Kate loves cake."

CHAPTER TWENTY-FOUR

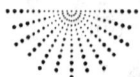

*B*en knocked on the door for the third time. "I know you're in there, and I'm not going away." The door unlatched and cracked about as wide as a reluctant clam shell. Ben pushed open the door to see Kate sweaty and panting her way through a vigorous routine with a set of barbells, her lean firm muscles handling the twenty-five-pound weights with ease. She stared straight ahead as if unaware of his presence.

"I've known you long enough to know that look. You've been perfecting it since you were a little girl. It's the same one you'd use when I'd make you do your homework. You're going to pretend to ignore me and not respond," he sighed.

"So, I'll say what I came to say and leave. You can pout and mope until you feel adult enough to finally come and talk to me."

Kate never raised her eyes from the weights. Breathing in with every lift and breathing out with every return, her concentration locked.

"You're too close to these kids and their circumstances, Kate. You've allowed yourself to be drawn in and your judgement suffers. I need someone in the field who can remain unattached and level-headed. I can't risk the safety of the team on someone who is acting unpredictably. Working from pure emotions is a bad strategy."

Frustration creeping into his voice, Ben blurted out his words as if they were hot coffee burning his tongue. "I know finding out about your mother has been difficult. Then losing her again. I know you have some issues with Tim about that, but damn it, Kate. You're not the only one who lost something. You're not the only one who loved her. We all lost. We're a small community. We all knew Jess and loved her."

Ben rubbed his stub. "Your emotional outbursts have been so frequent and intense lately, I feel sometimes I don't know you. If you can't hold it together, then you've just got to sit things out until you can."

Ben threw his arm up in the air in frustration. Kate stopped in the middle of her rep and stared at him with eyes he had never seen before. There was anger and indifference in those eyes. The power of her gaze caused him to take a step back and rebalance. Steeling himself, he pressed on.

"During the last rescue, you could have gotten yourself killed. Against my expressed instructions, you ran into that building. Not securing the perimeter, not checking for ambushes, not caring what the situation was for your team. Overwhelmed by your emotions you put yourself, everyone else, and the mission in danger. I want to save these kids as much as anyone, but if we get ourselves killed, we can't save anybody. Surely you can see this."

He ran his hand over his face trying to wipe the anger from his voice. "Yes, you understand better than most what these kids are going through, but you're reckless about it. I can't have that." Ben sighed. His chest deflated like a leaky balloon.

"Get it together Kate, or you could be off the team for good." He turned and left the room.

Kate let her weights crash to the floor. *"So, what,"* she thought. *"I'm passionate. I care. Is that wrong? Just because I don't do things by his stick-to-the-rules book doesn't mean that I'm reckless. It's not about me. It's about the kids."*

Every time she saw one of the kids her blood would boil. It made her relive the hell of those years in Poland. Looking into their eyes Kate felt every hurt and every pain they had suffered. It was like looking into a broken mirror into the past; the images distorted and fragmented, slicing into a familiar nightmare. She placed her elbows on her knees and buried her face in her hands. Her passions wedged up inside her like a bite of unchewed food.

Dark thoughts swirled and mingled haphazardly in her mind. *"Kelp, Kelp was my mother."* A wave of nausea and shame washed over her. Kate wasn't sure if she was ashamed of Kelp or ashamed of herself for feeling as she did.

"She killed so many. She tried to kill me. Damn it. I wanted to kill her." A confusing mixture of guilt, anger, and heartache engulfed her. Learning the truth had brought up long buried memories, turned old feelings upside down, and tossed them into the sky to rain down on her like hot ashes from a volcano she thought was long dead.

Feelings she believed she'd dealt with and buried away resurfaced to poke holes in her new reality. Seeing what her mother had become and knowing what she had done made her angry and sad all at once. The sight of her dead body made everything so cold and so real. Real in a painful way. Real in an angry way. Real in a crazy way. She was an orphan again, helpless and alone. At the mercy of whatever happened around her. The scab had been pulled off the sore and it hurt like hell.

The chaos of her feeling swung wider and faster when she thought of Tim. *"You took her away from me again. You killed her."* Kate picked up the weight and heaved it across the room. It crashed into the wall leaving a jagged hole. *"I know it was Kelp, but I can't forgive you for doing it."*

Kate panted and sweated like a marathoner approaching the finish line. Leaning back on the weight bench, her rage turned into a headache. She glanced at the bed with the thought of laying down to sleep it off. On the bed was a slice of yellow cake with caramel icing. Her favorite. She cried.

CHAPTER TWENTY-FIVE

ate walked into the warehouse fully ready to be dressed down and denied. A turbulent night of unsettling dreams and unpleasant introspection left her emotionally drained and humble in a way she hadn't felt since she was in training.

"Hey Kate, you ready to go?" Jacob asked, wearing a smile too big for his face. His sparkling blue eyes brighter than usual.

"I'm not going, remember? My assignment is here with Titus."

"I guess you haven't talked to Ben yet. Well you better get in there. He's in the office," he winked. "You're going. Don't let on that you know." Calling over his shoulder as he walked away. "I'll see you later."

"Hey Jacob, do you know where Tim is?" Kate asked.

He yelled back. "He's long gone, Kate. Left early this morning."

Kate felt relief; she wasn't sure if she could face him. She knew she had to, but later was better. Approaching the office, Kate rapped on the door and entered. Ben looked up and returned to his writing. "I was just about to send for you. It seems there has been a change in plans. Mary was going so that she and Jacob could escort the child back, but Mary's needed in Vancouver. I will need you to take her place. We leave in two hours." Ben never raised his head from his work.

"Okay, I'll be ready," Kate said softly, not sure why she wasn't more elated. She turned to leave but turned back. "Ben, I want to…"

He stopped writing but looked down at the paper as if he was reading the words. "Don't apologize. I can see that whatever is going on with you runs deeper than I thought. Don't say things now that you don't mean just to smooth things over. Let's get through this job. You wrestle with your demons. Then and only then, we can work on getting back to where we were." He went back to his writing.

Kate closed her eyes and the words fell out of her mouth. "I owe you and Tim and everyone an apology. I haven't wanted to face my demons. My own truths. It was too hard to look in the holes in my life. I'd just jump over them and ignore what was brewing inside me. It's been easier to blame it on everyone and everything else. I've spent the last few hours kicking myself in the butt." Kate bit her lips. "I'm sorry. I don't know what else to say. She turned and left the office.

Ben looked up at the closing door, smiled and lit a cigar.

CHAPTER TWENTY-SIX

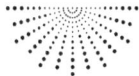

*E*arly that afternoon Ben, Jacob, and Kate left the warehouse heading down I-75 away from Detroit and into Ohio.

"It will take us the better part of 20 hours to get to Houston. We'll get there tomorrow around noon. By nightfall we should have the girl and you two can be on your way back. I'll continue down to Corpus Christy, take the plane to the island and meet up with Tim. Hopefully he'll have found the boy and we can all be back home in about 4 days. Everybody got that?"

"Why does it take two of us to bring the girl back?" Kate asked.

"It'll look less suspicious and will be safer if it's a couple traveling with their daughter." The warmth hadn't returned to his voice.

"Yeah," said Jacob. "Things are messed up out here on the roads. Since everything went to hell, it's not safe to be out here alone. Militias and gangs are everywhere looking to cash in and take advantage of anyone they can."

"I'm hoping we don't run into any that. We don't need the distraction," said Ben. "Some of the reports I've been reading are making pretty wild claims. Everybody is practicing their own brand of justice. Law enforcement is coming back on line, but it's a slow process."

"If we have to take some of the back roads to avoid trouble it'll take us longer than 20 hours to get to Houston," Jacob added.

"Better that than the alternative," Ben said.

Kate hunkered down in the back seat. "I'll get a little sleep so I can be ready when it's my turn to drive. I assume we don't want to stop."

"That right, just restroom breaks. We won't be stopping at every sign post that says food..." he looked to Jacob who hunched his shoulders proclaiming his innocence.

Kate laughed. It felt good to laugh. There hadn't been much to laugh about lately. As Ben and Jacob squabbled, she closed her eyes and drifted into the hum and sway of the car.

Several hours, one gas stop, and one restroom break later, Ben pulled the car into the parking lot of road side sandwich shop.

"Wake up sleeping beauty," he said, rousing Kate from her slumber.

"Where are we?"

"We're in Missouri. In about an hour we get to Arkansas. We're making good time." Jacob said.

"Let's stretch our legs, get something to eat and one of you can take over the driving." Ben headed to the men's room without waiting for a response.

"Turkey with light mayo and an iced tea?" Jacob asked, his eyes broadcasting his delight.

"That sounds good." Kate answered as she stepped from the back seat reaching for the clouds to release the stiffness in her back. Jacob took off for the sandwich shop. Kate headed to the ladies' room. Meeting back at the car they decided to sit at a picnic table and eat. "Are you going to eat that whole thing?" Kate asked Jacob, looking at the large pepperoni pizza he ordered. Jacob smiled and shoved another slice into his already full mouth.

"I need another pop. Anybody want something?" Jacob asked, heading for the soda vending machine.

"Kate..." Ben started.

She cut him off. "You were right. I've been off my game lately. Everything you said was true. With what's been going on, I've been unsettled. I promise I'll do better." Ben reached across the table and squeezed her hand.

Fifteen minutes later they were back on the road with Jacob at the wheel.

"You ride shot gun. I need to drive. After seven hours of listening to Ben and every country station between here and Michigan, I need the relief." Ben ignored him and dove head first under the blanket in the back. He was asleep in minutes.

"Did he sing?" Kate asked jokingly.

"If you can call it that. Sounded more like a moose mating call. Waa- woo," they laughed. "Kate, I don't mean to pry, but is everything alright? I mean you haven't been yourself lately."

Kate leaned back in her seat and let out a long sigh. "I know I've been a real handful lately. Things just haven't felt right. I've got so much racing around in my head. I can't seem to find my balance. It's been hard to stay focused."

"I understand. If you ever need somebody to talk to or just talk at, you know that I'm here for you. Just say the word and you can talk until you're all talked out."

"Thanks Jacob. I'll keep that in mind. Right now, I just need to think things through."

"Okay, whatever you want. I do mean whatever. I...I miss the way we used to be. You know how we were growing up. We used to talk and laugh and have fun together. When's the last time you went anywhere and just let loose? Everything has gotten so serious. There's never any fun anymore." Jacob said.

"I know things have really changed. Looking back, it seems like another world. Maybe this is the new normal. Maybe we just have to find our fun and laughs where we can." They rode on in silence watching the orange red sun lower itself into the horizon.

Just after dark, on a flat desolate stretch of West 30 near Texarkana between the Arkansas and Texas border, Jacob began slowing down.

"Time for a bathroom break already?" Kate asked.

"No," Jacob said, staring concerned through the front window.

"There's something across the road up ahead. It's a semi. Maybe he's in trouble or maybe we're in trouble. Stay alert." Kate shook her head and felt to make sure her weapon was within reach.

"Should I wake up Ben?"

"No, hopefully that won't be necessary. We should let the old moose sleep. We can handle this. Stay in the car while I see what's going on."

The car stopped fifty feet in front of the truck. A half-dozen burly unshaved men stepped into view. Jacob survey the group as he exited the car. Two of the men leaned on long planks of wood. One held a baseball bat, another lingered, half hidden in the shadows dressed in a long black coat. The other two sported a collection of muscle that said they didn't need weapons; they were weapons.

Using his thumb, the leader tilted back his straw cowboy hat and eyed Jacob. Ending his appraisal with a gap-toothed smirk. "Welcome to the I-40 inspection station. This is where you pay for the privilege of driving on our road." He stepped forward.

"I didn't realize this was a toll road."

"'Tis now. Thangs have changed lately."

"What's the toll?" Josh asked crossing his arms.

"Everything you got that we want." He sneered looking around Jacob at Kate. His cohorts laughed.

"Look man, we just need to pass through. We don't have anything of value and we don't want any trouble."

"We'll decide what's of value," said the big man. "Just do what you're told. Start by telling that pretty little woman of yours to come out here and join the party."

"Jacob, is everything alright?" Kate asked stepping from the car.

"Everything's alright, Kate. Just stay in the car."

"Hey Kate. Come join the party!" The leader yelled moving toward the car. Jacob moved to block his path.

"You're not being very friendly, Jacob," he said, reaching out to grab him. Jacob dodged his powerful claw, grabbed his wrist twisting his arm and brought him to his knees. He cried out as Jacob forced him to the ground and put his foot on his back.

Kate appeared at his side. Her sword to the ready. "I told you to stay in the car."

"Thanks for the chivalry, but I think you may need a little back up."

The gang started moving forward forming a circle around them. The leader groaned in pain.

"You made a big mistake, Jacob. Both of you are gonna pay and you're gonna pay big."

"Are you ready for this?" Jacob asked looking at Kate.

She nodded. "I'm afraid we don't have a choice."

Jacob nodded and kicked the arm of the leader. At the sound of breaking bone and the primal scream of pain that followed, they sprang into action. Jacob caught the end of the bat that was aiming for his head and wrenched it from its wielder. Swinging it back he downed the man and began a bat and board battle with the other. Kate ran at one of the muscle men. She ducked under his swing and sliced his thigh causing him to crash to the ground screaming in pain. The other hulk managed to graze her with a swipe of his massive hands and she fell to the ground and rolled to a crouching position. As he charged her again she pivoted, swung her sword opening a long gash down his arm. "Aw...you bitch!" he shouted.

A scream and a shotgun blast brought the scene to an abrupt end. All eyes turned toward the sound at the rear of the truck. Two figures stepped out of the shadows. One supporting a bloody hand and a grimace. The other was Ben with a shotgun and a frown.

"You boys need to gather up your wounded and get out of here so we can be on our way. I'll skip the part about what low life's you are. I'm sure you already know that. Just be glad I'm letting you leave with your sorry lives." The group stared at each other, nobody moved.

"I won't make this offer again." He cocked the gun. Limping and hopping, the bandits grumbled their way to the truck. Climbing inside they yelled curses and sped off down the road.

"Where did you come from?" asked Jacob,, brushing dust from his clothes.

"Somebody has got to watch you youngsters." He grinned. "And you know how protective us old moose are." He raised his brows.

Jacob blushed and gave a weak smile. "You heard that...huh?"

"Haven't you learned by now," Kate chimed in. "He hears everything."

"Enough laughing," Ben faked a Texas accent. "We got to get back to getting." Cradling the shot gun, he said to Jacob. "You grab some shut eye. Since I now own a shotgun, I'll ride shotgun. It's less than 500 miles to Houston. Kate can drive us in."

"I'm wired up. I don't know if I can sleep."

"You better try," said Ben. "We don't know for sure what we may encounter when we arrive. Don't forget we're racing to beat the Primae. This little incident has put us off schedule. We'll need everyone rested and ready for whatever."

"That didn't take long," Kate commented on the sounds of Jacobs snoring in the back.

"Jacobs' a good man. One day he may lead this merry band of ours."

"I never considered anybody else but you leading us."

"Things happen. Life changes. I may not always want to lead. The day may and probably will come when I just want to relax and live out the rest of my days in quiet bliss. You'll have to put this old moose out to pasture." Kate smiled. He cut a sideways glance at her. "Some grandkids would be nice."

"Who...who me?" he nodded. "I don't know if I'm cut out for that. Besides I'm not planning on getting married any time soon."

"Well you know Jacob would marry you tomorrow if you'd agreed."

"Jacob?"

"Aw, come on Kate. Don't pretend that you don't know Jacob has always been in love with you. Even when you were kids he was your biggest fan. Why do you think he co-signs everything you do and say? Why he is always there whenever you so much as stub your toe? Who do you think is behind those birthday parties you get each year?" He shook his head. "If you don't know, you're the only one who doesn't."

Kate flushed. "I've just never thought about things changing. I guess. I like Jacob. I even love him in a way. I just..."

"I know your plate's pretty full right now, but that is something you should give some thought to. Life is precarious, especially ours.

Don't miss out on its pleasures. You can pretend you've never thought about it. I know better." He laughed.

"What's so funny?"

"His father asked me when you two were going to stop playing footsie and tie the knot." Ben turned on the radio and began yodeling, while Kate drove wide eyed and blushing. Every once and while he would yodel aloud a pertinent lyric from a love song and laugh. Kate tried to tune him out.

CHAPTER TWENTY-SEVEN

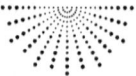

"*H*ave you found the location of the child, Micken?"

"Yes Ikayla, she was adopted by a wealthy couple in Royden Oaks. It's a suburb of Houston, a few miles north of our present location. Security is high, but we should be able to act with a minimum of difficulty."

"Good, we must continue the purge. These contemptuous hybrids must be eliminated. The fools do not realize what they are unleashing into the human gene pool. If we don't put an end to this theft of our genetic superiority, we will be breeding our own destruction. The humans could one day prove to be a credible rival. It is better for the monkeys to remain as they are, controlled and used as needed. But, these wretched hybrids will upset that delicate balance. They must be eliminated. The old order of things must be reinstated and maintained."

Ikayla was a porcelain doll crafted out of steel. Her cold black hair was molded into a tight bun and her piercing brown eyes balanced out a flawless face that looked like the parts were ordered and assembled at her request.

"Have the others sanctioned this more aggressive approach?" inquired Micken. "My understanding was that after the failure with

Hayden and his cohorts, there would be a secession of all actions. A period of reflection."

"Reflect on what? How wrong it was to use such an inappropriate method as global warming to accomplish our goals?" Ikayla scowled. "Have they realized how wrong it was to allow that over-confident Hayden and his collection of self-indulgent underachievers to guide anything? After their failure we have to be more aggressive, not less. Hayden and his ilk choose elimination when subjugation is the best answer to this situation."

Micken averted his stare; his soft features blushing and melting away as the conversation became more intense. "There is a faction among us who feel the equaling of our species is inevitable. They advocate engaging and merging. Some believe we should openly present ourselves and act as mentors for the humans. It has been said that in the big picture this will prove to be mutually beneficial to us all."

"Are you proposing acquiescence, Micken?

"Not I. I was just..."

"You were just sounding like that milquetoast Milborne. Shall I begin to call you Reverend Micken?" Do you also feel that we should breed with them? Do you feel that by weakening and depleting our gene pool we will be doing the moral thing?"

"No, not at all. I was just concerned because there has been so much dissension among us. So many opposing groups have formed. I fear that our position could be diminished if we continue to be so polarized." He hesitated and swallowed. "I was concerned."

"I don't wish to hear any more of that talk. There is a new realization coming, Micken. Our brethren have accepted the ridiculous idea that we are no longer the most favored. That we have been demoted to the status of just another face in the crowd. If we behave as such, then of course it will come to be. I am not willing to accept second class status. We are not like the humans. We are and always will be their superiors. There are a growing number among us who agree with me. Our demise is not yet written."

"I dare say, those beliefs are considered heretical to some, to say the least. This is very rocky ground you are plowing, mistress. There may be many who agree with you, but there are more who do not."

"It is true there are detractors, but the growing consensus shall be on my side. We just need a few...occurrences...to convince the skeptical." She paced around the room studying him with rapacious eyes. "Are you on our side, Micken? Does our present mission make you uncomfortable?"

He hesitated before answering. "I am obligated to your house. Your opinion is my opinion. I feel it is my obligation to perform as expected. I only speak out of concern for your well-being."

"Indeed," she said warily. "You know your place."

"The boy child," stated Micken, looking away and changing the subject. "His whereabouts still eludes us?"

"He has proven a bit harder to pin down, but his general location is known. Jackan is securing the details." Unsure if she wanted to share more information Ikayla hesitated giving Micken another look, but continued. "This boy is believed to have shown some aptitudes we may wish to harness."

"He has been touched? How can that be possible? He is a half blood. Only the purest have ever possessed the gift. And their births are exceedingly rare."

"His mother no doubt possessed some aberration of the ability. A pity this was not known before her elimination. She could have been of use for bree..."

Ikayla halted her thought. "Oh well, it does not matter. It is spilled water now. Whatever she possessed, has been passed to the boy. It is not known to what extent." Ikayla strutted her lean muscular body to the balcony doors and peered out.

"This boy will be turned to serve us. We must be careful and not risk damaging his mind. Without his cooperation, his abilities, whatever they are, would become useless. In that case he might as well be turned out with the rest of these malcontents. When our business is concluded here we shall retrieve him."

"I shall check on the preparations" said Micken, exiting the room.

CHAPTER TWENTY-EIGHT

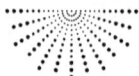

"*I*t's a gated community with a private security patrol. We should park outside of the neighborhood and walk in to avoid being detected," Ben suggested.

"The time has passed."

All heads turned toward the sound of the voice. Obscured in the shadows, a cloaked figure emerged. Weapons were drawn, muscles tensed; all senses went on high alert.

"Who's there?" Ben demanded, stepping forward balancing on his toe and ready to deflect any attack.

"I am no threat," The form moved forward and lowered the cowl Lifeless black eyes stared in their direction. "The child has left this plane of existence." The voice echoed around itself as if each word was repeated twice.

"She's dead?" Kate cried out.

"Yes, and those who cared for her." The voice was low and placid, just above a whisper and void of any emotion.

"You bastard!" Kate yelled.

"Are you bragging about your handy work? Killing helpless children?" Jacob yelled, raising his sword as he raised his voice.

"I had no part in these events," the figure calmly answered.

"What did you do? Sit and watch?" Jacob spit out, swiping his sword at the air. "I bet that got your jollies off."

"Why should we believe you? If you weren't involved how do you know she is dead?" Ben asked, his face contorting with concern.

"I glimpsed her essence as it moved forward."

"You're part of the Primae. We can't believe you. This is a delaying tactic," Jacob said, turning to move down the block.

"I am not one of those you call the Primae. I do not wish to delay you, but to redirect you. Time is short. The girl child is lost. The boy is not. Not only because he still lives, but because he is important."

"What do you mean, important? And who are you?" Ben asked.

He paused. "I am Dowan. I observe."

"Observe? Who observes the murder of children?" Kate screamed.

"If that is what occurs. I do not interfere. I do not judge. That is beyond my sphere."

"Convenient," Jacob said.

"What of the boy?" Ben asked, waving the others to silence.

"The boy child still lives."

"I thought you didn't interfere?" added Kate sarcastically.

"I am approaching my limits."

"Then why do it?" asked Ben.

"I do this because it is needed." A hint of sadness trailed from the words.

"Needed? Needed by whom?" asked Ben.

"By life," Dowan answered as if the question was absurd. "In everything there is something exceptional. If only because life itself is exceptional. This is so common it goes unnoticed. It seems unimportant. On rare occasions, one of these exceptional lives has unlimited potential. This child is one. His continued existence must be assured."

"Why?" Kate asked. "Who are you working for?"

"My actions are singular."

"If the kid is so important why don't you do something about it yourself? Like stop the ones who want to kill him?" Asked Ben.

"My abilities…" Dowan paused. "…are limited."

"You don't believe this, do you?" Jacob asked. "It's got to be one of them who did this. This could be a trap. How do we know we're not being set up? We know they want us dead."

"He has a point," Ben agreed. "There is too much bad blood between the Primae and us. We can't go on your word alone."

"I cannot compel you. Do not let the boy perish. More is at stake than you know." Dowan stepped back into the shadows and faded away.

"You're not trusting that thing, are you?" Asked Jacob.

"I'm not trusting anyone but us." Ben insisted.

"It's true," Kate whispered. "I don't know how I know, but it's true. She's dead."

Ben rubbed the stump of his arm. "Don't lose it, Kate. Let's just remain calm. We'll go to the house and ..."

"Find the body," whispered Kate.

Silently they proceeded to the house, a cloud of apprehension hanging over them. Each member of the group steeled themselves for what they feared was true.

CHAPTER TWENTY-NINE

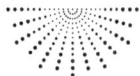

"Thanks for letting me come along. I would have found it hard to just turn around and go home."

"After what we found at the house Kate, I think we all may be needed," Ben said, his hand gripping the steering wheel so tight he could feel his fingers pulsing.

"Why did they do it, Ben? They didn't just kill those people. They savaged them. It's as if they scarified them."

Kate closed her eyes, fighting back a lingering sense of sorrow.

"And that poor little girl. She was just a baby, a complete innocent. I don't know who we're dealing with, but they are ruthless and heartless, even for the Primae. It would take a monster to do what they did." Kate pounded the dash board. "I wonder what humans would think of Angels now if they knew they were the ones who did this?"

"I'm not sure who or what exactly we're up against this time. This group doesn't seem to have any filters. We all are in great danger. If they will ravish a child like that, imagine what they would do to us?" Ben swiped his stump before his face, forgetting there was no hand there to wipe the brow he missed.

Catching Kate's worried look from the corner of his eye, he turned his head in frustration. "I forget sometimes. You would think I would be used to it being gone by now."

"It takes time," Kate said as she placed her hand on his shoulder.

"Yeah, I know. 'Phantom limb' syndrome," Ben looked into the rearview mirror at a restlessly sleeping Jacob.

"I'm a little worried about him," he said, with a swish of his head. "He took the sight of the girl pretty hard. I was really surprised. I thought I would have to restrain you, not him."

Kate lowered her head balling up her hands and locking them between her knees. "I was ready for it. At least as ready as I could get. Somehow, I believed that Dowan. At least the part about her being dead."

"Yeah, Dowan; I don't know what to make of that one. Do we have an ally or are we being set up for some kind of betrayal?"

"What is 'Dowan' anyway? I've never seen anything like…it before. I don't know if it's male or female, Angel or Nephilim, or something in between, or neither? It looked like it was blind, but those eyes seem to know and see everything."

"I don't know for sure what to call…" Ben shrugged his shoulders, "…him, but I have heard about those that are as much one thing as the other. They are considered blessed by some and cursed by others. Touched with senses beyond our understanding. Whatever it is, it is powerful and probably dangerous. We have to stay on our toes. I have a feeling this mission may be…" he searched the road ahead for the right word and came up with "…costly."

"What about the boy? What do you think Dowan meant by what he said?"

"I don't know."

"Has Tim found him yet?"

"Communications are spotty. We haven't been able to get in touch with him. I'm not that worried. Tim's very capable. He's used to working on his own. I know that he'll come through for us." Ben sighed.

"Why don't you lay back and get some rest. I've got about four hours of fast driving and some serious thinking to concentrate on. I'll wake you when we're almost there."

"I thought we were to meet our ride in Corpus Christi?" Kate asked.

"Calvin will meet us at the Austin airport. He had to evacuate the coast. Corpus Christi is underwater. The gulf had a sudden surge again. The waters are claiming coastal land and not giving it back." He shrugged. "We knew this could happen."

"I'm getting worried we may not survive this. Things don't seem to be improving. I talked to Chris last week. He's working at the United Nations now. He said they're evacuating people in coastal lands all over the world. The refugees are in the tens of millions. He sounded really worried."

"We have to give it time and hope the planet can right itself. Since the damage we were doing has basically stopped, hopefully things will start to improve."

"What about the island? Do you think Tim will be alright there?"

"Tim will be okay. The island isn't going anywhere right now. There are reports of some lost costal land, but Puerto Rico is a big place. It should be alright for a while longer. Calvin is a little worried about flying out there. Things are so unpredictable. We don't know how bad it may get. The ocean currents and wind patterns are erratic and sometimes violent. Whatever we're going to do we have to do it now."

The car raced forward as if Ben was trying to out run his frustrations. "Look, lay back and get some rest. I'll need you at 100 percent."

Kate closed her eyes, laid back in her seat, and tried not to picture dead children and drowned cites.

CHAPTER THIRTY

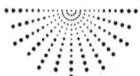

*T*im pressed himself against the wall and slid around the corner of a cantina. Drawing a stiletto, he hoped his pursuer was far enough behind not to have seen him step into the shadows. He gripped the hilt firmly, but loose enough to angle the hold for a slash or a thrust. When his pursuer rounded the corner, Tim threw his free hand over the man's shoulders and pulled him off balance. Using his weight, he spun him in a half circle. The man crashed face first into the wall. With the flick of his wrist he adjusted the hold and raised his blade.

"Stop! Stop! It's me Kaplan."

"Kap!" Tim shouted as he spun him around and snatched the cap from his head. A cascade of dred locs fell in his face. "What the hell are you doing here? You fool I could have killed you."

Gasping like a man just pulled from drowning, he panted. "I've been following you ever since you arrived on the island." Looking down at the knife, he said, "I just want to help. I couldn't just sit around and do nothing. Jairo is my son, remember." He tweeted his nose checking for blood. "I think you broke my nose."

Tim slapped his hand down. "You can't be here, Kap. This is not fun and games; this is serious. You could get yourself killed, man." He held up the knife and gestured to it. "The ones we are dealing with are dangerous. They would think nothing of ending your life. You aren't equipped to handle this kind of situation. Now I want you to turn around and go home. We'll bring your son to you. I promise."

"No. I'm not going anywhere. You'll have to kill me to stop me. Jairo is worth the risk."

"What if you get killed, how will that help him? You'd be more help if you stay out of the way."

With eyes full of sorrow, a voice full of determination, and a face drawn and weary from lack of sleep, Kap stood fast to his declaration. "I'm here to stay. There's nothing you can say or do that will make me leave. If you won't take me with you, I'll go it alone. Either way I'm going to find my son."

Tim stared at him with sympathy and exasperation. Shaking his head, he sheathed his knife, throwing up his hands in surrender. "Alright, there's nothing I can do to convince you otherwise." He shook his finger in his face. "You have to promise to do exactly as I tell you without argument. If you don't, I'll hogtie you and put you on a slow boat back to the states."

Kap half smiled and eagerly nodded his agreement.

"I'll have hell to pay," Tim said, running his hand across his hair. "Ben is not going to be happy to see you."

Kaplan shrugged and ignored the statement. "Have you found Jairo yet?"

"Haven't you been following me? Don't you know the answer to that question?"

"I lost you yesterday and had to wait for you to return to your room last night before I started following you again."

"Huh. Some bloodhound you are."

"I don't know if you know this, but you move pretty fast. I've never seen anyone move in and out of shadow like you. It took everything I had to follow you in the day time. At night, you're like chasing smoke."

Tim cracked a smile. "That's the whole idea to move quickly and not be seen."

"What about Jairo, Tim?"

"I've found him, but it's going to take a lot to get him back."

"What do you mean? Where is he? Is he okay? Is he hurt?

"He's alright so far. He's in the southwestern part of the island in a hilly region near a town called Yauco. He was bought…"

"Bought!"

"Yes, bought like a bag of potatoes along with a half-dozen other kids as laborers. It's an agricultural region. You know coffee, tobacco, plantains; that kind of stuff."

Tim hesitated and took in a deep breath. "It's a drug cartel. They're using the kids to grow and harvest marijuana. The kids are cheap expendable labor. They don't have to worry about them running off because they have nowhere to go; no one to run to."

Kap grew pale. His weary expression twisted into angst. The intensity of his anger could be felt like the heat from an oven. He cupped his hands against the side of his head as if he was keeping it from exploding. "But, he's only eight years old. I'll kill them. I'll kill them!" he whispered, gnashing his teeth like a mill grinding grain.

"Hold yourself together, Kap." Tim gave him a strong jerk. "Now is not the time to fall apart. He's relatively safe and we know where he is."

"Safe? You call being a slave of a drug cartel safe?"

"I mean he's not in danger at the moment. As soon as Ben gets here we'll figure out a way to set him and the other kids free. Ben should be here…" he looked at his watch. "…in about three hours unless the weather holds them back. We'll go get something to eat, then go wait at the airport till he arrives." "*That will give me some time to figure out a way to explain you to him.*" he thought.

CHAPTER THIRTY-ONE

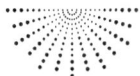

"*T*here've been inquiries about the boy. We are not the only ones to seek his whereabouts," Micken offered sitting on the edge of his seat.

"The Ceteri no doubt," Ikayla said, looking up from the desk. "They are like bedbugs. Parasitic, always where you don't want them and hard to get rid of. I suppose their encounter with Hayden gave them a false sense of competence. The fools, we'll have to turn that confidence on them. It will give me such pleasure to crush those half-breeds," she smirked, sending a wadded-up paper sailing into the trash can. "*Score*," she thought. "We will need to move quickly to thwart their intervention."

"It would be prudent to take them a little more seriously," Micken offered. "After all you would not want to make the same under estimations that Hayden did. We should accept the fact that these individuals are quite capable."

I am not Hayden," Ikayla said, rising to make her declaration. "Our goals are different. His was genocide. The eradication of the human race. He was short-sighted, wasteful, and sadly predictable. Why would you acquire a mansion and kill off all the servants? Who would do the menial things that must be done?" she smiled, a gurgle of laughter in her throat. "There are many ways to clip troublesome wings. You don't have to kill the bird to keep it from flying away. That is what cages are for."

She paused a moment enjoying her private humor. "I simply want a return to the proper order of things. The way it was before the darkness." Ikayla sauntered to the window and flung back the curtain flooding the room with diffused light.

Micken arched his brows at the gesture. "Will the others intervene? I am concerned. You seem so confident in your assertions."

"Not likely. They don't have the will. The insignificant dolts adhere to the old code. A system that is both antiquated and useless; not fit for modern times and modern problems. I have some new ideas about the way things should be done."

Ikayla moved to the mirror and began mindlessly primping. "Let's get this thing done. There are other pressing issues I wish to focus on. Where is the boy?"

Micken opened his notebook. "He's been located at an estate near the town of Yauco. Our intelligence says that he is one of the laborers in the drug fields of the Aceveda Cartel." He looked up from his paper. "Shall we attempt to bargain for him, or risk going in and extracting him?"

"Bargain? Ha. Your sense of humor Micken, is so pedantic." There was no laughter in her steely brown eyes.

"A tree does not argue with the wind it simply bends to its will. Prepare to move at first light." She smirked. "The wind is coming."

CHAPTER THIRTY-TWO

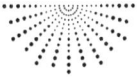

"Ohat the hell is he doing here?" Ben grumbled approaching Tim and Kaplan.

"I might ask you the same thing," Tim pointed at Kate and Jacob.

Ben's bluster softened. "We were too late. They got there before us. Massacred the mother, father, a nanny and two children. The girl was one of them."

Kaplan's eyes grew wide at the realization. "Does that mean they're coming after Jairo?" His head was bouncing back and forth between Tim and Ben, searching for an answer. "We've got to get moving!"

"You're not moving anywhere, but out of here. I don't know how you ended up here." Ben cut his eyes at Tim. "This is the end of the road for you."

Kaplan pushed forward, meeting Ben face to face. "The hell I am! He's my son and no one, not you or your murderous friends are going to stop me from saving him!"

Sliding an arm in and wedging himself between them, Tim pushed them apart. "Fellows, fellows. Let's calm down. We're on the same team remember? We've got enough obstacles against us without being against each other. Let's just focus on the task before us."

"Why did you bring him along Tim? I thought it was understood that this was too dangerous for him to be involved?"

"He didn't bring me along. I got here before he did," Kaplan spit at him. "I came on my own and if necessary, I'll find Jairo on my own. I'm not as helpless as you think. And I'm not part of your fan club. I don't take orders from you."

"Fan club!" Ben yelled waving his stump like a club.

"Mr. Kaplan," Kate stepped in. Her voice was calm and flirty. "Why don't you come with us." She elbowed Jacob.

"Come on Jacob, let's take Mr. Kaplan and go get some something cool to drink. This heat is about to drop me." She linked arms with a reluctant Kaplan. Jacob followed suit and linked with his other arm. They hustled him off toward the airport terminal. Kaplan's head darted about, trying to figure out what was going on. Tim mouthed a "thank you," over the shoulders of an animated Ben. Kate acknowledged it with a wink.

"Okay Ben, you can calm down now. I know you don't like Kap being here, but I've known you long enough to know that something else is bothering you. You would never blow up like that just about him being here. Whatever it is, spill it."

Ben grabbed his stump and began rubbing it. His expression was a combination of worry, fear, and exhaustion.

Tim sensed his anxiety and placed a hand on his shoulder. "Ben, what is it?"

"Dowan."

"What's a 'Dowan'?"

Ben relayed the facts of their encounter with Dowan on the streets of Royden Oaks. "He's the only thing I can think of. I think Dowan is an Anima. I know it sounds crazy, but I feel it in my bones, Tim. Dowan is an Anima."

"That's not possible. Anima are just legend, aren't they? I've only heard stories, but...They're to us the way angels are to humans."

"I'm telling you, Tim. Dowan is an Anima." he said the words as if he needed to hear them aloud to believe them.

"The pupil-less black eyes, indistinct gender, the ethereal coming and going, the knowledge of things outside time; and there is just an aura about him." Ben walked in circles panting as if he was running to catch up with his breath.

"Those eyes, Tim. You're never seen such sad haunted things in your life."

"I don't know Ben," Tim pushed the hat back on his head wiping his brow. "If this Dowan is what you say, are we dealing with a friend or a foe?"

"I don't know. Legend says that they only appear at times of great trouble and things are never the same when they leave."

"Well the timing is certainly right." Tim said. "With the reports I've been hearing, and the way things look, these would definitely qualify as troubled times." Tim took two steps away and turned back.

"If this Dowan is an Anima that means he's an avatar, a spirit of something, but of what?"

Ben threw up his arms. "I don't know. I wouldn't tell anyone but you this, Tim, but, I'm...I'm scared, man. I have a bad feeling in my bones."

He stared Tim in the eyes. "You have to promise me Tim, that whatever happens on this mission you'll be around to take over and make things right if something should..." He bobbed his head. "You know..."

"Ben, don't talk like that..."

Ben grabbed his arm. "Don't brush this off, Tim. I've got a really, really bad feeling growing inside me. Promise me." A note of panic was in his tone.

"We've been brothers for a long time. I trust you more than I've ever trusted anyone. Please, promise you'll do this for me."

Tim laid a hand on Ben's shoulder, feeling the tension pulsating through his friend. "Of course, Ben. You know I'd do anything for you. You don't even have to ask."

Tim felt his muscle ease. They shared a strained smile. "Relax, man. Things will be alright. Come on let's get the others and go find Jairo."

As they neared the terminal, Tim asked, "Ben, could you play nice with Kap?" Ben gave him a glance out of the corner of his eyes. "He's here and there is no way we're going to convince him to just go away." Ben started to respond. Tim silenced him with a tilt of his head.

CHAPTER THIRTY-THREE

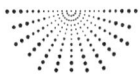

"That's a lot of security just to watch a bunch of kids weeding a garden," Tim adjusted the focus on his binoculars that were pointing to the west side of the valley. "Those shacks must be where the workers live."

"If you can call this living. We'll have to wait until it gets dark before we go in. There's no way we can get down there without being seen in the daylight," Ben passed his binoculars to Kaplan. "I want you to point out which one is your son."

Kaplan zeroed in on one flock of the dozens of children toiling in the midday sun. They were pulling weeds, planting young sprouts, and carrying bundles as large as themselves. Their clothes were dirty and ragged. Most wore no shoes and those that did had them tied to their feet by cords of rope. The little farmers shuffled about like weary old men. None looked up or spoke. They hung their heads and moved along prescribed routes. Working from dusk to dawn, the laughter of childhood was replaced by the grunts and groans of forced labor.

Heavily armed men dressed in camouflage gear watched over the workers. The black metal of their automatic weapons gleaming like the skin of a snake. Salacious eyes and malicious sneers studied the vulnerable young bodies, picking out which would have "night duties" to perform for unscrupulous men.

"There he is!" Kaplan started to rise. "That's him. The one in the green t-shirt."

Timothy grabbed his arm and pulled him back down. "Stay down. They've got lookouts. We're trying to sneak in remember?"

"Let's go. We've got to get my boy out of there."

"Not now," insisted Ben. "We have to wait until dark. When we've got some cover, we'll take out the guards, go in and scoop up the children."

"Why wait?" asked Kaplan. "He's right before our eyes. We can rush in and grab him."

"Not just your son, but all of them," Ben insisted.

"Hey guys, something's going on," Tim interrupted. "Look over there." He pointed to the east.

A black SUV was barreling across the field. The vehicle followed no road. It mowed a path through the growing crops straight toward the children. Gunfire rang out as the guards began firing at the speeding interloper. Bullets ricocheted off the body of the truck, sounding like hail on a tin roof. The armored buffalo charged forward undeterred. A cloud of dirt and plants swirled through the air making the vehicle look like it was propelled by its own personal tornado.

Some of the children fell to the ground hiding behind rocks and wooden crates. Others ran screaming for the shelters. Jairo stood undeterred staring upward into the sky.

The passenger side window of the SUV lowered. A double-barreled silver shaft emerged like a silver arm. The boom of a jet breaking the sound barrier echoed over the field. A small missile shot across the field blowing a hole in the ground and setting off fires. Like miniature fighter jets, a barrage of missiles flew as if they were an attack squadron. Crashing and exploding, they upended earth and bodies, flinging them around like leaves in a wind storm. The guards ran for cover as bombs rained down turning the landscape into a disaster zone. The wind began to gust. Dust swirled up from the sun baked soil. A dark cloud tented over the field adding an ominous backdrop.

"Jairo, get down!" Kaplan shouted, trying to rise. Tim and Ben held the struggling man while staring down at the spectacle.

"Let me go. Get your damn hands off me. I've got to get down there. They're about to kill my son."

"No, they aren't," Ben said. "That not a kill squad. That's a smash and snatch squad."

"It's the Primae. They're after the boy," Tim added.

"Yeah, they're trying to kill him!" Kaplan shouted. "Jairo, Jairo!"

"No, they aren't. Those missiles are aimed at the guards. It's the Primae, alright. They never have been subtle." Ben said.

"Come on," yelled Kaplan, fighting to free himself. "Let's stop them. They can't have him."

The winds continued to rise obscuring the view. The young boy stood unmoved by the commotion around him, while everyone around him was running and screaming.

The SUV shrieked to a stop. Two black clad figures emerged from the front seats. Jackan sprayed a cover of missiles in a circle devastating anything that remained standing. An expression seen only on children at play plastered his face. The other figure marched over to the boy in the green t-shirt, standing in the middle of a war zone. "I've got the boy," Micken said, and hauled him back to the vehicle. One last missile, a throaty laugh, and Jackan sped the SUV back across the field amid the cloud of dust and smoke.

Kaplan rolled over on his back in tears. "They've got my son. He was right there, and you wouldn't let me help him."

"Look Kaplan," Ben said, his voice strong and clear, but gentle. "I know this looks bad, but you've got to keep it together. We'll get Jairo back. Work with us and this will turn out alright. I promise."

Kaplan pressed his lips together, shook his head, and beat his fist against the ground. "Good man," Ben said. "Let's get back to the city. We've got to get Jairo before they can leave the island. I hate to leave the other kids, but we'll have to come back for them another time."

"You do have some people skills after all. You may get the hang of this leadership thing if you keep this up." Tim said, nudging Ben with his elbow.

"I'm not all asshole. The guy's scared and nervous. We all are."

"I'll call Kate. The Primae doesn't know we're on to them; for once we've got the upper hand."

Tim looked at the field. "Why do you think they kidnapped the boy and didn't kill him?"

Ben cupped his stump. "Dowan said he was important. The Primae seem to already know this. We have to find out why."

CHAPTER THIRTY-FOUR

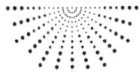

"The Primae have Jairo," Kate said. "Tim called; he says there are probably three of them. Two men for sure. He thinks there may be a third one. They want you to case the hotels and find out where they're staying. I've got to get in touch with our pilot and have him here and ready, so we can get us off this rock as soon as we have the boy."

Jacob shook his head. "They want him alive. That Dowan said the boy was important. I guess that part was true."

Kate shuttered. "Ugh, I don't think I'd want the Primae to want me for anything. What do you think it means?"

"I don't know, but it can't be good," They shared a moment of uncomfortable silence.

"I'm heading out. I'll call soon as I find them," Jacob said.

"Keep a low profile. Don't let them make you and don't play the hero. Call when you find them."

"Wow," Jacob smiled. "You sound like a wife already, giving orders like you care. And I haven't even asked you to marry me yet."

"Yet? I didn't know you were planning too."

"Of course, you did." He casually waved his hand. "I've been planning that since we were 12 years old. I've just been waiting on you to grow up. I always heard that child brides were a pain in the ass to deal with."

Kate put her hands on her hips. "I'm glad you finally informed me of my future. I was wondering what I was going to do when we got back home."

"Come to think of it," Jacob crossed his arms over his chest and placed a finger to his chin. "It's probably a good idea for you to go shopping for a wedding dress. I heard it takes months to make those things." He kissed her on the cheek. "See you later."

CHAPTER THIRTY-FIVE

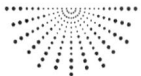

*J*airo sat silent in the back seat of the SUV, staring straight ahead.

Ikayla crinkled her nose and cracked the window. She moved closer to the window. Giving the boy a half-hearted glance, she said, "Jackan, are you certain this is the one?"

"Yes, Ikayla this is the son of Helen. His name is Jairo."

"Perhaps when some of this filth is washed from him I will be more impressed." She ventured another glance and gave him a dismissive turn of the head. "You've made sure we won't be followed?"

"Several explosive devices were planted at the main house. They will be kept quite busy dealing with that situation. When we return to the road a car will be waiting for us. So, as you can see all is in hand."

She fanned the air and lowered the window.

CHAPTER THIRTY-SIX

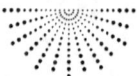

"*U*nder no circumstances are you to leave this vehicle. No matter what is happening," Ben leaned in the window of the van.

"Keep the motor running. When we run out of that door we need you charged up and ready to go." He added. "Stay sharp." His voice as rough as sandpaper. "Do you know the route?"

Kaplan shook his head. "Turn right, then left onto the highway. Four miles to the air field."

"Good man..."

"But, I want to..."

"Look Kaplan. Your job is as important as any of ours. Don't argue man. Just do your part," Kaplan deflated and fell back into the seat.

Ben nodded and slapped his hand on the door before joining the others at the rear of the hotel.

"He worries me, Tim. Maybe you or Jacob should stay here with him?"

"We can't Ben. It'll take all of us to pull this off. Don't worry about Kap. He knows how important this is. He'll come through for us," Tim answered.

Jacob chimed in."I'm with Ben on this one. The guys too unsteady. What's to keep him from going off halfcocked?"

"Not you too, Jacob? Tim said. "We better get inside before you two start doubting me."

CHAPTER THIRTY-SEVEN

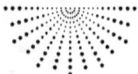

"*K*nock, knock..."

"Who is it?"

"I bring fresh towels?" The voice yelled through the door.

An immaculately dressed Micken opened the door. "We did not order towels."

"I do not know, Señor. I was told to bring fresh towels," the maid pleaded.

Annoyed, Micken said, "Come on in and get to it then." He turned his back and returned to his desk.

Cradling several towels, the chamber maid proceeded into the room leaving her cart angled in the open door.

"This is how you repay me?" An angry male voice was shouting in the hall.

"Baby, it's not what you think." A young woman and man appeared with their backs to the door.

"Hey man, I just met her. I didn't know she was married," Jacob said, his hands raised in surrender.

"You expect me to believe that? What kind of an idiot do you think I am?" Ben replied.

"Come on baby. Let me explain. It's not what you think," Kate offered, backing her way around the cart and through the doorway.

"Shut up, you lying whore. I gave you everything and this is how you repay me? Banging this pimply-faced washout?" Ben shouted.

"Hey, wait a minute," Jacob protested, moving backward into the room and standing behind Kate. His head bobbed up and down following the movement of Ben's gun.

"Shut your A-hole, punk," he raised the gun to Jacob's head.

CHAPTER THIRTY-EIGHT

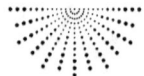

*T*im was positioned on the balcony of the hotel room above the Primae's' suite. With the skill of a seasoned mountain climber, he secured a rope to the post of the railing and repelled down to the balcony below. The high winds caused him to sway and swing more than he liked.

Ikayla circled the boy, studying him like a specimen in a jar. "Do you know what you are?"

Jairo remained silent and unmoved. If not for the slight rise and fall of his chest, he could have been mistaken for a statue.

"My patience is not known for its length. If you will not cooperate freely, there are ways of making you more agreeable."

"It appears that he is deaf and mute or just obstinate beyond measure," Jackan wondered aloud.

"He is neither. It is one of the attributes of the touched. The ability to be outside of their existence, to exist in a singularity. I would surmise that since the spectacle of his mother's death there have been few moments he has been fully in this world. History says that trauma can bring on the transformation. Some begin the transformation immediately, becoming detached and distracted. For others, the change is gradual, leaving them open to..." She gave a catty smile. "... to other influences."

"How do you know so much about this?" Jackan asked.

"I make a point of knowing where the pillars of power stand." She took a moment to enjoy the thought. "We'll have to be careful with him. I don't want to damage him and lose access to his talents."

Ikayla cupped Jairo's chin and turned the placid young face up to hers. "Look at his eyes. They're already starting to turn." She pivoted toward the door at the sound of yelling.

"What is going on out there?" Ikayla moved toward the door. "Keep an eye on him. I will return as soon as I deal with whatever this is." She stomped out of the room slamming the door.

CHAPTER THIRTY-NINE

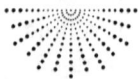

*B*en moved in, forcing the cart out of the doorway and Kate and Joshua further into the room. "Which one of you do I kill first?" he asked, waving the gun between them.

"Get out of our room!" Micken yelled, "Or I will call hotel security."

"I think you better sit down and shut up little man. I'm in no mood to deal with another pansy ass." Micken bristled.

The maid began crying and ran into the bathroom, locking the door behind her.

"What is going on out here?" Ikayla demanded, charging into the room. She stopped short when the gun caught her eye.

"We're having a session of 'Divorce Court'. Glad you could join us," Ben answered casually, scratching his chin with the gun.

"Get the out of my room. Take your domestic squabbles to the trash bin where they belong," Micken insisted.

Ben stepped forward. "I told you to shut the hell up before I dump you in a trash bin."

"He's crazy," cried Kate. "He's going to kill us all."

"Micken, call hotel security." Ikayla ordered.

Ben pointed the revolver at him and cocked the trigger. "I wouldn't do that if I were you, Micken. These bullets don't care who I give them to. Besides," he smiled, "...court is still in session."

Micken reached for the phone. Ben reached over and banged him on the head with handle of the gun. The phone fell to the floor. Micken pulled back cupping his head and fell into a chair.

"I call the shots around here," Ben growled. "Nobody does anything unless I tell them to."

Ikayla fumed with indignation. "What do you want? We have nothing to do with this sordid affair of yours."

Jacob slid near the door.

"Back over there, lover boy, where I can see you," Ben said directing him with a swish of the barrel.

"Look man, I just picked her up at the hotel bar. I thought I could get in a little afternoon quickie. I didn't bargain for nothing like this."

"Maybe you should have thought of that before you started thinking with the wrong head."

Ikayla moved to charge him.

"I'd think twice, stop and then think again, if I were you, lady." Ben smirked aiming the gun at her face.

"Too bad," he said, looking her up and down. "...since I'm soon to be a single man." He sneered at Kate.

"I would consider asking you out. But, I can see you're just like the rest; too much of a bitch to get along with."

CHAPTER FORTY

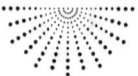

$\mathcal{T}$im peered around the curtains and saw Jairo sitting in a chair in the middle of the room. Jackan was standing with his ear to the door, listening to the commotion in the other room. When the noise reached a fever pitch, Tim slid open the balcony door and crept in behind the curtains. He froze when the breeze swayed the fabric. Jackan didn't notice. Like a bug, Tim skirted along the wall. The slight tilt of the boy's head signaled that he sensed someone else had entered the room. Jackan reached for the door knob. Grabbing a small statuette, Tim lunged for Jackan and struck him on the back of the head. He collapsed back into Tim's arms.

Tim deposited the dead weight of Jackan's body against the door before approaching the boy.

"Jairo, I'm Tim. I'm here with your father to bring you home."

The boy looked up at him. His eyes were as empty as a well without water. His face was expressionless. Tim felt a foreboding pass over him as he looked into those blank eyes. Shaking off the uneasiness, he said, "Okay, let's go. We haven't much time." Jairo rose, moved to the door, then onto the balcony and stood by the railing as if he had been instructed to do so. Tim hunched his shoulders and followed him.

"Okay you're going to get on my back and hold on to my neck for a few minutes, so we can get to the other side. Okay? Don't be afra..."

Before he could finish his sentence, Jairo had moved into position.

Tim started to feel his words were useless and unnecessary as the boy acted without instruction or resistance. Tim bent down, Jairo climbed on his back and wrapped his arms around his neck. He grabbed the rope and stepped onto the railing. *"At least the winds have died down,"* he thought.

"Here we go," Kicking off from the banister, they swung over the five-foot expanse and landed on the opposite balcony. With a flick of his wrist, Tim flung the end of the rope up, landing it on the railing of the upper balcony.

"Okay, come on," he said, taking Jairo's hand. Moving through the room, they exited into the hall and headed for the stairs. At the door to the stairwell he stopped and pulled the fire alarm. The siren blared to life. Bright red lights began flashing, filling the hall and stairwell.

"What the hell is that?" Ben said, moving to look into the hall. He saw Tim and Jairo at the stairwell door. Tim signaled him with a salute and they disappeared through the door. Hotel room doors flew open and the hallway began filling up with panicked guests. Ben re-entered the room. "It's your lucky day. But, don't think I'll let this go." He ran out the door and entered the stairwell.

"Oh my God," Kate cried. "I just knew he was going to kill us. I got to get away from here before he comes back." She took off running.

"Hey, what about me?" yelled Jacob, following behind her. They both entered the stairwell merging into the gathering stampede.

Ikayla turned to Micken, her face twisted with anger. Still dazed from the blow to his head, he leaned over, hanging his head between his legs.

"Get the boy," she ordered through clenched teeth.

Micken struggled to his feet and moved to the door. He turned the door handle and pushed on the door. "It won't bulge. Jackan, open the door!" He banged on the door.

"Jackan, something is blocking the door," he beat on the door again. The scream of the siren raised the tension in the room. Trampling footsteps moved in a rush in the hall. Shrieks and hurried conversations filled the air.

The maid peeked out of the bathroom. Seeing no one in her path, she bolted for the door and disappeared into the crowd.

"What is going on?" Ikayla asked.

"Something is blocking the door."

"Jackan," she shouted. "Open the door." Together they forced the door open until it was wide enough to enter the room. Bending over the half-conscious Jackan, she asked, "What happened? Where is the boy?"

"Somebody hit me," he said, sitting up and rubbing the lump on his head.

Ikayla turned an intense shade of red and screamed with a rage that dwarfed the sound of the fire alarm. "We have been had!"

Micken looked around confused.

"Those people were the Ceteri. They have the boy. That ridiculous display out there was just a distraction." Her eyes burned with fury. "We have to catch them before they get away."

Marching out of the room, Ikayla stopped at the console table by the front door and retrieved a revolver.

"Make a fool out of me, will you?" she asked into the air...

CHAPTER FORTY-ONE

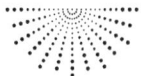

*T*he stairwell was packed with anxious people. Scores of hotel guests and employees made their way down the crowded escape route. Frightened parents shielded their scared children. Elderly patrons cautiously hugged the walls, moving at a snail's pace, trying to navigate the hectic crowd around them. Jacob and Kate struggled to stay together as they were jostled and pushed by the unsettled mass of people.

Ben burst out of the rear door and raced to the van on the other side of the parking lot. Tim was standing nervously outside the vehicle scanning the area, a look of anxiety on his face.

"The boy. He's in the back of the van."

"With his father?" Ben asked?

Tim swallowed. "Kaplan isn't here."

"What! I told you that guy was trouble! We can't stay here and wait on him to come back! Our little ruse will be discovered once they know the boy is gone!"

"I know. I'm sure he'll be back before Kate and Jacob get here," Tim palmed his forehead. "I'm sorry, Ben. I thought he could be counted on. I don't know what to say."

Ben closed his eyes and took a deep breath. He fingers clamped his stub like the jaws of a shark.

"Get in the van and protect the boy. When Kate and Jacob get here, keep them in the van, out of sight. I'll try and find Kaplan."

"Maybe I should go. I want... " Tim pleaded.

"No! Get in the van and protect the boy. I'll be back." Ben dashed off into the crowd of hotel guests, onlookers, and emergency responders.

"Kaplan, you've stepped both of our feet in it," Tim mumbled and entered the van.

Jacob threw open the door. Tim sprang to life, greeting them with the barrel of his gun. He and Kate fell in, breathing heavily. "Where's Ben and Kaplan?" Jacob asked, looking around.

Tim lowered his head. "Kaplan's missing. Ben went to try and find him."

"I knew that guy couldn't be trusted!" Jacob shouted, slamming his fist into his seat. Kate nudged him with her elbow, tilting her head toward Jairo.

"Oh...uh..."

Tim rose from his seat and opened the door. "You two stay here with Jairo. I'm going to find them. We can't stay here much longer."

Kate grabbed his hand. "Be careful, okay?"

"I will, kid. Just be ready to leave as soon as we get back." Tim climbed on the top of a dumpster and scanned the crowd. Near the hotel entrance, he spotted Kaplan. Jumping down and parting the crowd like a bulldozer, he reached him and snatched him by his collar.

"What the hell do you think you're doing here?"

"I heard the fire alarm and I got worried. I came to see if I could help," Kaplan answered.

"You were told to stay in the van. Now you've jeopardized everything. If you would have done like you were told, we could have been out of here by now."

"You found him!" he shouted.

"Shut up, man. Keep your voice down!" Tim resisted the urge to hit him.

"Get back to the van. Give Jacob the keys and tell him to be ready."

Kaplan started to speak, but saw the anger in Tim's face, turned, and ran back to the van.

Tim skirted around the crowd., standing on car hoods searching for Ben. The familiar face of Jackan appeared on the edge of a group of fire fighters. Their eyes met. A moment of connection passed between them. Jackan move toward him. Tim turned in the opposite direction as a black Ford Taurus screeched to a halt in front of him.

"Get in." Tim recognized Ben and slid into the passenger seat. "I told you to stay with the boy."

"Kate and Jacob are with him. I found Kaplan and sent him back to the van," Tim said, peering around the visor and seeing Jackan coming toward the car.

"Let's go." he pointed. "That's one of them. He was the one guarding the boy."

Ben shifted the car into gear and sped off. Jackan jumped into the passenger seat of a waiting red Chrysler 300 with Micken at the wheel.

"Call Jacob and tell him to head to the air field. We'll lure these guys away and meet them there," Ben said.

Jacob, with the phone to his head, watched the Chrysler take off after the Ford. The scowled-faced passenger checking the clip of his gun caught his attention. A cold chill brought goose bumps to his arms. Jacob winced and consider pursuing them. Instead, he mouthed a prayer and eased the van out of the lot and onto the highway.

Ben wove down the narrow streets. Up hills, through alleys, and across weeded fields. The car bounced over pot holes and uneven pavement. Skidding down gravel road, Ben struggled to maintain control. The pursuer in the red car continued on their tail, gaining and losing ground with ever twist and turn.

"Let me drive," Tim said.

"I can drive!" Ben shouted, frustration evident in his voice.

"Come on, Ben. I know you're a capable guy. But face it, man. There are just some things that two hands are better at than one."

Ben looked at the stub on the end of his arm, cursing the missing hand.

"Come on Ben, you're a better shot than me, even with one hand. You can take out one their tires or something."

Ben swallowed his pride. It went down hard as a falling brick. He slammed on the brakes. Like acrobats at the circus, Ben slid down and over as Tim rose up and hopped into the driver's seat. Two seconds later, they were careening down a winding stretch of road.

Shots banged out, bouncing off the truck of the car. Tim swerved the car as if the bullets had stung him in the back side. Ben lowered the window and drew out his 9mm Glock. He leaned out the window and returned a barrage of shots that caused the red car to slow down and lose ground.

Having gained ground from their pursuers, Tim executed a 180 turn and sped directly at the Chrysler. Both cars raced toward a head on collision. Ben leaned forward and sent several rounds in a deliberate line across the Chrysler's windshield. The shots shattered the windshield. The glass cracked into a blinding mosaic of a thousand pieces. Micken reacted to the damaged glass by jerking at the wheel, sending the car swerving to the right. They skidded off the road, blowing both front tires.

As the Taurus sped past, Jackan rose up through the sunroof, his face speckled with dots of blood from the flying shards. He cursed and swore like a mad man. Taking careful aim, he willed his bullets at the car. "Bang, bang."

The bullets flew as true as if they were attached to a rubber band springing back on itself. Ben's head snapped back. His Glock fell from his hand and landed on the gravel. His head and arm hung limply out the car window. Blood from the hole inside of his head ran down the car door.

"Great shooting!" Tim shouted, as his concentration on the road eased. "I knew you could do it." He slapped Ben on the knee. Ben didn't react.

"Ben are you alright?" Tim looked over at his friend. He slammed on the brakes.

"Ben, Ben. Oh my God. No, Ben!" Tim pulled him back into the car and pressed him to his chest. A torrent of anger, sadness and tears erupted from him.

"Do not weep for him. He knew the end was near. He is resolved."

Tim was startled out of his grief. He whipped his head around at the sound of the voice.

"What?" he shouted. "Who are you? How did you get back here?"

"I am..."

"Dowan," Tim interrupted. Dowan nodded. "What do you want? Why are you here?"

"The boy is still in danger."

"Why are you so worried about the boy? What is he to you?"

"He is..." Dowan paused. "...essential."

"Essential how?" Dowan did not answer him. He just stared at him with ominous black eyes.

Tim stared back, looking into eyes that unsettled him. Empty eyes that showed no reflection, nor refracted any light. They were like looking into a tiny black hole. Like looking into your own grave. He could feel himself being drawn into their endless expanse. Feelings of anxiety and doom surrounded him. Tim felt lost and vulnerable. The hopelessness continued to drag him down.

"All is not lost," a voice whispered from the depths. Tim closed his eyes and shook his head. When he looked up Dowan was gone. Only the stark reality of his dead friend in his arms remained.

CHAPTER FORTY-TWO

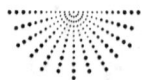

*T*he plane rocked and bounced as it winged its way across the gulf. The unpredictable winds howled and screamed like a banshee, squeezing the plane through the sky like toothpaste shooting out of a tube. The engines groaned as they fought to traverse the gloomy expanse. The waters beneath rose and churned in violent rebellion creating a challenge to the pilot's skill and endurance.

Kate, teary eyed and inconsolable, rested her head on Jacob's heaving chest. Wrestling to stifle his own grief, Jacob bit back his sobs until he could taste the salt in his own blood. Locked in an embrace of sorrow the two silently rode the erratic dips and sways of the plane, only occasionally engaging in a conversation of tears.

Kaplan and Jairo sat on the opposite side of the plane. Not allowing the boy an inch of freedom, Kaplan remained glued at his side. Holding his hand, an arm around his shoulder, he remained in constant contact with some part of him as if he was afraid letting go would mean losing him again. Jairo was unfettered, sitting oblivious to his surroundings.

"I'm going to check on Uncle Tim," Kate said, removing herself from Jacob's arms. She looked into his red eyes and kissed his lips. "I'm glad you're here."

Jacob stoked her auburn hair. "There's no place I'd rather be."

As she passed, Kaplan started to speak. Kate's cold reproach halted the effort. He pulled Jairo closer, hiding behind him. In a rear section of the plane, behind a stack of boxes, Tim sat on the floor next to the body of his dead friend. Kate moved in beside him, taking his hand and laying her head on his shoulder.

"He knew somehow this would happen. He made me promise to take over if something happened to him. I told him he was just being silly and now..." Tim's voice trailed off.

Kate squeezed his hand. "Whenever someone that I cared for died, Ben would wrap his arms around me and tell me to remember their life. A life is something that you make. Something that you do on purpose, something you create. Something to be proud of. That is what matters. All our beginnings have an end. Death, he said, is just like birth, it just happens. They are part of the same thing. But, what they leave behind is what's important." she almost smiled. "Silly I know, but somehow it made me feel better."

"If I had just..."

"Don't," Kate looked him in the eyes shaking her head.

"Don't do what I did. Don't get caught up in feelings of guilt and regret. I tried to blame you for what happened to my mother. I needed someone to drop all those feelings on." she sighed.

"That thing was no longer my mother. My mother died a long time ago. You did what you had to do. You didn't kill my mother. You stopped Kelp. You helped her to escape what they had turned her into. You gave her peace. It wasn't you who killed Ben. As mad as I am at Kaplan for leaving his post, he didn't do it either. The Primae did."

Tim closed his eyes, sighed, and released a long slow breath. "He was closer than a brother. We have been through so much together."

"He was a father to me," Kate added.

Tim wiped his eyes, sat up and dry washed his hands. "Wow, sensitive and smart. Maybe you should lead this group."

"You forgot beautiful." Kate joked, wiping her eyes.

"No, I didn't. I thought that was a given."

Kate tilted her head. "It never hurts to tell a woman she's beautiful,

Uncle Tim. Maybe I should lead this group. It seems you still have a lot to learn about some things."

"Huh, I've missed you, kid. Since you've been on the outs with me, I haven't had anybody to connect with."

"I've missed you too, Uncle Tim. I'm sorry I was so..."

"None of that. You had good reasons to be upset. I'm just glad we finally got through it." He spread his arms. Kate fell into his arms. "I love you kid."

"I love you too, Uncle Tim."

Tim stiffened. "We have company."

Kate turned to see Dowan standing on the other side of the body.

"It seems where ever things go wrong lately, you turn up" Kate spit at him.

"What do you want?" Tim asked. "The boy is safe with his father. There is no reason for you to be here."

"Can't you just leave us alone and let us grieve in peace? Ben died saving the boy. Isn't that enough?" Kate said.

"She's right. Enough already. Go away and leave us be."

"There are others, " Dowan responded.

"Other what? Other children? Kate asked. Dowan nodded.

Tim struggled to his feet. "Why are you so interested in these children? What's so special about them? What do they have to do with you?"

"They are parts of the whole," Dowan answered.

"Part of the whole *what*? What are you saying?" Tim asked. "Why don't you just say what you have to say. This cryptic crap is getting on my nerves."

"The balance must be restored."

"What the hell are you talking about? What balance?" Kate asked, crossing her arms.

"We have dealt with children like him before. We can handle it," Tim answered, waving him away.

Dowan shook his head. His expression darkened. "You don't understand. They are three. He is but one."

"Two other children?" Kate asked, her face twisted with annoyance and frustration.

Dowan took a deep breath. "You do not have understanding." His eyes lit up like windows letting in dark sunlight. The eerie glow drew them in.

"In the beginning, the universe was sentient. All things were conscious. All things had a duty to existence. Every planet and star pulsated with their own individual possibilities. Every being, every particle, every point of energy lived."

A picture swept across the blackness of his eyes. Tim and Kate clutched at each other as they looked into eyes that overtook them and pulled them in.

"As with all things, change happened. Life morphed again and again, changing, altering, into an infinity of diversity, giving birth to new and spectacular forms. The planets, like all things, lived and died. The ones that survived and flourished became fewer and fewer. Most turned into barren lumps of stone or orbiting globs of gas. This world, this Eden, is one of the few that has continued to live and thrive. Now it is dying. Its essence has been wounded and is bleeding away."

"You talk as if the planet were a living being. Almost a person..." Kate said.

Dowan nodded. "The boy is needed. He holds a part within."

"Needed for what? Look, you have to talk plainer than this. How are we supposed to understand what you're trying to say?" Tim asked.

Dowan shook his head in frustration. Taking a step backwards, he began to fade into the shadows.

"He lives in the wind." He answered, and then he was gone.

"Lives in the wind?" asked Kate. "What is that supposed to mean?"

"I don't know what's going on. But, I'm going to get to the bottom of this."

Tim stormed out of the rear compartment and entered the main part of the cabin. Kate followed close behind. He stooped down in front of Jairo. The boy was staring straight ahead.

"What is it?" asked Kaplan. "What's wrong?" He pulled Jairo closer.

"Nothing Kap. I just need to talk to Jairo for a moment."

"About what? He's traumatized. He can't…"

Tim held up a hand. "Just relax, Kap. I'm not going to hurt the boy." Kaplan firmly held his grip.

"Jairo, look at me." The boy turned his head to meet Tim's gaze. His eyes were dark and hollow like two entrances to a cave. Tim reared back at the sight. He shook his head to clear his thoughts and fought back the desire to fall into the spell cast by those eyes.

Clearing his throat, he asked, "Jairo, do you know Dowan?" The boy flinched.

Kate looked at Tim and shrugged. "Was that a yes or no?"

"I don't know." Tim said. "Jairo, what about the wind?" One corner of Jairo's mouth twitched. Tim looked back to Kate. "*I can't believe I'm doing this.*" He thought. "Jairo, what do you know about the wind?"

"What are you asking him, Tim?" Kap said. "This is crazy? He's just a little…" His words faded as the howling around them abruptly stopped. Heads raised and looked around. Everything was calm. There was no wind. The plane suddenly dropped as if someone opened their hand and let it fall. Everything inside the cabin was sent tumbling.

Tim stared gaped mouthed at the boy from the floor on the other side of the cabin. "*What the hell. What are we supposed to do with that?*" he thought. Jairo sat unmoved and unaffected. The rest of the flight to Austin was smooth and uneventful, except for the hysterical rantings of Kaplan.

CHAPTER FORTY-THREE

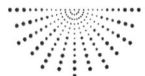

*B*ack in Austin, Tim and Kate rode in the van transporting Ben's body. Jacob followed with Kaplan and Jairo in a sedan with dark tinted windows.

"Okay stuff, what do you make of all this? I didn't want to talk about this in front of Kap. The way he freaked out on the plane, I'm afraid if I breach the subject again in front of him we'll have to tie him down."

"I can't blame him. You were there. You saw what the kid did. I mean, he did do it, didn't he?" Kate asked.

Tim shrugged. "Your guess is as good as mine. I'm more worried about this Dowan. What do you know about Animas?"

"'Animas?'" asked Jacob.

"Ben believed Dowan is an Anima and I have to admit I do too." Tim answered.

"That would explain a lot, but it raises more questions than it answers. Like if it or he is an Anima, what is he doing here? And why now? What does he really want? I could go on for hours."

"Yeah, I know," Tim brushed his hand through his hair. "I don't know much about Animas, but isn't an Anima supposed to be an avatar for something?" Kate nodded her head.

"And aren't they supposed to appear in times of great turmoil and strife?" Kate agreed. "Well, the timing is right. With what the world is going through, I would say this is a time of turmoil and strife. We have to figure out what Dowan is the spirit of. And why now. And why is he so interested in these children."

"Dowan did say they are very important. But, important to whom? To him?" Kate leaned back in her seat. "There's always the possibility that Dowan is in league with the Primae. This could be an elaborate rouse to draw us out into some kind of a trap and finish us off."

"I thought about that, too. I guess it could be a possibility, but my gut tells me this Dowan is the real deal. Ben thought so too," Tim continued.

"Ben..." Kate whispered and closed her eyes. "Okay, maybe you're right. If so, why? And how do we find the other ones he spoke of?"

Tim hunched his shoulders "I got nothing. After we take care of our personal business..." he looked over his shoulders at Ben's body, "...we'll have a meeting and see what the others think."

"Sounds good to me. Maybe somebody else has some insight." Kate twisted in her seat to face Tim. "You don't think Dowan could be...?"

"What?" Kate shook her head and waved off the thought.

"What is it?" Tim insisted, "We're trying to brainstorm here. I've got you here because I like the way you think, so out with it."

"Okay, okay, Kate said, "just thinking out loud. I know it may sound farfetched, but could Dowan be an avatar for...the planet? With all that talk about everything being sentient. I told you it would sound crazy but..."

Tim eased off the gas and leaned back into his seat. "That one went over my head, but I guess anything could be possible." Tim thought for a moment. "Until we can better understand what we're dealing with I don't want to dismiss any possibilities. Right now, I'm willing to accept that anything could be true."

Kate extended her hand against the dashboard as the ground shook, causing the van to sway. "These tremors are unnerving. They're so frequent and they feel like they're getting worse."

"Yeah, with all the reports of storms, floods and quakes, I'm beginning to wonder how much more the planet can take before it splits in two." Tim said.

"We woke the world up by exposing Hayden and his henchmen, but it may have been too late," Kate warned.

"Don't lose hope. This could just be the symptoms of a course correction," Tim said, wishing more than believing.

"If Dowan is the avatar for the planet, maybe he's trying to heal things? Maybe that's what this is all about. Maybe we should be helping him?" Kate wondered.

"Maybe, but that doesn't explain the children. The only thing I'm sure of right now is if we run into any of our friendly neighborhood road warriors, they'll be very sorry. I've got some serious pent up tension rumbling through me right now. It's a long way from Austin to Detroit, and I need to work some of this off."

Kate smiled and nestled back into her seat, hoping no one was foolish enough to get in their way.

CHAPTER FORTY-FOUR

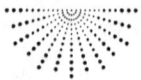

*T*he Cessna touched down on a private section of the Baton Rouge Metropolitan Airport. "Refueling and an engine check, and we'll be back in the air in no more than forty minutes," Micken said.

Ikayla looked up from her paperwork and gave him a look of contempt with the flick of her lashes.

"When we land," she said in a frosty voice, "you and Jackan are to scour Detroit until you find the Ceteri. I want to know where they are and what they are doing with the boy. Use whatever resources are needed. I have had my fill of theses miscreants. It is time we put an end to their meddling once and for all." She sank back into her papers.

Half smiling and half grimacing, Micken returned to his seat on the other end of the plane with Jackan.

"You are positive you killed one of them?" he asked.

"With the amount of blood on the road. There is no doubt," Jackan boasted with a smile, while mindlessly opening and closing his knife.

"Well, there's that at least. We have been given instructions to locate the Ceteri, with all due haste."

"It appears their little drama in the hotel room has bruised some one's ego." Jackan snickered.

"I'd show a bit more discretion," Micken looked over his shoulder. "Ikayla possesses a considerable amount of power and ability; not to mention she has considerable backing from some powerful elements."

Jackan noisily clicked his knife closed. "So, do I."

Micken turned and gave him his full attention. The implications of his statement struck him full in the face. He didn't know whether to smile or frown. A slight tilt of the head, a knowing grin, and he said, "I find it to be the bane of our species and maybe even our eventual downfall, that we only give birth to Caesars."

Jackan shrugged his shoulders. "Do you expect water not to be wet or a star not to shine? We are what we are."

He smiled. "By the way, you do whatever it is you do. I will deal with the Ceteri." He leaned back in his chair and closed his eyes.

"I would refrain from repeating your actions in Houston. I believe Ikayla did not approve."

Jackan smiled and turned onto his side.

CHAPTER FORTY-FIVE

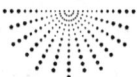

"*T*hat was a nice service," Titus said. "Ben would have been pleased that you kept things simple."

"Losing Ben has been hard on the whole group. I thought something small and simple would be best," Tim responded. "...with the state of things outside, the upheaval going on around the world, and this thing with the Anima and the kids, we're all stretched a little thin. Nobody is sure what is going to happen next. A long emotional service would have been too much of a burden."

Titus leaned in toward Tim. "I looked into what you asked me about," he pulled Tim into a corner of the room.

"There's not a lot in the archives, and most of what is there is speculation and hearsay at best. Not a whole lot more than what you already know."

"Animas are our equivalent to the humans' conception of Angels. The main difference is we don't think they are messengers for God. You could call them the Angels of the Angels, but they're free agents." He laughed. When Tim gave him a dry response, he flushed red. "Sorry, I couldn't help it."

"Animas are an anomaly, more myth than anything else. According to legend and that's all we have to go by, they appear very rarely and for a limited time. It seems they are more spirit than flesh but are considered very powerful. They are connected to whatever is happening when they appear.

"Some have speculated that they are really just physical manifestations of our anxieties; our fears made tangible. Some say they move between dimensions as easily as we walk from room to room. They are supposedly time-fluid and they have the ability to move anywhere in space and time."

Titus blew out a breath. "It got way too metaphysical for me. I couldn't understand all of it. As far as this Dowan is concerned, I can't say whether he's friend or foe. They have been known to bring good and bad fortune in their wake. In our history they have been considered bringers of retribution and delivers of judgement. Sound like Angels, don't they?" He raised his brows.

"Take your pick. I think a lot of what's said about them is wild speculation trying to explain what nobody understands." Titus shook his head. "That's about all there was," he added.

"Oh yeah, there was this passage: *Creation serves. Life endures.* It was in big bold letters on several pages."

"What does that mean?" Tim asked. Titus shrugged his shoulders.

"What about the children? Did you find anything about them?"

"That's the one bright spot," Time explained. "...they're prodigies, little Einsteins and Mozarts, only greatly enhanced by their blood line. The talents, or power, or whatever you want to call it, transfigures them. Those are their words not mine."

"What do you mean transfigures, like a caterpillar to a butterfly?"

"No, it bonds with them, allowing them to become one with whatever skill they have. Like Jairo could become a great aviator. He is connected to his element on a primal level. They become a genius at it, an innovator. They change things."

"So, it's like an enhanced talent they are born into?" Tim asked.

"Yeah, like that, but more. That is as long as nobody messes with it. There were some stories of some trying to control and use their gifts. The results were disastrous."

Tim raised his brows and asked. "Do I want to know?"

"There was one story with some kid who was connected to fire." Titus shook his head. "Burned nearly a whole continent before they realized the mistake they made."

"Okay. Thanks for looking. You're right, that more or less confirms my suspicions. It coincides with what I've heard through the years. Look, keep this to yourself. I don't want the fact that we have an Anima hanging around to become common knowledge. It might spook the others. We can't have the group freaking out," Tim warned.

"Got you. I wouldn't know what to tell anybody, anyway. I'm not sure if I totally believe all this." Titus responded.

Tim patted him on the back. "Believe it, Titus. This Dowan is real."

CHAPTER FORTY-SIX

"*I* was wondering when you'd show up again," Dowan moved out of the shadow in the corner of Tim's room and stood beside the bed. Tim leaned back on his pillows.

"Let me say this up front. I don't particularly trust you. I have doubts and lots of questions." Dowan nodded. "Are you an Anima?" Dowan did not answer. Tim sighed.

"Alright, in some way are you connected to the planet?" Dowan nodded. "Can you fix what's going? I mean, repair the planet. You know, make it right again?"

"I can aid, but, I am only a part, a nexus."

"The children you spoke of are the other parts?"

Dowan nodded again. "Together, we are one."

"How are you one?"

Dowan stared straight ahead and did not answer.

"Whatever," Tim mumbled. "Okay, just tell me what we can do to make this right and where the other children are."

Dowan moved closer and placed his hand against Tim's head. His hand became translucent and sank into Tim's head as if it was entering a pool of water.

Tim jerked into an upright position. His eyes fluttered and rolled back into his head. He tried to speak, but the words died in his throat. Tim felt his mind being ripped wide open. Images and sensations rushed into his head, appearing before him like photographs in an album. He felt he wasn't just seeing these things, but that he had become a part of these visions, as if he had stepped through a window and entered these places.

The wind, the sun, and the odors were real. He became part of what he was seeing. Names, faces and all manner of information became known to him, as if his mind were a notepad and the knowledge was being written directly onto it. Dowan moved and Tim moved along with him, jumping from place to place. Quicker than an eye could blink, they moved across space and time, living days in seconds and years in a heartbeat, going from place to place like water running through a pipe.

Dowan drew his hand back. Tim collapsed like a rag doll. He was pulled back into his body.

"You now have understanding," Dowan said, his cold blank eyes gleaming like black marbles.

Tim leaned forward, his head in both hands. "What did you do to me? That was intense. My brain is still spinning in my skull."

He blew out a long slow breath. "Where were you when I was trying to learn algebra?" Tim threw his legs over the side of the bed and sat massaging his temple.

"Let's not do that again, okay? I feel like I've been drinking jet fuel. It seems I got what you wanted me to know. That and a whole lot more," Tim panted to slow down his breathing. "We'll go find the children. What do we do once we have them?"

Dowan moved back into the shadows. "I will be there."

"Of course, you will," Tim said throwing his hands into the air.

CHAPTER FORTY-SEVEN

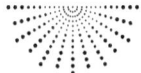

*J*ackan sipped a cup of strong black coffee. He turned his back to the three Ceteri members talking at the next table. With the concentration of a safe cracker, he listened to their conversation.

"An Anima is involved," said the first man.

"I don't believe it. They're not real. They're just legends," the second man said.

"It's true," interjected the woman. "All four of them saw it, including Ben, before he died. What I want to know is what the Anima has to do with what's going on? And what about this talk about three touched children? Three of them," she repeated as if she didn't believe her own words.

"Three?" asked the second man.

"Yeah, that's what I heard too" the first man agreed.

"I don't like this," the woman said. "The world is tearing itself apart: an Anima; touched children; Ben being killed; this does not look good for us. I have to admit I'm worried. I thought after Hayden was stopped things would get better, but they haven't. If anything, they're getting worse by the day. Are we going to survive this?"

Puzzled looks ran around the table.

"What are they doing about all this?" the second man asked.

The first man perked up. "Jacob and Kate are leaving soon to pick up one of the children. Tim and who ever are going after the other one."

"That's all fine and dandy," the second man said, "...but, what are touched children and an Anima going to do to improve things? What do they plan on doing with them?"

"Beats me," the first man said. "Maybe, they've got something worked out and these kids and the Anima are part of it."

He paused and mumbled. "Why else would they be wasting time doing this if they didn't?"

The building began to vibrate. Everyone grabbed the sides of their chair and looked up at the ceiling as if the rumbling was coming from the sky and not the ground. The three grabbed their mugs as they began dancing across the table. The tremor lasted 5 seconds, but felt like an hour, leaving them speechless. The trio shared a silent nod in solidarity and hugged their mugs even harder.

Jackan left the coffee house and returned to his car parked down the street from the Ceteri's warehouse.

"An Anima," he thought. *"Three children who are all touched."* Jackan leaned back and contemplated the possibilities.

They probably have the one boy locked away. I'll never get near him again, but maybe I can get my hands on one of the others, he said, thinking aloud.

CHAPTER FORTY-EIGHT

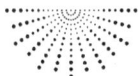

"You two are going to Toronto and get the boy." Tim said to Kate and Jacob. "It appears that the Primae aren't aware of these kids yet. He's still with his mother and father. I want you to bring the whole family here. Tell them as little as possible. Just let them know that you're bringing them in to protect them. We'll fill them in once they are here, okay?"

"What's this boy's special ability? Jairo connection is to the wind; what does this boy do?" Kate asked.

"His name is Simon, and water is his element. The girl's name is Charlene, and earth is her domain. From what Dowan showed me, the children somehow embody earth, wind, and water. He seems to be the fire that melds them together. How? I don't exactly know. He showed me a lot of things. I will admit, a lot of it I don't understand. With the way things are spiraling out of control, I don't have time to understand. I don't need to understand. I just need to know enough to do something that helps."

"I just talked to Chris last night," Kate piped in. "He'll be in town tomorrow. He sounded pretty low. Chris says the UN Commission that has been coordinating the rescues and relocations around the world are working non-stop. They've nearly gotten to the point where they've accepted the fact they're fighting a losing battle."

"What do you mean, fighting a losing battle? Are they throwing in the towel and giving up?" Jacob asked.

"Their scientists say despite what we tried to do, we may have been too late. We may have crossed that threshold. Things are only going to get worse. They're just not sure how bad it's going to get. It's like the planet is having seizures. It's tearing itself apart. They don't know if there's anything they can do. Thousands, hundreds of thousands, have already died. Soon it will be millions, then billions. When it reaches that point we can stop worrying about rescuing and feeding and housing everyone and start to worry about the unstoppable famine and disease."

"That makes what we are trying to do that much more important," Tim said. "This Anima and these children maybe our only hope."

"We're putting an awful lot of trust in someone we don't even know. Are you sure you can trust this information you got from Dowan?" Kate asked.

"I know," answered Tim. "But, do we really have a choice? I don't know anything else we can do."

He looked from face to face. "If anybody has any other ideas of what we can do, speak up. Now is the time before we commit ourselves to this."

The room remained silent. Nervous heads turned away from making eye contact. "He's been right so far. I can't explain what he did to me. The way he gave me this information. For a few moments, I was a part of him. We were one entity. I can still feel what he felt, his sorrow, his despair, maybe even a little fear."

Tim paused and shook his head like a swimmer breaking the surface of the water.

"I don't totally understand it or like it. Do I trust the him? I can't say yes. But, I do trust the information."

"What if they don't want to come?" Jacob asked.

"That is not an option. I don't care what you have to say or do. Get them here." Tim responded.

"When do we leave?" Kate asked.

"An hour ago," he waved goodbye to them. They turned and left the warehouse.

"Titus," Tim said, turning to the man at his side. "I'd like to take you with me to pick up the girl, but with losing Ben I need somebody here that knows what they're doing, someone I can trust. That, my friend, is you."

"I'm kinda getting used to being left behind. You're starting to make me feel like the ugly red-headed stepchild," he laughed and slapped Tim on the back.

"It's okay, I understand. Why don't you take Samson? That boy needs something to do other than cleaning out the vehicles and making pizza runs."

"Find him and get him ready then. We leave for Arkansas in one hour," Tim said.

CHAPTER FORTY-NINE

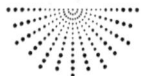

"*N*ormally we could make this trip in 4 or 5 hours, but with this weather it's going to be more like 7 or 8. That is, if we don't encounter any problems." Jacob reached over and squeezed Kate's hand "Are you alright? I don't like to see you like this."

Kate brought herself back to the moment. "I'm sorry. I don't mean to be such a downer. It's just that I'm really worried."

"Talking to Chris last night really upset you didn't it?"

Kate nodded. "When we stopped Hayden and his crew I thought we had really done something to make a difference. I thought we had bought ourselves some time to fix things." Kate leaned back in her seat and sighed. "But, look at this." she said pointing out the car window. The rain was falling down in unbroken sheets, alternating with sporadic volleys of golf ball sized hail. Small tremors rumbled so often it felt like the ground was on a conveyor belt.

"What is it, the end of August? You can't even tell what season it is. Half the trees have leaves, half don't. It's freezing one day, then sizzling hot the next. Earthquakes where there never were quakes before, floods, hurricanes, tornadoes, and fog so thick you could hide a mountain in it. I just don't know..." the words seeped out. "I'm scared."

"That's why we're doing this, isn't it? We're going to fix this. We've tried all the regular ways of doing things. The scientists have exhausted their tool bags. This is a little extra ordinary intervention."

He forced a half smile. "I haven't been big on this Dowan, but it seems like he's offering us something we can use. Something we can't turn down. A way out of this mess. There's no doubt we need some kind of help. If he's got something we can use, I'm willing to go the extra mile to make it happen." He paused. "I think we're going to have to just have a little faith that things will be alright."

"Do you really think so? Do you honestly believe these children will make a difference? What if this Dowan is just looking out for himself and the hell with the rest of us?" Kate asked anxiously.

Jacob squeezed her hand tighter. "I don't know, Kate. I hope more than now. I'm counting on the world having a future; on us having a future. Please don't give up. Don't give up on us," Jacob swallowed the lump in his throat. "I love you, Kate. I won't let that future die."

"Me neither," Kate whispered.

Jacob slapped the steering wheel. "I'll have to admit, I'm a little worried about Dowan getting into Tim's head. Could he be manipulating him? What if he's putting things in his head he wants Tim to believe? I trust Tim. I trust him with my life, but I do wish we had a backup plan."

"I trust Tim, too. I know he wouldn't do anything to sabotage us. I have to believe he knows what he's doing." Kate leaned over and kissed him on the cheek. "You're a good man, Jacob. If you keep this up, I might have to marry you after all."

He shrugged his shoulder. "That's a foregone conclusion. I'm just waiting on you to order that dress." The car swerved on the slippery road. Kate reached out and braced herself against the dashboard. Jacob smiled at her. "See how you upset me?"

Kate forced a smile and stared out anxiously at the raging storm.

She and Jacob took no notice of the gray sedan that had followed them out of the city. Jackan followed behind, never letting the tan colored car get too far ahead.

"Three children touched? How can that be? If it's true, this is really something special. Just what I need. If I can get my hands on one, two or why not all three. And an Anima," he said to the gathering storm. *"Think of the power."* Jackan drove and planned, matching the gray sedan turn for turn.

CHAPTER FIFTY

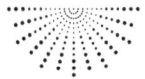

"*W*ho is it?" came the response to Kate's knock on the apartment door.

"I'm looking for the Campbells."

A short waifish woman with wispy black hair and large sad gray eyes peeked out through a crack in the door. "What do you want?"

"Sybil Campbell, my name is Kate and this is Jacob. Can we talk? This is very important."

" Go away. We don't want to buy anything."

"We're not selling anything," Jacob added. "We just need to talk to you about…" He looked around and whispered. "The Primae."

Her eyes jumped wide open and she slammed the door.

"Nice going, Mr. Smooth," Kate said. "You want to go find some puppies to drop kick?"

Jacob shrank back. "I didn't mean to frighten her."

Kate shook her head.

"Sybil," she said to the closed door. "We aren't the Primae. But, we know they're looking for you. We've come to take you and your family somewhere safe." There was no answer.

"Sybil, you know if we were the Primae, we would just knock down the door and take you. Jacob and I are part of the Ceteri. We were sent to help you." Still no response. "Please. Sybil, we want to help."

The door cracked open. Kate pushed it and it swung all the way open. Sybil was standing, trembling, in the middle of the room. Kate moved to her.

"Don't be afraid. We aren't going to hurt you. You're safe, I promise." Kate looked around the sparsely furnished room. "Why don't we sit down?" Kate guided Sybil to the sofa. "Where are your husband and son?"

"They're at the park. Simon loves the swings. They'll be back soon."

Kate smiled at her. She hesitantly returned it. "Sybil, have you noticed anything unusual about Simon lately?"

Sybil tensed and clutched her hands. "Simon is autistic. He's different from other children."

Kate and Jacob looked at each other.

"Sybil," Jacob said, "Simon isn't autistic. He's touched. Do you know what that means?"

She nodded "But he can't be. I'm a half blood and that makes him only one quarter. Only pure bloods are touched."

"That's what we thought too, but he's not the only one. There are two more just like him. We need to get you and him somewhere safe before the Primae find you." Sybil went stiff at the mention of the name.

The door opened and a short man with curly hair and a lost expression walked into the room. A pudgy cheeked young boy preceded him, running to the waiting arms of his mother.

"Sybil what's wrong? Who are these people?" the man asked cautiously.

Sybil looked up at him with relief in her eyes. "It's alright, Alexander. They are here to help."

An hour later, the group was on the road to Detroit.

The rain had held back, though the skies looked ominous and menacing. The wind swept a steady carpet of leaves and brush crisscrossing the road. Jacob, Simon, and Alexander sat in the front seats talking cars and land marks. Kate and Sybil sat in the back huddled together.

"Are you two married?" Sybil asked.

Kate flushed and quickly answered. "No, no we're just good friends."

"Oh, I'm sorry. I just thought…"

"Just thought what?" asked Kate.

"If you don't mind me saying. It's kind of obvious that he cares about you. I mean, the way he looks at you. You know, the way a man looks at a shiny new car or a new power tool."

"Nice to know I at least rate up there with new appliances."

"I didn't mean it like that. It's just that men have a limited range of emotions."

"I don't know what men you've been hanging around with, but the ones I know have an overabundance of emotions." The two women looked into each other's eyes and laughed.

"Kate, what's this all about? I appreciate you coming to look for us, but I know this is about more than protecting us from the Primae. Though Alex won't say it, I know he's relieved. He's been walking on egg shells ever since I told him the truth. The poor man is looking over his shoulder so often it's a wonder he doesn't have whip lash. He's afraid he won't be able to protect us if they come for me. I don't have the heart to tell him he's right." She locked eyes with Kate. "This has something to do with Simon, doesn't it? With his," she paused, "…condition."

Kate looked away. "Yes," she said softly. "I don't know totally what's going on, but it's important. I'm asking you to trust us. When we get to the warehouse everything will be explained. We have only positive intentions for you and your family. As a matter of fact, we think you may be able to help us all." Sybil opened her mouth to ask how.

"Bathroom break," Jacob announced. "Mr. Simon has made a request."

"Sounds good to me," said Kate. I would like to stretch my legs. We've been cramped in a lot of cars lately.

Jacob pulled into a rest area and parked in front of the concession stand. "Anybody want anything special?" he asked. "I'm going for chips and sodas."

"Is there anything you like better than eating" asked Kate.

"Yes," he said and winked at her. Kate blushed. Sybil gave her a smiling glance.

"Some 'Sour Worms,'" yelled Simon, as his father led him skipping to the rest room.

Kate and Sybil stepped inside the building lounge area out of the wind. "He's got it bad." Sybil said smiling. Kate blushed and moved to look at the map.

Jacob returned with an arm full of sodas and sweets. "Where's Simon and Alexander?" he asked.

"I don't know," said Sybil. "They have been gone a while. I'll go check on them."

"No, let me," offered Jacob, handing over his load of snacks. "They are in the men's room after all." Jacob headed toward the lavatory.

A loud crash broke the peace of the rest stop. The sound of a child's screams filled the area. Thunder cracked, and sheets of rain rushed down like stampeding horses. Jacob took off running with Kate and Sybil following behind. A car barreled out from the side of the building that housed the rest rooms. Jacob dove out of the way as the vehicle sped directly at him. In the car, he saw a man driving with one hand and struggling to hold down a screaming child with the other.

"Simon," he shouted. The car wove through the lot and headed for the freeway. "That guy has Simon." Jacob started to run to the car.

"Simon!" Sybil screamed.

"Where's Alexander?" Kate shouted.

"Alexander, what happen to Alexander?" Sybil screamed, grabbing her hair in terror.

Jacob stopped and turned back to the men's room. He burst in the door. Alexander was lying bleeding on the floor. Streams were shooting out of the broken faucets, flooding the floor, creating pools of crimson water as they mixed with Alexander's blood.

Kate rushed in and knelt beside him." He's been stabbed, but he's alive. We have to stop the bleeding." Sybil stood in the doorway screaming. "Jacob get the car while I try and stop the bleeding. We've got to get him to a hospital."

Jacob looked at Kate. "The Primae have Simon." I recognized that guy. He was one of the guys in the car when Ben was killed. The one with the gun.

Kate's eyes danced in their sockets. Alexander's moan made her decision for her.

"We have to save Alexander. That has to be our priority right now. We'll go after Simon once we take care of this." She looked down at the still bleeding wound. "Get the car."

Jackan raced down the highway. He slapped the struggling child, sending him crouching down on to the floor of the car. Simon cried and screamed.

"Shut up," he shouted. "Do as you're told, and I won't do to you what I did to your father."

Simon's screams dissolved in a weak whimper. He sat on the floor and hugged his knees to his chest. The skies cried with him, pouring out buckets of rain.

Jackan sped away, imagining the power he could syphon from the young body at his feet.

CHAPTER FIFTY-ONE

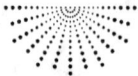

*S*amson eased the SUV up the wooded pass. "Are you sure anybody lives way out here? We haven't seen a house or a farm for 40 miles, just acres of trees."

"This is timber country. These trees are the farm." Tim lowered the window. "These guys are intent on staying off the grid. I'd bet we're the first ones in these woods in years."

"At least the tremors have stopped. Or maybe you just don't feel them up here."

"I have a sneaky suspicion that little girl may have something to do with that. Remember earth is her thing."

"What, she's controlling the earthquakes?"

"Maybe not controlling them, but her being around has some effect on them."

Samson gave him a skeptical look.

The SUV crested a plateau and came onto an open field. In the distance a small one-story house sat between a trio of giant oak trees. As the vehicle crept closer to the house, a man in corduroys and a flannel shirt stepped out from around the back of the building. He was tall and muscular with piercing brown eyes and a 12-gauge shot gun slung over his shoulder.

Samson and Tim exited the car and approached the man. "How are you doing? We're looking for the Hinkell family. Are you Gerald Hinkell?" Tim asked.

"Might be, might not be. Depends on who's asking and what they want."

"Does the name Ceteri mean anything to you?" The man frowned and maintain his dead eyed stare. "How about the Primae?" Tim asked. The man lowered the shot gun from his shoulder.

"I guess he's heard of them." Samson said, taking a step back.

Tim held up his hands "Hold on, Mr. Hinkell; Gerald. Do you mind if I call you Gerald?" He didn't respond. "I'm Tim and this is Samson. We are part of the Ceteri. If you know what that means, you know we are no threat to you or your family. We're on the same side. You have nothing to fear from us."

"I don't have a side."

Tim ignored the comment. "We just want to talk to you. I promise, we'll explain everything."

"You can explain the hell off my place. We don't want no part of you or what you're offering." He raised the gun to face them. "We're already safe and we plan on keeping it that way. As long as we stay away from the likes of you," he said. "The Primae are no concern of ours. We stay off the grid. They'll never find us out here."

"We found you, didn't we?" Samson asked.

"We'll just get lost again. And this time I'll make sure nobody finds us."

A voice came from an open window. "You might as well let them come in Gerald. If they know we're here, I'm sure there are others that know as well."

Tim nodded. "Come on Gerald, you must know that if the Primae wants you, they'll find you. And they do want you. They have an extra incentive..." Tim paused for effect. "...your daughter."

Gerald reared up and took a step forward. Both men took a step back. "What about my daughter?"

"We know that she's touched. They probably know it too. They will want her and her abilities."

The door of the house swung open and a tall slim woman with high cheek bones and long flowing black hair stepped out. The frightened expression in her eyes, mirrored the alarm in her voice. "How do you know about our Charlene?" At the mention of her name, a young girl who was the duplicate of her mother, but in miniature, peeked from around her dress.

"Go back into the house, Darla. I'll handle this." Gerald said, irritation in his voice.

"No, Gerald. Ever since you told me about this, we've been running and hiding and pretending we were safe. Now that people are showing up we have to rethink things." Gerald rolled his eyes and let out an audible sigh.

The little girl frowned and pouted her lips at the tension in the air. She stood with her arms folded and anger in her eyes. The ground began to rumble. The house shook. The old oak trees swayed. Darla reached down and picked up her little girl. "It's alright, sweetie. The men are just here to talk to mommy and daddy. Everything is okay." The tremor subsided.

Samson and Tim shared a nervous look. Gerald narrowed his eyes and grinned. Darla waved them in before turning and disappearing into the house.

Gerald waited for Tim and Samson to enter before following them in and taking a seat on the sofa next to Darla and Charlene. The gun at his side. "Alright," he said. "Speak your piece, so you can be on your way."

"This is such a fantastic story I almost don't know where to start," Tim said.

"How about just telling the part that concerns us." Gerald said.

"The whole thing concerns you." Samson said. "It concerns you and me and them," he pointed at his family. "And the whole darn world."

"Easy Samson," Tim said before turning back to Gerald. "The story is complicated, but it involves your daughter, two other kids that are touched, and an Anima."

Gerald jumped to his feet. "Do you think I'm an idiot? Anima aren't even real. And as far as two other kids, one child is born like Charlene in a thousand years. I don't..."

Tim interrupted. "How do you think we found you? How do you think we even know who you are? Dowan, the Anima told me." Tim shook his head. "Well, he didn't really tell me. He showed me...but, that's another story all together."

"Dowan," Charlene said perking up and jumping out of her mother's lap.

Tim looked at Darla. She and everyone else was looking at a joyful Charlene. "Do you know Dowan, sweetheart?" Tim asked.

"He's my friend. He comes and plays with me." She said.

Tim turned to Darla. She shook her head and shrugged her shoulders. "I didn't know." Turning Charlene around to look at her, she asked. "Is Dowan your imaginary friend?"

"He is real. He comes at night to play with me." Charlene smiled.

Darla grabbed her daughter and pulled her to her breast not knowing exactly what to feel. "What is an Anima and why is he visiting my daughter?"

Gerald sat with his mouth open. "This can't be. Animas aren't real."

"That's what I thought too, Gerald. But, this one is real, and he is connected to these children. I didn't know he had visited any of them." He turned to Samson. "That was a yes from Jairo. He has visited the other children too."

Tim bit his lip before continuing. "Like I said, there are three of them; Charlene and two boys. Each one has an ability with one of the elements. Charlene, the earth, Jairo, the wind, and Simon, the water. Somehow these kids and this Anima are connected to the planet. Dowan has said that if they are all together they can do something to help heal the world. You see how our world is tearing itself apart. Charlene may have some control over keeping the ground still, but I know you've experienced the storms. These children and this Anima might be our last chance to save the planet and save ourselves."

"What are you asking? That we bring our daughter to this thing?" Darla asked, hugging her daughter and looking form Gerald to Tim and back again.

"Look, folks somehow these kids and this Anima are connected. As time goes by, I think she will become more and more connected to him. She'll end up like Jairo, despondent, and almost catatonic."

"No way," said Gerald. "There is no way I'm taking my daughter near this thing. You can just get in your car and head back to where ever you came from."

"You're not listening, man. She's already near him. They're connected. He's been visiting here." Samson said.

"Mommy, what's wrong? Don't you like Dowan?" Charlene asked.

Darla stumbled with what to say. "It's not that sweetheart. It's just..." She looked to Gerald for help. He just stared blankly.

"I don't know what else to tell you, but come with us. One way or another you'll have to face this. I don't know how or even if you can break the connection between them. At least with us you'll have some help. People who are on your side. If you turn away, you'll have to deal with this on your own. You'll be working in the blind. I don' t think you want that. Then there is the Primae to think about. Sooner or later they'll come for Charlene. They don't sit down and talk. Do you really want to face them alone?"

"Gerald..." Darla's said her voice shaky. "...we can't do this on our own anymore. I know you've always kept us safe, but things have changed. We can't turn away their help."

Gerald looked at his family. His eyes dropped to the floor before he raised his head and stared at Tim. "I'm not turning my little girl over to no Anima. We'll go with you." He looked at Darla for her agreement. "But if things start happening we don't like, we're leaving. And that's final."

"That's all I can ask."

Charlene walked over to Tim. "Is Dowan your friend too?"

Tim took her hand. "I certainly hope so, sweetheart. I certainly hope so."

CHAPTER FIFTY-TWO

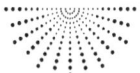

$\mathcal{T}$im walked into the building with Charlene skipping at his side, holding his hand. The others trailed behind them. The warehouse complex was a collection of inter-connected buildings spanning two city blocks. Reconfigured and rehabbed, the Ceteri had turned the old industrial structures into an all-encompassing living and working environment.

Titus met them as they were checking in. He leaned down, putting his hands on his knees, looking the little girl in the face. "And who do we have here? A princess, I would suspect?"

"Titus, this is Charlene. Our honored guest and these are her parents Gerald and Darla Hinkell."

"Welcome, I'm pleased to meet you. I'm Titus. If there is anything you need, I'm the man to see. And that goes double for you, little princess." Charlene giggled and hugged Tim's leg. "It seems you have an admirer."

Tim shrugged. "What can I say. The women love me."

"Samson," Titus said. "Why don't you take our guest and get them settled in." He looked at Charlene out the corner of his eyes.

"I believe if you hurry there might be some cake left in the galley." Charlene lit up at the mention of sweets.

"Come on folks, this way," Samson guided them into another section of the building.

"We'll talk after you get some rest," Tim yelled after them.

"I'm glad you're back," Titus said after they were out of range. "I'm afraid we have a problem. A big problem." He pointed his head toward a door in the far corner. "Kate and Jacob are in the meeting room. You'll want to talk to them straight away."

Tim walked in on a distressed-looking Kate and Jacob. His heart sank when he saw the looks on their face. "What wrong? Didn't you find Simon and his family?"

"We found him alright and convinced them to come back with us." Jacob said.

"Then everything's' good?" he asked, pressing for the answer he wanted and not one he was afraid to hear.

"Not quite," Kate said. "When we were on our way back, we stopped at a rest area. Alexander, that's Simon's father was attacked and stabbed. His attacker kidnapped Simon."

Tim closed his eyes as if by not seeing them he could stop the news from being true.

"It was the Primae," Jacob blurted out. "I got a look at the guy driving as he was speeding away. It was the guy in the car that chased you in Puerto Rico. The one with the gun. The one who killed Ben."

He pounded the table and huffed like a steam engine. "Bastard."

Tim clenched his fists as a picture of Jackan filled his mind.

"We couldn't chase him. We had to get Alexander to a hospital. He was hurt really bad. He almost died." Kate added, embarrassed at the admission.

Tim slid down in a chair. "No, you made the right choice. You couldn't let the guy bleed to death. The Primae want Simon alive. He should be alright, at least for now." He massaged his temple.

"How is he now, the father? Will he be alright?"

"He lost a lot of blood, but he'll make it. We left him and his wife in a hospital about half way between here and Toronto, in London, Canada. They'll join us here when he's able to travel."

"How did they know?" Jacob asked. "We just found out about these kids ourselves a couple of days ago." He looked sideways at Tim.

"Could Dowan have told them where the boy was? Could he be playing both sides here? After all we don't really know what his end game is."

"I don't know," Tim said. He took a deep breath. "Look, Jacob I know you don't trust him and believe it or not I share some of the same concerns, but I think you're way off on this one. They must be watching us. That's the only other explanation that makes sense. I think it's a safe bet to assume you were followed. I can't be sure, but I don't think Samson and I were. Were there more than one of them? "

"I only saw one," Jacob said looking to Kate for confirmation.

"Well there's that. At least we don't have a *Perdidi unum* to deal with this time," Kate looked up at the reference to Kelp.

Jacob reached over and squeezed her hand. Tim bite his lip when the thoughtlessness of his comment struck him. The room fell silent for a moment.

Tim cleared his throat and returned to business. "I'll get with Titus. We'll have to beef up security. They may try to acquire the other children."

"We have to get him back. I promised they would be safe if they came with us. And all we did was almost get Alexander killed while we stood around and watched Simon be taken." Kate said, almost in tears. "We led them straight to him."

"Calm down, Kate. You're didn't put them in harm's way. The Primae just took advantage of the situation. We will get him back." he added, more as a thought than a statement. "We have to."

"How are we going to find him? The Primae could have him anywhere. We have no idea where they are or what they're doing with him." Jacob said. "I'm sorry Tim. We..." he let out a deep sigh. "...we blew it."

"No, you didn't. I want you two to stop beating yourselves up. You're two smart and capable members of our group. I would trust my life to either one of you. This could have happened to anyone of us. We've had set backs before. We just have to fix it, that's all." Tim answered firmly.

"Do you think Dowan would help again?" Kate asked. "He found him before, he can probably do it again. Can't he?" Jacob looked at her and frowned.

"Whenever he shows up, I'll ask him. I don't see any reason why he shouldn't help. He seems to want the children as badly as we do." Tim leaned on the desk. "Things out there are getting worse by the day, by the hour. I just hope we have time for this." Tim pinched the bridge of his nose.

"Kate, I want you and Jacob to question our guests, call Simon's parents, and talk to Kaplan. Don't interrogate them, just talk to them and see if you can put some pieces together. Find out what you can about these kids. Try and find out what they have in common. Find a reason why these kids were chosen. I don't believe this is just random. I don't like that we've been acting in the dark for so long. Let's see if we can get ahead of things for once.

"Don't dismiss anything. We don't know what could be important. We're losing more than we're winning lately. We can't afford to keep doing that. Let's turn this thing around." Tim blew out a long breath.

"I'm really beat, I need to try and get some rest before it's time to go after Simon. Besides, our friend doesn't seem to like coming around when there's a crowd." Giving them a weak smile, he slowly made his way to his room.

CHAPTER FIFTY-THREE

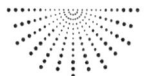

*J*ackan locked a collar around Simon's neck and chained him to an iron bedpost. Simon sat in the middle of the bed and whimpered like a scared puppy. Rain pounded against the windows turning the view into a washed-out water color. The downpour ebbed and flowed with his flow of tears, going from sprinkles to torrential storms.

"Cry all you want to. No one will hear you. No one can find you. We're all alone until you give me what I want." Jackan's phone chimed to life. Micken's name flashed across the screen. He ignored the request, along with the dozen others he had dismissed.

"When I return," he said looking at the shivering child, "...you will give me what I want, or I will take it."

Simon jumped at the sound of the slamming door. He yanked and pulled on the chain, howling and weeping. The rains increased.

Jackan slipped into the Primae's apartment and headed for a stack of obscure tomes tucked away in a vault in a back room.

"You have been out of touch for the last two days. What do you have to report?" Jackan spun around to see Ikayla standing in the doorway.

Trying to hide his annoyance and surprise, he responded. "I have been following your instructions,"

"And…" she raised a doubting brow.

"They are well-hidden. I haven't been able to make contact…yet."

"But, you are making progress?" The casualness in her voice was disconcerting.

"Yes," he hurriedly said. "I have all my contacts on alert. We should have what we need soon."

Ikayla walked over to him and stared deep into his eyes. "Good."

Jackan was so distracted by the intensity of her gaze and her close proximity that he did not notice the small device being dropped into his jacket pocket. Ikayla pivoted and exited the room without further acknowledging him.

Jackan heaved a deep breath and proceeded to the vault. Removing a slender book from inside it, he slipped it into his pocket. Silently he made his way out of the apartment, making sure to inspect his path before proceeding.

'Give him fifteen minutes," Ikayla said to Micken from behind drawn curtains. "The tracker will lead us to him."

"What will you do once we find him?"

Ikayla smiled. "Knowing that he has disobeyed my directives and instituted his own agenda, I will be magnanimous and give him the chance to redeem himself. Knowing Jackan, he will deny any duplicity and try to explain his way out of this." Her laughter was deep and throaty.

"I can smell the ambition reeking from him like musk on a sweaty dog." She paused and tilted her head as if she needed the thought to go to a certain part of her head for analysis before she could speak on it.

"It has been a while since I have performed a reading. I hope I'm not too out of practice."

"It's true you are a reader?" Micken asked.

Ikayla fixed him with an imperious stare. "Yes, it is not commonly known, but you will find, Micken, I have many skills."

CHAPTER FIFTY-FOUR

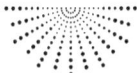

$\mathcal{T}$im laid in his bed dozing in and out of sleep, waiting for Dowan to make an appearance. The heavy rains outside pelted the building like a barrage of stones. Worry and frustration raced through Tim's mind like a rat in a maze. He tried to relax, when in reality, he was calling out for to Dowan. Doubts about the Anima kept floating to the surface. Was Jacob right? Were they being manipulated? Had Dowan told the Primae where Simon was? What does he really want? Were they being played? Was he putting the children and his team in harm's way? Could they really do something to save the planet? Or was this just the latest wasted effort in a string of useless efforts? Tim snatched his pillow and threw it across the room. The pillow flew through the air and passed through the figure stepping out of the shadows.

"It's about time you showed up," His voice dripped with sarcasm and anger. "Why didn't you tell me that you had been visiting Charlene and the other children?"

"They have always been with me, we are one."

"What do you mean, we are one? They're mortal. You're...whatever you are."

"From the time of their conception we have been joined. They complete me. They are mine."

"Yours, what are you saying? Are you planning to take the children?'

"They will be with me."

Tim leapt out of the bed. "You can't take them. They have families, people who love them."

"They are already with me. They have always been with me. They are part of me and I am part of them." For the first time something close to a smile crossed his lips.

Tim felt a ripple of fear at the reaction. "I won't let you take the children."

"You cannot stop what is already done," Dowan's voice echoed like the sounds from the mouth of a cave. His face remained expressionless. His eyes blank and mysterious.

Tim marched in place as if he was going to rush him. He waved a balled fist at him. "I don't care if the planet goes to hell. I'm not going to let you take those kids!" he yelled.

Dowan remained mockingly silent.

"We've got a problem. You're not taking those kids and that is final. There has to be another way," He swallowed the growing lump in his throat, trying to rein in his anger.

The Anima wobbled slightly like a three-legged table.

"What is wrong with you?"

"Time is limited. There is chaos. Forces are…" Dowan grabbed his head and let out a throaty groan like a dying animal.

"What is it?"

"He is in distress."

"Who is in distress?"

"The young one."

"Do you mean Simon? That is our problem. The Primae have him. Do you know where he is?"

"I am with him."

"Tell me where he is, damn it." Dowan raised his hand and moved toward Tim.

"Not again." Tim said bracing himself.

Dowan's hand reached into his mind and Tim stiffened like a board. Images rushed at him. This time it was different, more intense. Pain coursed through his body, He saw Simon, chained and despondent. Jackan stood scowling down on him.

Dowan faltered. His eyes flashed red. Something was wrong. He seemed to come apart and spread in all directions like spilled water. Tim felt as if he was being dragged by a rudderless speed boat over choppy water. Countless images poured into Tim's mind. Pictures of the children. Their eyes as black and lifeless as the Anima. The same emotionless expression on their faces. They stood around Dowan like the legs of a tripod. The children seemed to have become a part of him rather than separate beings, as if they were grafted to him and shared the same body. An aura of energy radiated from them that was both brilliant and terrifying.

Dowan looked down on a vicious play of destruction. A sneer of delight on his face. Angry storms bared down sending down torrents of rain and hail. Plumes of magma erupted from craters in the ground as violent quakes shook the ground as if a giant hand was shaking the earth like a snow globe. The winds swirled about ripping trees from the ground, leveling buildings and whipping blinding plumes of dirt and debris through the air.

The land was a smoldering heap of chaos and devastation. Dowan reveled over this play of devastation with a frightening glower of delight. Mounds of dead and dying bodies laid scattered about like random piles of pebbles. Tim wrenched from the smell of death around him. The screams of the dying masses caused him to press his hands over his ears and turn away in horror. Tim collapsed in on himself, screamed, and fell onto the floor.

His consciousness floated in a void. A foreboding emptiness surrounded him.

"Save the children," the voice said. "Don't give him the power. Don't let him use the children." Tim saw the image of Ben come together before him, an image taking form in the nothingness.

"Ben, is that you? How can this be?"

"Dowan opened the door that allowed me to reach out. The whole planet is in danger. He has been unleashed. All that you know it is in danger. Dowan will destroy all life. He is a never-ending cycle of death and rebirth. His only desire is to destroy in order to recreate. Only to destroy again. You must stop him. He must not be allowed to redefine his fate. He is the spirit of the planet, the embodiment of life. He must not be allowed to have control. His duty is to serve." The image started to fade.

"Ben, don't go! Help us, please!"

"Creation serves, Life…" The words faded with the image.

Tim awoke in the morning, curled in a ball on the floor at the foot of his bed. Dowan was nowhere to be found. He sat on the side of the bed and tried to make sense of what he remembered. What was real and what was a dream. His mind struggled to determine the difference. The images were fractured, blurry and incomplete, but an ominous sense of dread lingered in his mind. As the pictures of the night before took shape, Tim fear of the Anima grew. He dressed and ran to see the children.

Kaplan was looking haggard and spent as if he hadn't slept in days. His eyes hung heavy like rain clouds. Jairo sat, crossed legged on the floor like a yogi, silent and detached.

"What's wrong with him, Tim?" Kaplan asked, as Tim came into the room. "He just sits here. Never saying or doing anything. I have to force food down his throat or he'd just sit there and fade away. And his eyes, his eyes are…dead." He dropped his head into his hands.

"I don't know Kap, just hang in there we're working to solve this." Tim sat down and faced the boy. "Dowan," was all he said. Jairo tilted his head toward him. Tim stood. "Just as I thought. Dowan is in contact with him as well." Dowan's words came back to him. *We are becoming the same*".

"What does it all mean? Kap asked again.

"I'm not totally sure, yet. Just make sure you stay close to him. Don't let him out of your sight."

Tim met Kate in the hall on his way to see Charlene.

"I've been looking for you." Tim wasn't sure if it was agitation, fear, or surprise that was in her voice. "These children are special, alright. They are definitely connected. I'd even say they were chosen." Her eyes were as wide as a full moon, as if she couldn't believe what she was saying.

"All three were born the same year, same day and at the same time. All three were breach births and still-born."

"You mean they were born dead?" Tim asked.

Kate nodded her head. "All three were certified as prenatal deaths, but without intervention they all three spontaneously began breathing." She leaned in closer.

"And get this, all three have the same birth mark. On the heel of their right foot; it looks like three interlocked circles with a flame in the middle. I saw Charlene's and Jairo's. It looks like a tattoo," Kate fell back against the wall shaking her head." What are we into?"

Tim looked around as if the answer was written on the wall. "I know I'm the defacto leader right now, but I don't have any answers, just a whole lot of questions and a lump of doubt that's about to choke the life out of me. We've just got to figure this out together."

"Sorry," she said, "I know you're under a lot of pressure. I didn't want to add to the load. But, this is…I don't know." She closed her eyes and let out a long breath.

"It's alright, kiddo. Let's me check on Charlene while you find Jacob. We have to go rescue Simon. After we have all the kids together, we'll deal with Dowan. I'm afraid our friendly neighborhood Anima, may not be as friendly and helpful as advertised".

"You've seen him again?" Kate asked. Tim nodded as he hurried away.

CHAPTER FIFTY-FIVE

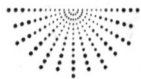

"*W*ho the hell are you?" Jackan shouted, walking in and seeing the stranger with the boy. "How the hell did you get in here." He dropped the book into a chair and produced his knife.

Dowan turned to face him. A grimace of pain and anger was on his face. His dead eyes gleamed like dark stars. Simon sat entranced and emotionless, his bonds laying at his feet.

"You're that Anima, aren't you? Step away from the kid. He is mine." He flipped out his blade and waved it like a warning flag. Jackan circled the Anima and moved toward the boy. Dowan followed his movements like a cat watching a mouse, pivoting to block his path. The rains increased, and lightening flashed washing the room in stark light. Jackan sprung forward and swung down. The knife passed through Dowan like a rock falling through air.

Jackan stumbled forward, regain his footing and stepped back in frustration. He looked from the Anima to Simon and made a decision. "If I can't have him then nobody can." With those words, he raised the knife and lunged for Simon.

Dowan stretched out his arms and caught Jackan in mid-stride enclosing him in an embrace. When his arms closed around him, Jackan's body jerked and twisted like a flag in a wind storm. His eyes grew wide and for a moment he understood everything. He teetered between life and death, this world and the next. Jackan dropped to the ground as if he was a bird shot out of the sky. The smell of charred flesh filled the room. Dowan's image flickered, and he slumped over before turning to face Simon. The boy raised his eyes to meet him. His eyes were lifeless and unfocused. "Soon," Dowan said. Something passed between them. The Anima stepped back and faded from the room.

CHAPTER FIFTY-SIX

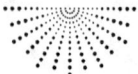

*I*kayla raised her foot and kicked in the door. She brushed at her clothing, patted her hair and walked in as if she was entering a tea party. Micken followed her in, accessing her with a growing respect. The smell assaulted her nose and she put her hand to her face. Jackan's body laid at the foot of the bed, charred and blackened like a lump of coal. Ikayla studied the boy sitting crossed leg on the bed wondering if he could be responsible for the body that laid before him.

"What happened?" Micken asked.

"Jackan obviously exceeded his capabilities." She smiled.

"The boy, do you think he did this?" Micken asked backing away from the bed.

"I doubt it. There's something else at play here."

"He's not the same one. But, look at his eyes. They're the same as the other one. He's touched. How can that be? There are never more than one born every millennium."

"I don't know. There are many things going on here that I do not know, and I do not like that. Hopefully there is still time for a reading. He can't have been dead for very long." Ikayla moved to the body, never taking her eyes off the boy.

"Watch him," she said pointing at Simon. Micken nodded and cautiously moved closer to the bed. Ikayla bent over the body, twitched her nose at the foul scent, and placed her hands above his head. She closed her eyes and concentrated.

Snatches of information began entering her mind. Her eyes shot open and she leapt to her feet.

"An Anima," her head jerked about, scanning the room.

"That's not possible. What would an Anima be doing here?" Micken said, fear creeping into his voice.

"Apparently a lot. That is what is responsible for this." She pointed at Jackan. Ikayla slowly lowered herself back to the body and resumed her work. After several minutes, she rose, wiped her hands on the bed linens, and clapped them together.

"There is no more here for us. Gather up the child and let's be out of here."

"What did you learn?"

"That there is more going on here then we realized. This child… and the others two are more important than I would have believed."

"Other two? But…"

"Not now," she insisted. "Just gather the child. The Ceteri must be looking for him as well."

"What about Jackan?" Micken asked, picking up Jackan's phone.

"What about him?" she said, stepping over the body and heading for the door.

CHAPTER FIFTY-SEVEN

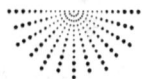

"Okay, we don't know what we're going to find in there are, so lets' stay extra sharp. Look for Simon. Whoever finds him, get him the hell out of here. We'll regroup back at the van. If for whatever reason we get separated, meet back at HQ. Got it?" Samson, Kate and Jacob nodded.

"Let's go," Tim ordered, exiting the van and taking point.

Like shadows, they crept along the walls of the building, slowing every few yards to listen for impending danger. Jacob's shoes squished and sloshed with water from the heavy rains. Everyone turned and looked at him. He gave a nervous grin and mouthed, "Sorry."

Within feet of the door, Tim stopped the band and signaled for them to maintain their position when he saw the door standing open. Alone, he crept forward and called out for the rest to join him as he stood at the opening looking into the sparsely furnished room. The smell of Jackan's torched body hung in the air. "We're too late," he sighed. "He's not here. Damn it!" He punched the wall.

"What happened?' Samson asked.

Jacob rushed in and stood over the body. He clenched his teeth and balled his fist into knots. "It's him. The one who kidnapped Simon and killed Ben." Jacob raised his foot daring to kick him. Kate moved to his side to stop him.

"Where's Simon?" Kate asked in a panic. "Does the Primae still have him?" Her eyes desperately searched the room. "What would make them kill their own man.? You don't think…"

She looked at Tim. "…Dowan had something to do with this?" She could tell he was thinking the same thing. "Could he have Simon?"

"My money's on Dowan. What reason would the Primae have for offing their own man? I knew that Anima was trouble." Jacob added, his face crunched into a scowl.

"Let's not jump to conclusions. We don't know what happened or where Simon is. Until we have the complete picture let's keep our heads," Tim rushed to say. "Look around for anything that might tell us something about where they are, or what they were doing here; anything." He avoided Kate's doubting gaze.

"Look at this collar and chain," Jacob said moving to the bed, his chest rising and falling like a bellow. "They had that little boy chained up like a dog. I just want to…" He pounded his fist into his open palm.

"Come on, reign it in. Keep your focus. We don't need anger right now. We need clear heads," Tim insisted.

"His parents are going to be here in a couple of days. What am I going to tell them?" Kate asked.

"We'll get him back," Tim offered.

"Tim," called Samson. "There's nothing but this book. It looks kind of strange. I've never seen this language before. And…" Samson stared at the book. He held it out for Tim.

"Can you feel it?" he asked. "There's something strange about this book."

Tim held the book and nodded. "There is something there. I can't explain it." He stumbled over the title. "*In Ministerium Dei Sapientiam*, in service of wisdom, I think that's what it says. It's something like Latin. But, it's an older variation, I think." He scanned a few of the pages.

"It's old, that's for sure. I can't make out much of it, maybe Andros can help us out." The others crowded around him. "There must be something in here that interested the Primae. We'll take it with us; hopefully it'll give us a clue to what they were up to. There's nothing else for us here."

Looking around the room he could feel it. In the back of his mind he knew Dowan had been here. Tim looked at Jackan and shuttered. *"Dowan did that."* Kate's eyes met his. He knew she felt it too. They kept the thought to themselves.

The rain poured down on the already flooded city as if the sky were a bucket with a hole in it. The large drops beat against the metal of the car in an avalanche of punches. Tim and the company rode in silence, each unable to muster enough breath to speak through the fog that hovered in their minds.

The End of Part II

PART III

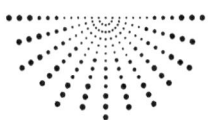

CHILDREN OF A NEW EDEN

CHAPTER FIFTY-EIGHT

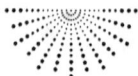

The winds churned and twisted, creating a thick cloud of dirt and garbage that made putting one foot in front of the other a game of chance. Every mile traveled was worse than the last. Rain gushed down, flooding the city, and inundating the sewer system with more water than it could handle. Black flows of human waste, trash, and slug turned the pavement and streets into a sickening swamp that rolled over the curbs and settled on the sidewalks, coating the cracking cement with layers of stagnate filth. The majority of the city was shrouded in mind-numbing darkness. Here and there a private generator or a lone transformer provided power to the lucky few for a time until electric sources sputtered to silence once the fuel ran out. Scant sporadic traffic lights and business signs that refused to die, flickered and flashed like warning beacons. The city power grid was in a constant state of failure. As soon as the repairmen fixed one section, another would falter and plunge an additional section of the city into darkness. Teams of utility workers were scattered about the city trying to maintain essential services to hospitals, rescue centers, and government buildings, all in a vain attempt to aid the frightened citizenry. They were losing the battle.

Hordes of people braved the elements trying to escape the city, seeking safety away from the crumbling infrastructure. Some ran, not knowing where they could run to. Escape was the only thought in their mind. Many who left the cities were washed off the roads by sudden flash floods or died in their cars on impassable freeways and under passes. Others were crushed by falling debris, collapsing trees, and dislodged hunks of cement, or they simply fell victim to the terrible ferocity of the sporadic storms; dying of exposure. The devastation was wide spread and deepening. Depression, suicide, and mercy killings claimed an ever-growing share of the populace. People who had seen too much loss and destruction lost hope. After the constant string of betrayals and sad revelations of the past few months, they huddled in their homes waiting to die. There were those who just didn't have any strength left and had already succumbed to the emptiness they saw life to be. Their rotting corpses scented the city with a stench of doom. Talk of faith and salvation was whispered by a scant few, but even fewer still believed. Those that looked "On High" for rescue were beginning to only see sad, clouded skies. The hardiest hunkered down in their homes with meager supplies, hoping they could out last whatever was coming. The quakes, thunderstorms, and tornados intensified and alternated with stretches of eerie calm. Everywhere around the city, around the country, around the world, the same scenario, in varying degrees, played out.

Micken eased the car down the road, skirting abandoned vehicles and avoiding viaducts and underpasses that held chest-high lakes of water. He squinted and refocused, trying to see his way through the ever-increasing maelstrom.

"Why is he smirking like that?" Micken asked, catching peeks at the boy through the rear-view mirror. The unsteadiness in his voice revealed his nervousness.

Ikayla took Simon's chin and turned his face to hers. She reached out to him with her mind. Closing her eyes, she sought to invade his thoughts. Her eyes sprang open and she drew back away from him. "That face," she shouted. "The Anima has shielded him from me. Somehow, he is with him. I could feel him, even see him looking back at me."

"What do we do if we encounter it? Your power can't match his. We can't hope to stand against it. We should contact the others for assistance," Micken pleaded.

"No," she protested. "The others cannot be involved in this. Their interference would be counter-productive. Besides, this is my find and I don't intend on sharing it or losing control of it. From what I gleaned from Jackan, these children are more powerful than we could imagine. If the others find out they will try and take that control for themselves."

The rain stopped. The wind went still. The ground seemed to exhale and settle down like a baby going to sleep. The few sparse lights illuminating the cloudy night switched off. The world felt as if it had breathed its last breath and died.

"What's going on? What's happening?" asked Micken, searching the surrounding area for answers. Ikayla felt a change. She placed her hand to her breast and braced herself against her seat and waited. A chilling forbiddance surrounded her. She tried to pinpoint what it was, but it hung just out of reach.

"What is that?" Micken shouted, pointing past the windshield. Dowan stood there, blocking their path. A glowing bubble of energy was growing around him as if he was encased in a block off. A grimace of angst and anger on his face. His eyes were like lasers of dark light. His gaze bore down on the vehicle. A force pushed at the car, causing it to slow down.

"It's the Animal!" Ikayla yelled. "Why are you slowing down?"

"I'm not. Something is pushing us back. It's like I'm driving through wet cement." Micken's foot pumped at the accelerator.

"Speed up!" she screamed. "Run him down. Get us away from here."

Micken gritted his teeth and slammed his foot on the gas pedal. The engine revved and groaned. The vehicle lurched forward, struggling for speed. The car crashed into the shield of light and bounced back. The sound of screeching tires and crunching metal pierced the eerie silence. The front end of the car folded in on itself like a wad of paper. It spun in circles, jackknifed, and finally came to rest diagonally across the road, barely avoiding tipping over.

Micken slumped over the steering wheel, a deep gash on his forehead. Blood splattered across the dashboard and shattered windshield. He tried to sit up, but fell back depleted, groaning, and coughing up blood. Ikayla was crumpled half on the floor and half in her seat. She cursed and struggled to untwist the pretzel she had become. When she raised her head, Dowan was seated between her and the boy. Ikayla leaned away, pressing herself into the corner of her seat. She grabbed the door handle.

Dowan froze her with a stare of violent determination. His eyes drew her in, sucking her into their cold blackness. His insatiable anger overwhelmed her. Ikayla struggled to resist, to look away, but the pull of his gaze held her like a vise, drawing her in deeper, absorbing her. She gnashed her teeth trying to speak. Nothing came out. She tried to scream but had no control. Locked in place, her body struggled to open the door. One hand gripping the door handle, she dug deep within herself calling on all her strength to pull away. Her body convulsed in protest. Her arm jerked and flipped the door handle. It sprang open, spilling her backward out of the car. Crouched on all fours panting like a dog, she rose and stumbled backward away from the car.

"Micken, Micken wake up!" she shouted, moving further away. When he didn't answer, she hesitated and crept back to the car, peeking into the back seat. Dowan and Simon were gone.

"Wake up," Ikayla demanded, dragging Micken from the vehicle and dropping him on the ground. He roused and grumbled like an irritated drunk.

"If you can't function, I will be forced to leave you behind," Ikayla threatened.

Micken pushed himself up onto wobbly legs, stumbling back against a light pole. Blood smeared his face and coated the front of his clothes. In obvious pain, with one eye swollen closed, he mumbled.

"I will need time to rest and repair, but. I will recover."

Ikayla, her hand and knees blackened with dirt, her hair a

disheveled mess, stared into the blackness, a look of apprehension on her face, her voice full of anxiety.

"We are all in danger. This Anima intends to destroy all things, all life, everywhere, all of us. I saw it, there in those eyes. We have to mobilize the others. If we don't destroy him, he will destroy everything. There is not much time. I felt his power growing."

CHAPTER FIFTY-NINE

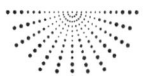

"*I* was wondering when you'd finally show up," Andros looked up from the collection of parts he was working on as Tim lumbered into the room.

"Quite a dilemma you have going," he added, closing one eye and examining a triangular widget in the light.

Tim plopped into a chair as if he had been dropped by an invisible hand. Andros couldn't help but smile, remembering the similarity to the young boy who used to come to see him pouting with the troubles of the world on his shoulders.

Peering over his jeweler's glasses, he said, "I haven't seen that look in…oh…a couple of decades. The last time, if I remember correctly, you had brought down a building. The wrong building as I recall." He chuckled. "What did you do this time. Bring down a whole city?"

"Come on Andros. I don't have to tell you what's going on. Nothing ever happens around here that you don't know about. I used to be amazed how you already knew what I had on my mind before I told you." His eyelids drooped like broken window blinds.

"We're in real trouble. This is bigger than I can get my head around. I need help." The sincerity in his voice was as clear as it was gut-wrenching.

"Sorry Tim. I can't help but see that rambunctious young fella who had a head full of schemes, eyes full of mischief and the confidence of a prize bull. Now you've grown up and you are leading this merry band." He laid down his work and gave him his full attention. "I couldn't be prouder of you."

"Hold off on the pride. I'm a long way from doing anything to be proud of."

"I understand that you've got yourself mixed up with an Anima?" Tim nodded. "That is troubling news. When I was still with the Primae, we had an encounter with an Anima. An unpleasant encounter if there ever was one."

Tim sat up. "You never mentioned that you've seen an Anima."

"There are many things I haven't mentioned," he winked at him and added as an afterthought, "...and many I never will." Tim gave the gray-haired man a wary look. Andros responded with a tilt of the head, then took the seat next to him.

"Animas don't see things as we do. They operate on a whole different plane of understanding. It's tricky, to say the least, to deal with them. Take the children, for one. What they are is called a, 'tria junc-ta in uno,' three joined in one. I believe he chose them at birth and instilled these elemental abilities in them. No doubt in anticipation of this time." Andros parsed his lips and nodded his head.

"This was not a random act. If he is not stopped, he will drain the life force from them until there is nothing left. This is part of a greater plan. You just have to figure out what he really wants."

"I think I know what this one wants." Tim said cradling his forehead.

"Oh, and what is that?"

"He wants to remake the world. During one of our encounters he was...imparting information to me. Something happened to him. It was like he was having a seizure or something. Anyway, his powers, abilities, whatever you want to call them went haywire. I got caught up in whatever he was going through and sort of entered his mind, his world or whatever. It created a new connection between us. It's as if he left a little piece of himself with me. I can still sense him in the back of my mind. When we were going through his episode, I started seeing images and knowing things. Things I'm sure he didn't want me to see."

"Images of what?" Andros scrunched his brow.

Tim hung his head down as if the information was too heavy for his head to carry.

"The first thing I realized was he's connected, he's part of this planet. I don't know, the life force, the spirit, the soul, or something. As bad as we've mucked things up, he is making them worse; on purpose. In this vision, he was hovering like a cloud on a mountain top, raining down destruction on the world. It was horrible. Earthquakes, tornadoes, floods; death and mayhem everywhere. Just like what's going on now. Everything and everyone was dead or dying. The whole planet was in a blender being chopped up, mixed up into something new."

Tim bristled at the images. "The children, he wants, he needs the children. They were at his side like little Animas; hollow eyes and blank expressions. They seemed to have become a part of him, as if they had been grafted onto him and were just little faces peering from his body."

Tim stood up wrapped his arms around his middle and began pacing. "What was most disturbing was how cold he was. I don't mean like temperature, but cold like empty. It's as if he was hollow inside. There was no anger or no hatred in him. No compassion. No warmth. There was nothing." He looked up at Andros. "And then there was Ben."

"Ben, what does Ben have to do with what you saw?"

"He came to me, Andros. He stood before me just like you are now. Dowan had inadvertently opened a door and Ben slipped through. He warned me not to let Dowan take the children. He said, 'Stop him or all is lost. Life itself is in danger.' Then he spoke those words in that book."

"What words?"

"Creation serves. Life endures."

Andros stroked his beard, stood up, and began pacing. "I've been studying the book ever since Kate brought it to me."

He pulled the book out of his tunic and handed it to Tim.

Tim's eyes brightened. "I knew you were on the case."

Andros cleared his throat. "Do you know what you have there?"

Tim shrugged his shoulders. "A book, an old book, I'll grant you, but it's just a book. We thought maybe it would give us some idea of what the Primae were up to."

"I wonder where they got it," Andros stroked his hairy chin. "You're right, it is really old. There probably isn't another one like it anywhere. That's not the kind of thing you just leave laying around. There's some valuable and dangerous information in there."

"All I care about is finding something that can help the children, help the the planet, and put a stop to Dowan."

Andros's voice took on a dire seriousness. "You don't understand, Tim. This book is older than anything I've ever seen. This is a sacred book. This is the original codex, the first language. There's no telling how old it is."

"That's nice," Tim said casually. "Hopefully you found something that will help us out of this situation."

"Tim, I can't emphasize how important and dangerous this book is."

"I'm not trying to make light of it Andros, it's just that I have more important things to think about right now. All I care about is if this book can help us or not."

"Alright," Andros said with a sigh. "But, believe me when I say this book is too dangerous to leave laying around."

"Okay, I promise," Andros gave him a wary look.

"How did you deal with your Anima?" Tim asked.

"She wasn't my Anima. I was just one of many."

"She?"

"Yes, she. I know Animas are androgynous, but this one was more she than he."

"How did you kill her?"

Andros pinched his nose. His voice dropped an octave. "You don't just spray them with a can of Raid and they die."

He looked into the distance. A grim expression crossed his face.

"The truth is, I'm not sure they can die."

"What do you mean they can't die? Everything can die." Tim blew out his frustrations with a snort.

"Look at it like this, Tim. God is a blizzard and everything is a snowflake; you, me, the planet, the whole freaking universe. You and I are a single flake. This Anima is a glacier. Its powers are primal and ancient."

"If they're so powerful how did you do it? How did you defeat her?"

"We didn't defeat it. We dealt with it."

"What is that supposed to mean?"

"It means the price was high. There was a lot of death and destruction. You're going up against a dangerous force. There are sacrifices that will have to be made." Andros tensed. "We will have to overcome much." Andros stopped Tim's questions with a raised hand. "He will have to be 'effected.'"

"'Effected?' What is that supposed to mean? And how are we supposed to do that, anyway?" Tim said, trying not to shout.

"I'm not sure yet, but I have some ideas. There are things in the book that may help. Things I have…" His words trailed off in a blank stare.

"Andros if we don't stop this thing, we're all are going to be sacrificed."

"Alright, Tim," Andros exhaled. "I'll do what I can."

"I know I'm asking a lot of you. You've done and seen things we can never hope to experience. I hate to admit it, but I don't have any idea of how to overcome this," Tim's expression softened. "Besides, you've always come through for me. I count on you. I trust you."

"Go and take care of what you can. I'll keep studying the book. When I have something concrete, I'll find you," Andros responded.

"Thanks, Andros. I knew you wouldn't let me down. Andros waved off the comment, took the book, and began leafing through the pages.

CHAPTER SIXTY

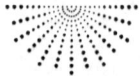

"Chris!" Kate yelled, running to greet him. Chris slipped out of his jacket, shook like a wet dog, and opened his arms to receive her.

"I'm so glad to see you," Kate looked him over. "You look tired, Chris."

"I'm fine. We've just been working day and night relocating people and trying to stay ahead of what's happening out there."

"What exactly is happening 'out there'? We see the storms here, but the news from the rest of the world is hit and miss or nonexistent. We can't be sure if what we hear is the truth or just wild rumors. All we really hear is fear. Is it as bad as people say it is?" Kate asked, more as a plea than a question.

Chris shook his head. "I'm afraid so and it's only getting worse. It hasn't hit the news yet, but we lost the Keys and part of southern Florida."

"What do you mean 'lost?'"

"Communications are spotty at best, but I got through to our staging grounds in Atlanta, at the CDC, just an hour ago. That's where I've been for the last week, working with the efforts to evacuate the eastern coastal islands and the lowlands. The report said a monster wave almost a hundred and fifty feet high and more than a mile wide swept in from the gulf and…Miami, Tampa Bay, Orlando…all deep under water. And it's not receding, it's growing."

He seemed to deflate as he spoke the words. "I don't even want to think of the number of people we lost."

Chris took a breath and closed his eyes. "The 'UN Council on Climate Change' predicts that by this time next week, most if not all of the coastal cities all over the world. will be washed away. We're trying to get the word out, but there are just so many of them and so little time."

"No," Kate fell back against the wall.

"That's not the worst of it," Chris continued, "…earthquakes in China and Nepal, all along the Himalayan region, have killed millions. The scientists say that the tectonic plates are shifting erratically. It's as if the planet is having seizures. We don't know what's happened to the Hawaiian Islands. The big volcano blew and that was the last we heard. Satellite images show the islands are no longer there. With these heavy winds, soon the sky will be filled with so much ash it will block out most of the sunlight. Between the faults and the ocean tides, we suggested the government totally evacuate California and all of the west coast. It's only a matter of time before New York and all of the upper east coast will be lost to us.

"In Europe, one minute there is rain, the next ice, then hail and wind storms," he paused and looked at the floor. "I guess we didn't stop things soon enough. It looks like the Primae are going to get their way." His voice became small and thin.

"I don't know what to do, Kate. I'm afraid we may be at the end of the line."

Kate wrapped him in a hug. "Come on, let's get some coffee. I need to fill you in on what's going on here. What's been happening here affects everything." Chris raised his brows. Kate gave him a half smile.

"My news is different, even for us," she made a nervous laugh. "I don't know if you'll find it hopeful or what." she gave him the other half of the smile. "Sorry."

Chris stopped and planted his feet. He fixed Kate with a determined stare. "I'm not back here just because I missed home. I knew something was going on here. What is it, Kate?"

Kate turned to face him. "What do you mean by that, Chris?" A look of surprise on her face. "You know us. You know what we're trying to do."

"Obviously I don't know everything." Chris gave her a sideways glance.

"That sounds like an accusation," the hint of an edge entered her voice.

Chris grabbed her arm. "I don't mean to sound like I'm accusing you of anything, but you know what's going on. Our scientists say the epicenter of all this activity is here, right here in this area. What is going on is most intense right here. Yes, there are occurrences going on all around the world, but everything seems to begin here and radiate out, striking points all over the planet. It as if this is the turbulent heart of all the destruction. It's like this is where the stone is dropped into the water and the waves are rippling out to the edges. They have tracked it and mapped it, but they can't explain it. When we put a stop to human contribution to the destruction of the planet we assumed things would start to ease off and get better. But, that hasn't happened. I have to think this has something to do with your people, with the Primae."

Chris turned away from her. "I haven't said anything about what I know or what I suspect. I'm not sure they would believe me if I did. I got myself assigned to the group that came here to track this. They're hoping they can find what is at the heart of this or at least something that will help."

He chuckled. "I still find it hard to believe myself sometimes. Besides, I wanted to talk to you guys first. I figured it might be something the Primae are doing and maybe we can stop them...again. At least I hoped that's what it was and not something worse. Though I can't imagine what could be worse."

"I can't believe what I'm hearing. Are you accusing us of doing something shady? Do you really think we're playing games?"

Chris hung his head. "No, I didn't mean for it to sound like that. It's just we're at our wits end."

When he raised his head, he had eyes full of desperation. "I'm scared, Kate. I don't know what to do. I don't think we're going to make it."

Kate took his hand. "Chris no, it's not the Primae. Well, not totally. There are things going on you don't know about. Come on, let's get that coffee and I'll tell you all I know. It may not make you feel better, but at least you'll know as much as any of us."

Chris nodded. Hand and hand, they walked to the cafeteria.

CHAPTER SIXTY-ONE

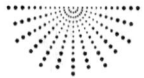

"*T*he fools!" Ikayla shouted. "They'll be the death of us all. First they put our fate in the hands of that incompetent Hayden and now they want to ignore the threat right before our eyes."

"I gather the council was not amenable to your proposal." Micken asked.

Ikayla assailed him with a contemptuous stare. She spoke through gritted teeth. "They had enough gall to say they are reviewing our status and feel that intervention at this time would be premature. I was ordered..." She gnashed her teeth and continued. "...*ordered* to stand down. The imbeciles!" She shouted. "I tried to make them understand the gravity of the situation, but they ignored my warning and dismissed me out of hand."

"What about your allies? We're you able to convince them to support you?"

Ikayla sat stiff-backed and ground her spiked heels into the wood floor. "They faded into thin air like smoke in the wind, afraid to test the resolve of the others. It appears that we are on our own."

Micken's voice jumped an octave. "Alone? We can't take on this Anima alone. Our one and only encounter showed us we're no match for him."

Ikayla's eyes bore down on him. He drew back regretting his frankness. "Go to the archives. In the vault is a book, *In Ministerium Dei Sapientiam*. Bring it to me."

Micken quickly limped out of the room, happy to put some distance between himself and the angry woman. Fifteen minutes later he returned with the look of a scared puppy on his face. "It is not there." he said, quickly moving across the room.

"It must be. Go and..." Her eyes darted around the room as if she heard something far off. "Jackan!" she shouted, reaching over and swiping everything off the top of the desk with one arm.

"The fool. That is what he crept back here for. I didn't give him credit for being that clever. It must still be in that hovel of his, unless..." Ikayla began, pacing around the room.

"Why would he take a book? What could he possibly do with it?"

"It is no ordinary book. I went to great lengths to procure it. It is timeless and ethereal. That book has been around longer than most of life has walked the earth. It contains some very powerful knowledge. He obviously meant to use it to try and take the boy's power." She answered her own question.

"The over-confident idiot. He didn't have the skill necessary to achieve such a thing. I am surprised he even knew it existed or what to do with it." Her pacing increased as the thoughts raced through her mind.

Plots and schemes began to take shape. She flicked a finger at Micken as if she was summing a pet. "Go to that place and retrieve the book. It is vital we recover it if we are ever going to overcome this Anima. If the book is not there, the only other possibility..." her thoughts became words. "The Ceteri must have it." *"I'm certain they won't leave it behind."* she thought.

"But...but," Micken, pleaded.

"Do as I say." Her tone was stern and final. "I will do the thinking."

Micken slinked toward the door.

"Hurry back," she yelled. "If the book is not there, as I suspect it will not be, I will need you to pay a diplomatic visit to our new soon-to-be reluctant allies."

CHAPTER SIXTY-TWO

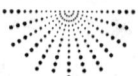

*A*n eerie calm had settled on the city. The wind was still as if the decaying stench in the air had weighed it down. Lakes of dank water still flooded the streets, gurgling up from over taxed sewer drains. The sky was full of clouds that looked like dirty cotton balls. Sporadically, the ground shivered like a scared child.

Using Jackan's phone, Micken retraced his steps back to the Ceteri's location. He parked down the street from the warehouse. Taking a deep breath, he walked to the entrance. Before he could grasp the door handle the tip of a sword was propped under his chin.

"I know you," Jacob sneered, a malevolent look on his face. "How thoughtful of you to come visit us. You saved me the trouble of hunting you down."

Micken swallowed. His Adam's apple rose and fell like his throat had tried to toss it into his mouth and missed. "I've come to deliver a message from my mistress." He stuttered. "It's about the Anima...and the boy," he added quickly.

"Deliver it to me" Jacob said, piercing his skin with the tip of his blade. "I'll make sure the others get the information."

"I was instructed to talk only to the leader," he insisted, the pitch of his voice rising with his fear.

"Then you should have held a séance, since you killed him!"

"It wasn't me. I've never killed anyone," Micken protested.

"Don't kill him, Jacob," Kate walked up behind them, breaking the tension. "Let's hear what he has to say. Think about Simon. We have to get him back."

Jacob lowered his sword but towered over the crouching man, his eyes staring like daggers down at him. His chest heaved with anger. Micken cupped his throat, his eyes darted about, hunting for a way to escape.

Kate led him inside and cloistered him in one of the meeting rooms before sending someone to find Tim. Jacob stood by the door whipping his sword in air as if he was swatting flies, while Kate paced back and forth before the table where Micken was seated.

Tim entered the room, followed closely behind by Andros, Chris, and Samson. "Put that thing away before someone gets hurt."

"That's the whole idea." Jacob muttered looking at Micken before sheathing his sword.

Tim took the seat across from Micken and sized him up. He noticed the prick on his neck and the smear of blood. He gave Jacob a stern look. Jacob returned a smile. "Who are you and what do you want?"

"He's one of the guys who killed Ben! That's who he is!" Jacob shouted. Kate grabbed his arm and held him back.

"You have a lot of nerve coming here." Tim gnashed his teeth. "What's to keep us from offing you and eliminating one of our enemies?"

Micken slouched and fidgeted in his chair. He wiped the sweat accumulating on his lip.

"Where's Simon?" Tim demanded.

"We don't have the boy," Micken said, his voice just above a whisper.

"Then where the hell is he!" Kate yelled.

"Ask the Anima," Micken sneered, sitting up in his chair trying to conceal his fear.

"Dowan has him?" Tim asked, a worried tone to his voice.

"If that's what you call the Amina. Yes, he does."

Tim stood up. "What did he do, take him from you?" He curled his lip in disgust.

"We don't have time to play games. If you don't have him, we have no need of you." He looked at Jacob. "He's all yours. Have fun." He turned away from the man. Jacob whipped out his sword and stepped forward.

Micken jerked back, scooting his chair from the table, a look of utter terror on his face.

"Find out why he's here before you do anything rash," Andros' words boomed over the ruckus. The authority in his voice stilled the room as if he had flicked a switch and turn off their ability to move.

Tim looked at Andros, nodded, and turned back to the table, retaking his seat. He frowned and narrowed his eyes. "Explain and you better make it worth our time. Why are you here?"

Micken swallowed and scanned the hate-filled eyes locked on him. "I was sent to offer a truce…"

"A truce?" Jacob shouted. "Forget it. After all that you have done we will never…"

Tim interrupted Jacob. "Quiet, or I will personally throw you out of the room!" Jacob shot him a cold look and turned his back. Kate took his hand and entwined their fingers, giving him a squeeze.

"You set the planet on a path of destruction, killed our people, kidnapped the boy, and almost killed his father, and you think we will accept a truce and trust you?" Tim asked, the astonishment obvious in his voice.

"Jackan killed your man. He was acting alone," Micken hurriedly said before he lost all his nerve. "He paid the price for his actions. The Anima saw to that."

Tim looked at Kate. They shared the thought. *"Dowan did kill him."*

"My mistress wants to meet with you and talk, no hidden agendas, no subterfuge, no tricks. We have a common enemy, and neither of us can defeat him alone."

Micken reached in his pocket and handed Tim a piece of paper with an address and a single sentence scribbled on it. "We are all in danger."

"Who is this mistress of yours?"

"Her name is Ikayla of the house of Avelar."

Tim read the note, pocketed it and stood. "Go tell your Mistress, we will be there this afternoon."

Jacob stomped his foot and stormed out of the room.

"Samson," Tim said over his shoulders. "Show our guest to the exit." As Tim was leaving the room, Andros stopped him.

"I need to be at that meeting."

"Why?" Tim asked surprised at the request.

"Trust me on this, Tim. I need to be there."

"Do you know something about…"

Before he could finish his question, the alarms went off. Sirens blared down the hall and screams could be heard bouncing off the walls. Everyone rushed toward the melee.

Arriving like a stampede of bison, the group crowded into the small room in the living quarters. A crowd gathered at the entrance. Tim and the other burst into the room. Kaplan was on his knees, wailing and screaming like a banshee.

"He took him! He took Jairo!" he shouted, beating on the floor as if he was trying to beat his way out of a box.

Tim knelt down to him and grabbed him by the shoulders.

"Kap, Kap," he screamed, shaking him like a rag doll.

"What happened? Where is Jairo? Who took him?" he asked, though an answer was not necessary.

His words drowning in tears and saliva as he cried. "Jairo was sitting here, right here." He beat at the floor. "I was lying across the bed. This thing appeared and held out his hand. Jairo took it. I yelled for him to not do it. No, Jairo! Get away for him!" I shouted.

"I was frozen in place. I couldn't move. My arms and legs wouldn't do anything. Jairo stood up and they disappeared into thin air like smoke." Kap collapsed onto the floor and cried into the carpet. "I couldn't stop him. He took my son."

Tim laid his hand on the man's heaving back. He looked at the startled crowd.

Micken, dragged along by Samson, drew everyone attention when he spoke. "It appears you need us as much as we need you."

Tim pushed his way to the door. "I'm going to check on Charlene. Get him the hell out of here."

CHAPTER SIXTY-THREE

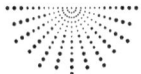

*T*im, Kate, and Andros inched down the streets. The devastation surrounding them left them speechless. A foreboding calmness hung in the air like an unspoken threat. The scene of impending doom drained the energy from their already taxed minds. The mournful groan from the engine, slurping pools of dark water, and an occasional gut-wrenching wail in the distance, were the only sounds.

"Are we really going to do this?" Kate asked, her expression screamed her disbelief. "I mean you can't really believe we can trust the Primae."

"We don't have a choice, Kate." Tim answered, his voice as ragged and choppy as the road. "We can't do this alone. The more allies we have, no matter how untrustworthy they are, the better our chances are."

Tim looked to Andros. "You've been awful quiet. What do you think?" He didn't respond. Tim bit his lip.

"Andros, at one time, you were part of the Primae. Do you know this Ikayla? Can she be trusted? Can we work with this her?"

Andros stared out the window, his eyes unfocused and cloudy. An awkward silence lingered like a foul odor.

"Yes," he finally said.

"You want to let us in on why you think so?"

Andros fixed him with an unreadable stare. A definite "No," was his answer, and he returned to staring out the window.

CHAPTER SIXTY-FOUR

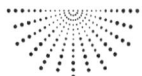

*M*icken led them into a room with chairs and a settee dressed in finely embroidered velvet and hand-woven rugs. A massive crystal chandelier hung in the center of room over a table set with an antique tea set and plates of fruits and pastries. The sweet spicy air had the subtle undertone of lilac. Ikayla posed before floor-to-ceiling red velvet drapery that looked like the trunks of giant sycamore trees. Her practiced smile greeted Tim and Kate as they entered the room. Extending an open hand, Ikayla marched toward them.

When Andros entered the room, lagging behind the others, she caught sight of him and froze in mid-step. Ikayla stood still like an over-filled glass, afraid of spilling its contents.

Andros planted his feet as if he was a boxer awaiting a punch. With a pained expression, he said, "Salve, Ikayla."

His voice confirmed what her eyes could not believe. The color drained from her face. Rubbery legs betrayed her. She deflated into a chair. Ikayla pressed a hand to her breast and gasped for a breath. She closed her eyes and let her head fall back offering her neck for sacrifice.

Tim and Kate exchanged surprised looks.

Fighting for control, Ikayla clenched her hands into fist, pressing so hard her nail nearly broke the skin. Composing herself, she slowly rose to her full height, smoothed her flowing silk dress, raised her chin, and locked a defiant stare on Andros. With words dipped in ice and acid, she said. "I see nothing has changed. You were always a step ahead of me." She uttered a weak laugh. "The last piece of the puzzle falls into place. Everything is finally starting to make sense."

The words fell from her lips like ice flakes chiseled from a glacier. Her eyes screamed at him in a language only they understood.

Tim interjected himself into the exchange. "I can see you two know each other..." He added behind a well-placed hand, "...very well."

Ikayla looked at the untouched tea serving and whispered to herself, "So much for civility." Clearing her throat, she launched into her objective. Turning her back on Andros, she spoke to Tim.

"This Anima of yours has got to be stopped. He is dangerous and will destroy us all if we don't join forces."

"He is not our Anima," Tim insisted, his eyes darting back and forth between Andros and Ikayla. Andros never took his eyes off Ikayla.

"Things wouldn't be as they are if you hadn't gone after the children," Kate added.

"That was business. This is life and death. Though I will grant you there is little difference," Ikayla replied.

"I guess you had nothing to do with Texas, or Puerto Rico, or Ben. Not to mention the fact you've been trying to kill us for years," Kate accused her, hands cross over her chest. Her eyes were shooting daggers.

Ikayla shot back a look of contempt. She turned her back, ignoring Kate and focused all her attention back on Tim.

"He was your man," Tim said, a hint of sarcasm entering his voice. "So, you will understand if we have some trust issues." He raised his brows. "Besides, how do you know what the Anima has planned?"

Ikayla's eyes bored down on him. She pressed her lips into an angry slit. "Jackan was over zealous. He had a tendency to take things too far. I was not aware at the time just how savage Jackan was, but…" Ikayla raised her eyes to the ceiling and exhaled a deep breath. "His savagery is nothing compared to your Anima. I saw it in his eyes. Those damnable soulless eyes."

She closed her eyes and shook off the image.

Tim opened his mouth to speak. Andros stopped him. "She's a reader," he said staring at the back of Ikayla's head. "She knows of what she speaks."

"A reader." Tim took a step back .eyeing her with new respect.

Ikayla turned to face Andros. Her eyes narrowed and she spoke slowly. "I did not need to read him. He read me, boring into my mind and showing me a hell I would not wish on anyone," she added, eyeing him from head to feet, "…not even you." Andros flinched as the barb struck him hard.

"What about Simon?" Kate asked, stepping forward.

"I do not know about the boy. He took him after we rescued him."

"Rescued?" Kate nearly laughed. "Was that supposed to be some kind of joke?" She turned to Tim. "You don't really think we can trust her? She won't even admit to what they've done."

Ikayla smirked and took a seat, crossing her long legs and smoothing a hand down her calf. She looked into Andros's watchful eyes and smirked again, whipping her gaze away from him with a dismissive swish.

"We need to rescue the boy. Will you help us get Simon back?" Tim asked.

After a moment's contemplation, Ikayla gave a reluctant nod.

"Don't you mean both boys?" Micken interjected.

Heads turned to face him. Ikayla silenced him with a look. He melted back into the background.

"We are undecided as of yet what to do. What do you have in mind?" Tim asked.

"I have been doing research," Ikayla said. "As of yet I only have vague notions. A valuable volume has been misplaced and…"

"We have it," Andros interrupted. All eyes fanned his way as he reached into his jacket and produced the book.

"In Ministerium Dei Sapientiam?" she asked. He nodded.

"Jackan," she gnashed her teeth. "Stealing from your new allies is not a good way to start a relationship, not to mention promote trust and cooperation."

"Let's not play games." Andros said. "It was found where your man died. Where you left him." The accusation in his tone was clear and severe. "We will deal with each other openly and sincerely or else our efforts are wasted."

Everyone silently shuffled in place. Andros gave each an accusatory glare and continued. "I have been studying this book. I believe I have an idea we can work on, together."

"You will return it," she demanded.

"After all this is over," Tim stepped in confronting her. "If we survive this, you can have your book. If we don't, it won't matter. For now, it is ours. Period."

"Oh, very well," she snapped. "I will not quibble with you but know that this is not settled."

"First things first, we have to get the boys away from him." Tim said.

"If they're still alive..." Micken said, drawing everyone's attention again.

"They are. He needs them. They are essential to his survival, to his strength, to his plan. In a way, they are parts of him," Andros offered.

Ikayla planted her hands on her hips. "And exactly how do you know this?"

"I have been studying the book and piecing together a plan of action. Remember, this is not the first Anima I've encountered. I believe I have started to understand what he wants and what he is planning to do."

"Have you become a prophet?" Ikayla quipped.

"I don't have to be a prophet to know that this Dowan plans on our destruction. He is a being an agent of change, an agent of destruction."

"Is he punishing us?" Tim asked, his brows colliding like dueling caterpillars. "Or has he just gone mad?"

Ikayla smirked. Andros cut his eyes at her. He cupped his forehead. "I believe in a sense he has." Andros blew out a deep breath.

"We have damaged the planet and in turn damaged him. This is his idea of retribution and renewal. He means to eliminate this tainted life and heal the planet; ergo heal himself. The book says even though the Anima travels between multiple planes of existence, he has a core and stays close to it; especially when he is in a weakened state as he is now."

"Weakened state?" said Kate to no one in particular. "I'd hate to see him when he's at full strength."

Andros continued, "One of the main reasons things are so chaotic is he is weak and unable to totally control the massive forces around him. Much of what has happened is due to his lack of control. Once he's absorbed the elements necessary to rejuvenate himself, to complete himself, then and only then will he act on his final objective. In the meantime, things will remain chaotic and he will need to stay close to his core."

"Absorb the elements? Are you talking about the children?" Kate asked, her face stretched with shock. Andros nodded. Kate sank into a chair.

"We have to not only get the two boys back right now, but we have to keep him from getting Charlotte," Tim said.

"She is the third child?" Ikayla asked.

"Yes." Andros answered. "He will need her to complete his triage."

"Then it is a simple thing." Ikayla said, taking a commanding pose. "We find this core, this hiding place and attack him before he's at full strength. Do you have any idea where this core may be?"

"Chris," Kate said, thinking aloud. "Chris said their instruments had things pinpointed to this area. He said somehow the disturbances were originating from around here and rippling out through the earth's core like waves."

"Where?" Tim asked. "Have they an exact location?"

"I don't think so," she said "All he said was in this area. I don't know how big of an area, but he was sure of it. That's why he came back here, to try and find out where and why."

"Tim," Andros said. "Since he is so close, with Ikayla's help you can zero in on him. He has a special connection to you. She also has been in direct contact with him, so together you two can focus those connections and it will lead you to him."

Tim and Ikayla shared a wary exchange. "I suppose we can do that," she said.

Ikayla raised a lacquered nail. "There is the possibility that we can bargain with this Anima."

"What kind of bargain?" Tim asked.

"He wants the children. What if we give them to him in exchange for his not destroying everything? It would be a small price to pay."

"You heartless bitch!" Kate shouted, her hand moving to her weapon. "There is no way we're going to sacrifice those kids to that thing!"

Tim moved in between the two women.

"Calm down, Kate. There's no way we're going along with something like that."

He turned to Ikayla. "If that's the best you can do, then we've wasted our time coming here."

Ikayla shrugged her shoulders and smiled. "It was just a thought." She sat and poured herself a cup of tea.

"Okay," Tim said. "Back to business. Finding him does us no good if we don't have a plan to defeat him. What do we attack him with? How do you defeat a being like this?"

Andros spoke up. "I have some ideas about that. I need you and Kate to return to the warehouse and pick up a few things. You'll also need to secure the girl. As long as he doesn't have all three, he can't complete his transformation. He'll remain in an incomplete and hopefully, weakened state. I'll stay here, and we'll work on ideas to defeat him."

"What kind of ideas, Andros?" Tim asked.

"I will have it fully worked out by the time you get back. I just need to go over a couple of things." His voice was soft, and his eyes held a plea in them.

Tim hesitated. He and Kate exchanged glances.

"Alright," he relented. "But how do you expect us to secure Charlotte? This guy can walk through walls, remember."

"We can't kill him, so we'll just have to slow him down. We have to use his own elements against him. Iron should work. He is basically an ethereal being made up of flowing energy. If we can hamper that flow, even for a short time it will give us the time we need to defeat him. Earth is the element he's missing." Andros stroked his chin and continued.

"Iron, it must be pure. No alloys, no contaminates, pure iron. That is the only thing that will provide the density we need. Even though iron exists in nature, pure iron does not, Hopefully, this concentration will do the trick. The composition of the pure metal will make it difficult for him to penetrate it. It will take a larger amount of his energy to breach it. Trying should weaken him even further. In his depleted state, he won't be able to take the girl. Encircle her in as much of the pure iron as you can. If I'm right it will frustrate his plans and give us a chance."

"You're sure about this?" Tim asked.

"I believe it will work."

Tim and Andros stared at each other for long seconds before Tim agreed with a shake of his head.

"We'll meet back in two hours."

"Thank you, Tim. Don't worry. I know what's at stake. I won't let you down." Andros rested his hand on Tim's shoulder.

"I'll write a list of the things we'll need. Andros leaned close to Tim. "In my room, in the back of the closet there is a gray bag. Bring it."

Tim grabbed Kate's arm and pulled her toward the door. She resisted, protesting the whole way.

CHAPTER SIXTY-FIVE

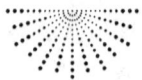

"**A**lright," Tim said, once they were in the car. "Let me have it. What do you have to say?"

"What does it matter? You've already decided. It no longer matters what I or anyone else thinks. It's obvious you've made up your mind."

"Look Kate, I know you're skeptical of the way things are going. All of us are, but I trust Andros. He's our best hope to get out of this thing in one piece."

"How do you know that? Do you have any idea what he has planned to do? Not to mention his connection with this Ikayla and the rest of the Primae. Do you really trust him that much? Are you really comfortable with putting the fate of the whole world in his hands?"

Tim laid his head against the steering wheel. His answer was slow to come, but it was definite. "Yes."

Kate looked at him in astonishment. "I hope you know what you're doing. We probably only have one chance at this. If we fail, it's game over. I don't need to be a psychologist to know that those two have some serious history together. I'm worried that a broken heart may trump common sense if you know what I mean."

"Yeah, the woman scorned thing is rather obvious. But, I don't think she'd sabotage things just to get back at an old lover. The stakes are too high."

"I hope you're right." Kate said with a skeptical tone in her voice.

Tim started the car but sat looking at the dashboard.

"Kate," his voice was barely above a whisper. "Ben once said to me that the biggest decisions you will ever make are not what to do, but who you trust. I'm not sure what Andros has planned, but I trust him just like I trusted Ben. Like I trust you and everyone one on our team. I'm not asking that you trust him. All I'm asking is that you trust me."

Kate swallowed the lump in her throat. "I do trust you, Tim. It's just that some back at the warehouse are afraid your connection with this Anima has affected you and you're not totally in control," she added quickly.

"You haven't been your usual self, it's shows, and people are scared. If you seem unsure, they are unsure too. They want..." she paused. "We want to believe in you like we always have. But the stakes are so high. If you tell me you're sure, I'll back you one hundred percent."

Tim swallowed a breath. "I am."

CHAPTER SIXTY-SIX

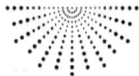

*A*ndros and Ikayla faced each other. Long intense moments of silence passed between them.

"Micken," she said, without taking her eyes from Andros. "Go and busy yourself."

There was no ambiguity in her tone, only the emotionless expectation of one who knows they will be obeyed. He silently scurried from the room, closing the door behind him. Ikayla sighed and laughed.

"She does not trust you," she shrugged. "Smarter than she looks." Raising a sarcastic brow, she sat and reclined deep into the chair.

"She is a lot like you," Andros shot back, "passionate and driven."

"Don't presume to know me."

"There was a time we knew each other all too well."

"Times change. What we were then has little resemblance to what we are now. Then we were naïve and grasping at shadows. We never truly knew ourselves, lest each other."

His eyes told her he knew that was a lie. "Alright," he said blowing out a breath. "Let us bear this out. There will be no time for recrimination later."

"There is nothing to discuss," she said, peering over her tea cup. "You made your choice. You redefined destiny. You rejected us."

She paused. "You rejected me." Her voice was as cold and sharp as shards of ice.

"I never rejected you," Andros blurted out. "You know why I couldn't stay."

"All I know is you chose to leave."

"I asked you to come with me."

"To what? To live like a savage among these humans?" Ikayla rose to confront him. "You were favored, ordained to be. You were blessed with the one true gift. We could have had it all. You took that future away with you."

She turned away from him. "I lost everything when you left. Your house fell. My house fell," she closed her eyes and let her head drop.

"Everything collapsed," she repeated. "I had to claw my way back from oblivion."

"I'm sorry. I never meant to harm you or anyone."

Ikayla knitted her brows, drawing her face into a sneer.

"I don't need your watered-down commiserations. We found a better way. I found a better me..." she spit out the words. "...without you."

"I didn't want it all. It was too much for me to imagine. I just wanted what we had. I could not bear what I would become if I stayed. What we would become. I would have become something neither of us could have lived with. It would have changed me. It would have destroyed me and eventually destroyed us."

"You were always so theatrical," she shook her head.

"Instead you abandoned everything, including me. You just turned your back and walked away. And now you are back. It seems you didn't do enough destruction the first time."

"I am here to help. To make things right."

She laughed. "Don't talk to me like I am one of the *Debitum*. If you wanted things to be right, if you wanted me, if you wanted us, you would have found a way long ago. You made your choice and we have both learned to live with it."

Ikayla jerked her chin up and clenched her teeth. "When you walked away you took everything with you."

Andros whispered back in a tender voice. "I left my heart with you."

Ikayla flushed red. Anger gushed from her like water from a dam. "I will tolerate your presence only because the threat is so extreme. If we survive this crisis, I expect you to die again. And this time to stay that way."

Andros flinched as if he had been slapped across the face. Sighing and closing his eyes, he said. "If that is the way you would have it, then so be it."

CHAPTER SIXTY-SEVEN

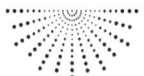

A shimmering kaleidoscope of blue, green, and red lights made the chamber alive with an iridescent slideshow. Energy surged through the walls, ceiling, and floor like blood racing through veins, growing and receding with ever increasing regularity. The air crackled and sizzled, humming with the power, as the ground and the walls expanded and ebbed, sending spears of sharpened stalactites crashing to the ground.

Simon, at one end of the chamber, stood buried, all but his face, in a tomb of crystalline rock. The cloudy crystals wrapped around him in an immobilizing cast. His skin was as pale as chalk. His eyes were as black as beads of tar.

Jairo, on the opposite end of the chamber, hovered just above the ground, surrounded by an electric storm of flickering sparks that danced around him like fire flies. He rose and sank as if he were riding an ocean wave. With each rise, he'd arch his back and flail wildly.

Dowan stood in the center of the cavern, his form expanding and retracting like a heartbeat, fading in and out of visibility. Hungry translucent tentacles of energy reached out from him engulfing his young captives, stroking and caressing them as you would a pet kitten.

"Soon," he thought, and a rumble reverberated through the ground in all directions as if the earth was agreeing with a belly laugh.

"When the joining is complete my little ones, we shall wash away all this and herald in a new reality. "

As the colors intensified, Dowan seemed to grow in stature. Images of Charlotte drifted through his mind and he reached out to touch her as if she stood before him.

"The last, the strongest," he thought.

Jairo floated toward the wall and settled into his charnel. The walls grew like freezing water and enclosed him, shrouding him in a blanket of opaque crystals. His face was ghost-like and drawn. He breathed in tiny convulsive gasps.

Dowan stretched out his arms and something close to a smile crossed his lips. He took one step forward and faded into the ether.

CHAPTER SIXTY-EIGHT

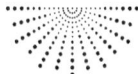

"*How* ow did it go?" Titus asked, as Tim and Kate stepped through the door.

Tim ignored the question. "Is Charlotte alright? Is she safe?"

"Yeah, she's back in her room with Joshua, Samson, and her parents. But Tim, she's starting to look and act the way Jairo did."

"I was afraid of that." Tim blew out a breath. "I need you to get these things Andros asked for," he handed him the list.

"Okay, but..." Titus said studying the list.

"We need them now!"

"Whoa, Tim. I'll get them. But, it will be kinda difficult to find pure iron, everything nowadays is an alloy."

"It has to be 100 percent pure." Tim insisted.

"Wait a minute." Titus said. "We have those iron bars from the smelt we used to have out back."

"Where are they?"

"They're in the storage locker out back. I'll have some of the boys clean them up and bring them in. Those things are heavy as all..."

Tim interrupted him. "Bring them to Charlotte's room," he yelled, running past Titus.

Titus looked at Kate. "What's going on? I've never seen Tim like this before. Is he alright? What happened with the Primae? And why are iron bars so damn important?"

"Come on," she said. "I'll fill you in while we get them."

CHAPTER SIXTY-NINE

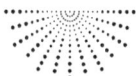

*C*harlotte was silent and still, staring straight ahead as if she was in a trance. Her mother and father huddled in a corner, drawn and weary, watching over her. Joshua and Samson were seated by the door; they jumped to attention when Tim rushed into the room.

Tim ignored everyone else and knelt beside the little girl. "Charlotte, Charlotte, sweetheart. It's Uncle Tim." She didn't respond. Tim took her chin and turned her face to him. Dark unfocused eyes looked back at him. He recognized the empty blackness of Dowan's influence and bit his lip. Wrapping his arms around her, he felt his heart thumping like an alarm bell.

"You promised you would protect her," Gerald, her father, yelled. Her mother whimpered, burying her face in his chest. "Now look at her. She's turning into whatever that little boy became. We should have sent you packing and went our own way. We'd still have our little girl."

Tim released the little girl. He pinched the crown of his nose and walked to face her parents. "I know things look bad, but don't give up on us yet."

"*Look bad?* You call what happening to her looking bad? What are you going to do when that thing turns up and wants to take our daughter? Can you stop it? Can you do anything?" Anger powered his voice, but a plea cried out from his eyes.

Tim took in the anger while trying to hide his own doubts and fears.

"We've got a..." Titus, Kate, and a crew of people, noisily entered the room hauling iron bands, four feet long and six inches wide. With a chorus of grunts and groans they dropped them to the floor.

Tim said a silent thank you and moved to assist them.

"Is this all of them?" he asked.

"There's a half dozen more. Soon as they're cleaned up they'll bring them in," Titus said.

"The more, the better. We have no idea how many of these we may need. I'm not even sure this will work. But this may be the only thing that can keep Dowan from taking Charlotte."

Tim grabbed at a band. The weight pulled him forward, nearly wrenching him off his feet.

"Help me," he yelled rubbing his arm. "We need to arrange these around Charlotte. If Andros is right, these iron bars will disrupt Dowan's powers, keeping him from taking Charlotte."

A skeptical grunt echoed in the room.

"I know," acknowledged Tim. "But, that's all we got for the moment. We've got to at least give it a try."

The bands were arranged around Charlotte like a battlement around a castle. Using two by fours and corrugated wire, Titus built the structure that rose above Charlotte's head. The young girl was unmoved as the cage grew around her.

"There's nothing more we can do right now but wait and hope this works." Tim said, trying to hide the doubt that was lingering in the back of his mind.

"Titus, you and the others stay here. If Dowan shows up, sound the alarm. Immediately! Don't try and stop him. Don't attack him. You don't want to end up burnt to a crisp like Jackan."

Tim walked to the cage and looked down at Charlotte. "Hang in there, sweetheart. Somehow we'll get you out of this."

He turned back to the others. "Kate, Joshua, Samson, and you too, Chris, come with me, we need to make some plans."

Tim and the others headed for the door.

"No heroes, Titus! If he shows up stay away from him," he yelled over his shoulder before disappearing around the corner. "Just sound the alarm!"

CHAPTER SEVENTY

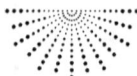

"I'm sure Kate has filled you in on what went on with the Primae," Tim said, scanning the questioning eyes focused on him. His gaze stopped at Kate, giving her a knowing nod. She blushed her confirmation.

"So, I won't waste time going over what you already know," he continued. "While Andros and Ikayla are making plans, I think we have to make some contingency plans of our own."

"Kate says you don't even know what they have planned, so how can we make other plans around what we don't know?" Joshua asked.

"Aren't you putting a lot of trust in people who were enemies just a few hours ago?" Chris added.

"Yeah," piped in Samson. "I know Andros is supposed to be one of us now, but who knows what may happen to him since he's been reunited with his old friends?"

"What are we supposed to do if the iron doesn't work? How can we believe that the Primae are on our side and aren't working against us? What's going to happen if this doesn't work? Will fire power have any effect? What about the missing boys?"

The questions poured out one after another, never waiting for answer.

Tim pivoted to Kate. "Do you have something to add to this happy chorus?"

Kate shrugged and gave a half smile. "I've said my piece."

Tim held up his hands and the room fell silent.

"The answer to all your questions is, I don't know. This is uncharted ground for all of us. We don't have many options and even fewer ideas. I'm willing to try most anything. Does anybody have an idea, a suggestion, a notion? Something other than a criticism?"

A chorus of "huh's and ahh's" was the feeble reply.

"Exactly," said Tim, letting them off the hook. "All we can do is stand together, count on each other, act as best we can and try to handle the situations as they arise. I know that doesn't sound like much of a plan, but it's what we got and it's worked for us until now. Our strongest weapon is our unity. Now, you three and Kate are going back with me to the house. We're going to break up into two teams of four and..."

The warehouse erupted with the wailing scream of sirens.

"He's here!" Kate yelled, and took off running. The rest of the crew followed close on her heels.

The agitated cries of the people in the room mixed with the shrill howls of Dowan. The warehouse sounded like a haunted forest. Kate and the others entered a scene of utter chaos. Titus worked to hold his group back as they waved fists and hurled insults. Two of the Ceteri laid unconscious on the floor.

Dowan, disregarding their presence, repeatedly approached the enclosure protecting Charlotte and was rebuffed each time. Each attempt to breach the iron wall was repelled by an invisible shield of resistance. Each failure was accompanied by a more furious howl. Coming in contact with the bands, Dowan would appear to grow faint and fade away as if the bars were erasing the parts of him they touched. Fury twisted his normally placid face. His eyes gleamed with the dark light of black fire.

Most of the onlookers in the room cowered against the wall frozen by their fear and covering their ears against the ear splitting screams the Anima was making. A few brave Ceteri move toward the Anima but were rebuffed by an unseen force.

"You cannot have her!" Tim yelled, confronting the Anima. "Dowan, no!"

Dowan turned and seized him with an angry stare.

"She is mine!" Tim heard the words in his head as the gaze of the Anima bore into his mind. Disjointed images of past and future worlds rising and falling apart, scenes of birth and destruction and then nothing but a void. Those empty black eyes drilled into his brain. Tim tumbled through darkness at the mercy of Dowan's rage. A chaos of emotions flooded over and through him. All the burning hot fury inside the Anima rushed at him like a blast of desert wind. The angers, the hates, the sorrows and the fears.

"Fear," he thought fighting to resist the onslaught. *"The other? The magi, joining."*

Images of Dowan being drawn into a golden light blinded him. Pictures of the children, weak and encased in a wall of crystal rushed into his mind. Dowan, angered by the breach, the intrusion, increased his rage, boring down even harder until Tim cried out in pain and collapsed onto the floor.

Dowan turned to reach for Charlotte again. Thwarted by the iron barrier and weakened by the encounter, he howled like a dying wolf and faded away.

"Tim, Tim are you alright?" Kate asked as she and the others rushed to him and crowded around him. Cradling his head in her lap, she stroked his face.

"Don't die. Please don't be dead," she begged.

Tim opened his eyes. A weak smile crossed his lips.

"Charlotte, did he take Charlotte?"

"No," Joshua answered. "The iron worked, this time."

"Yeah, this time," Chris added.

With the help of the others, Tim stood on wobbly legs.

"I'm alright, just a little unsteady." Tim placed his hands on his knees and shook his head until his vision began to clear. "We've got to get to Andros. I know where the kids are."

CHAPTER SEVENTY-ONE

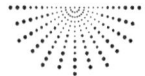

*J*kayla marched out of the room, vacuuming the air out in her wake. Andros plopped into a chair, sighing his frustration.

Like a self-conscious spirit, Micken, unobtrusively eased into the room and began silently collecting the dishes, his eyes stealing furtive glances at Andros.

"You need not be reverential in my presence. There is no need to avert your eyes. I am not the sun. You can look directly at me," Andros said through the fingers massaging his forehead.

Micken nodded an acknowledgement, gave a hesitant half smile, but none the less, hurried his dish gathering and turned to leave.

"You are from a fine house. The house Avelar has a long and storied lineage. You owe veneration to no one. You have earned your place."

"Yes, exalted one," he whispered. "But, I am *Debitum*. I serve however I must."

"Don't call me that," Andros frowned his disapproval. "I had hoped that antiquated practice of the obligated would have been cast out by now. The elders of your house should restore you and..."

"But sir," Micken interrupted, shrinking back at the impudence.

His voice was weak, but clear. "I had no choice. I have no house. The Avelars allowed me to serve. If they had not I would have been alone, an outcast in the world."

"What do you mean, you have no house. A house is a parent, a family. Everyone has one. To which house were you born?"

"My house no longer exists."

"What do you mean it no longer exists? Houses are forever. To what house were you born?" He asked again.

His eyes darted up and down. The dishes in his hands rattled as he reluctantly answered. "House…" He hesitated. "House Pantras."

"House Pantras? My house?" Micken nodded. Andros felt like Atlas as the weight of the world came to rest on his shoulders. His insides clenched and sieged up as if they had been turned to stone. Andros cleared his throat and swallowed. He looked away from Micken.

"I am beginning to see that my actions had consequences I had not anticipated. The decision I made was not meant to harm others, only to release a reluctant heart. I thought if I left, another would replace me, and things would progress with a more worthy suitor."

He exhaled a long breath. "It seems I was wrong about that as well. I am finding out that I have been wrong about a great many things."

Andros turned and stared intensely at Micken, who dipped his head a little lower. "I have wronged you. I have wronged many. It does not matter what my intentions were. There is much for me to atone for. I…I am sorry."

Micken parted his mouth to speak, but only wordless breaths came out. He bit his lip, dipped of his head, and scurried out of the room, the dishes rattling like loose change in a dryer.

CHAPTER SEVENTY-TWO

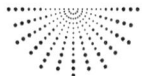

"*D*o you think the iron will continue to protect Charlotte from Dowan?" Samson asked.

"Mad as that bugger was, he'll be back and better prepared. I'd guarantee it," Joshua replied.

"I don't know how long those bands will hold him back, but Joshua is right. He'll be back." Tim said.

"What will happen if he gets the girl?" Chris asked.

"I hate to think about it." Samson answered.

"We just have to get him before he gets her," Kate added. "I hope Andros and Ikayla have come up with something we can use."

"I never thought I'd see the day we'd be allies with the Primae. This really must be the end of the world, everything is totally upside down," Joshua said, punctuating his remarks with a snort.

"Okay Tim, you said you know where the boys are. Where are they? And how do you know?" Kate asked.

"When Dowan first came to us, he...I don't know...bonded with me or whatever you want to call it. We became connected deeper than I think he intended us to. He's weak and so his guard isn't as strong as it might be. Anyway, I gained an insight into his mind while he was imparting information to me. When we are connected, I would see things and know things I don't think he wants me to know."

"You mean he's in your head?" Samson asked. "Like now?"

"Not all the time. He's not controlling me or anything like that, it's just that…it's hard to explain. It's like two people who have known each other for a long time and know what the other one is thinking. At least kinda like that."

"Sounds like you two are married," Joshua snorted a laugh. "Sorry," he said when everyone turned to look at him.

"Okay, you've got this psychic connection with this Dowan. Can you see a way to defeat him?" Chris asked.

"I didn't see a way to defeat him, but I did sense his fear."

"What could that thing be afraid of?" Samson asked.

"The joining. Something about a joining."

"The kids? Isn't that what he's trying to do, join with them? Why would he be afraid of that? Unless he's afraid it won't happen," Kate asked.

"I don't know," Tim said. "It's not all clear. Most of what I get is disjointed images and vague feelings. It's hard to make sense of it."

"But, you do know for sure where the boys are?" Kate asked.

Tim shook his head. "I saw them in a crystal cavern."

"A crystal cavern? Where is there a crystal cavern around here?" Chris asked.

Tim smiled. "They're in the salt mines under the city."

"The salt mines!" Everyone repeated in unison.

The salt mines, there's miles and miles of road down there. It'll take us weeks to search them all," Samson added.

"I'm hoping that since we know the general area, Ikayla will be able to use her powers to help me focus in on the exact location."

Joshua spoke up. "Alright, let's say she can. How are we gonna get the boys away from him?"

"I don't know, but we've got to. Everything depends on it," Tim said, pressing his foot down on the accelerator

CHAPTER SEVENTY-THREE

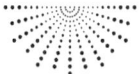

"**W**hat are you doing?" Titus asked, moving towards Charlotte's enclosure.

"I'm getting my family the hell out of here," Gerald said, ripping off one of the boards that held the iron bars together.

"You can't, man. That pen is the only thing keeping the Anima from taking your little girl," Titus insisted.

"She's my daughter and I'm taking her. Don't you try to stop me," Gerald waved a fist at him. "Ever since we came her she's been in danger. The longer we stay here the worse it gets."

Titus grabbed his arm. "Don't do this. You're making a mistake. We can't help you if you leave."

Gerald pushed him away. Picking up one of the boards, he swung it like a bat to fend off those approaching to stop him. "Get Charlotte," he yelled over his back to Darla.

"Gerald, I'm not sure we should leave," Darla pleaded.

"Don't argue. We take care of our own. We're getting the hell out of here. Gerald ripped off another board, causing four of the metal bands to crash to the floor. "Get her!" he yelled.

Darla reached into the opening and took Charlotte by her shoulders. "Come on baby," she said, pulling the child out of the opening.

"My sweet little girl," she whimpered, scooping Charlotte into her arms. "Gerald, look at her eyes."

"It'll be alright, Darla. We'll find a way out of this. Just not here. I'll get our things. Let's go."

"You're making a big mistake, Gerald. What if the Anima comes back for her? What are you going to do? How are you going to stop him?" Titus asked.

"If he comes back for her, he won't find her, because she won't be here! Now get out of our way!" Titus and the others stepped aside as Gerald guided his wife and child out of the room.

"Let them go." Titus said. "It's his decision. His choice. We can't make them stay."

"Damn straight!" Gerald yelled, backing out the door.

"Tim isn't going to like this," Titus said, as he watched them disappear out the door.

Darla shout broke the silence. "Stay away from my baby!" The alarm bells start wailing.

Gerald yelled over the sound of the sirens. "Get the hell away from my family."

Titus and the other rushed into the hall. "He's been here all along, waiting for something like this. Stay back! Don't let him zap you!"

Dowan floated toward Darla and Charlotte. Gerald rushed in to stop him. Dowan thrust out his hand and Gerald flew backward and crashed into the wall, landing in a crumpled ball. Darla screamed and wrapped her arms around Charlotte cradling her to her breast. Dowan spread his arms, a blast of bright light filled the hall. It was as if the sun had appeared in their midst. Everyone fell back screaming, turning their heads and covering their faces with their arms. As the light dissipated, Darla shouted.

"Charlotte, where's Charlotte? He's got Charlotte." She collapsed onto the floor, sobbing.

Gerald crawled over to her and folded her in his arms. He looked up at Titus with guilty pleading eyes.

"We'll get her back. We'll get her back," Titus repeated.

CHAPTER SEVENTY-FOUR

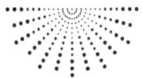

$\mathcal{T}$im rushed into the room yelling. "The iron worked. Dowan is mad as a swarm of wasps, but the iron managed to keep him from getting Charlotte."

Tim took a moment to catch his breath. "He has the boys in the salt mines."

"The salt mines under the city? How do you know this?" Ikayla asked.

"I saw it. When we stopped him at the warehouse, he turned on me and did that mind thing. I didn't just let him probe my mind this time. I pushed back and probed his. I saw things while we were connected."

"That was dangerous, Tim. He could have killed you," Andros said. "But I'm glad you tried. Did you see anything else?"

"It's fuzzy. I don't really remember everything I saw, but I felt he's worried about something; afraid of something."

"Afraid? Afraid of what?" Ikayla asked.

"I'm not sure, but he kept thinking about something called the mayus, the magus, the magi. I'm not sure. It was something like that. It was all jumbled up and unclear. I just got this overwhelming feeling he was afraid of it."

Ikayla and Andros looked at each other.

"What's going on?" Tim asked. "Does this mean something to you two?"

"No, nothing." Andros insisted, avoiding the question.

"The girl is safe; that's what's important."

"For now," Tim answered eyeing them both.

"Where are the others?" Andros asked.

"Waiting in the van," Tim replied, searching Andros' face for a hint of his thoughts. "We figured we didn't want to lose any time so they're ready and waiting to go."

"Right," agreed Andros. "When we get to the mines, you and Ikayla can join forces. Since you both have had contact with him, you will be drawn to him and can pin point the children's location."

Tim held out the gray cloth bag. Andros hesitated, closed his eyes and sighed deeply before he took it. "Did you get the other things I asked for?"

"They're in the van." Tim replied, trying to interpret Andros's expression. "What's the game plan?" he asked. "What have you come up with?"

"Let's go. I'll fill you in on the way." Andros replied.

Ikayla grabbed Andros' arm. They looked long into each other's eyes. Ikayla started to speak. Andros stopped her with a wag of his head and hurried out the door. Ikayla whispered to herself. "I see only dark light on this path."

CHAPTER SEVENTY-FIVE

*A*t the southwest corner of Detroit, bordering the suburbs of Allen Park and Melvindale, the entrance to the mines loomed like a wound slashed in the earth. The salt yard was littered with large trucks and containers for the distribution of the mined mineral. One hundred yards east of the entrance stood a boarded-up metal and glass building. A sign reading "Detroit Salt and Manufacturing Company, Public Welcome Center" hung above the boarded-up door. An additional sign on the door read, "Guided tours have been discontinued," reflecting the public's lack of curiosity and the company's lack of effort.

Like giant ant hills, dozens of mounds of rock salt dotted the landscape. Cargo trucks, backhoes, and drilling equipment occupied the spaces between the mounds like a child's discarded toys.

"What is that smell? It doesn't smell like salt to me," Joshua asked, pinching his nose. The dry medicinal air stung his nostril and caused his eyes to water.

"That's the chemicals they use in the mining process. Salt doesn't have a smell." Andros said, disregarding him and marching toward the opening.

"Things are too quiet," Kate drew everyone's attention to the eerie quiet and dark ominous sky above them. No one offered a response as if they were afraid to wake the possibilities that hung around them.

"Where to now?" Chris finally asked.

"Hey, Mr. Nose, you and Samson go over there to the visitor's center and see if you can sniff out a map." Tim ordered, shooing them away with a wave of his hand.

"Everyone else spread out and check those trucks. We're going to need flashlights and flares. Oh yeah, bring any kind of hand tools you happen to find. They might be needed."

"A city under the city, covering more than fifteen hundred acres with over a hundred miles of roads zigzagging through countless tunnels." Tim mumbled, before wiping his mouth with the back of his hand.

"Yeah," Chris added. "It'll take us days, even weeks to search all these tunnels.

"We don't have weeks, or days, or even hours," Ikayla offered. "You'll have to use your connection to him to get in and get out."

"Here's the map of the mine," Samson said, handing over the outstretched map. "These things go down over 1200 ft."

"Yeah, look at these pictures. This thing is huge," Joshua said, passing out souvenir cards with photos of the mines' interior on them.

"We don't have time for sightseeing," Tim grumbled. "Andros, why don't you explain to everyone how these things work."

Tim held up two black boxes that looked like transistor radios.

"These are scramblers, much like the ones used by the military to disrupt radio signals. I have modified these to hopefully interfere with the Anima's energy flow. The idea is to introduce a signal, set at a particular frequency, into his vicinity. It should disrupt his cohesion and cause him to become unstable; to virtually come apart."

Andros scanned the skeptical faces his devices were getting. "I'm not sure how close we will have to be in order for the signal to be strong enough to have the desired effect, but the closer the better. We will have our best outcome if we can get him between them, one on each side will have maximum effect. Any questions?"

Deep breaths and thumping hearts were his only response. "These will cause him to come apart?" Joshua asked, pointing at the boxes.

"In theory," Andros answered, getting a general moan as a response.

Ikayla moved to the front of the crowd and turned to Tim.

"Lay out the map and give me your hands. Look into my eyes," she instructed. Tim cautiously faced her and extended his hands. She intertwined their fingers and locked them together. Tim was surprised at the strength of her grip and the warmth he felt radiating from her hands. Ikayla stared into his eyes. "Concentrate," she whispered. "Think only of the children. Picture them. See where they are. See through his eyes."

Tim began to close his eyes. "Don't close your eyes," she insisted. "Look into mine. Look deep. Find what you are searching for in my eyes."

Tim felt them coming closer together. He looked into her eyes and saw himself looking back. A moment later he was looking through her eyes at himself. Another moment and they were both looking into his thoughts, walking through the images in his mind.

"I can see Jairo. There's Simon." A hint of joy was in his voice. "I can see them."

"Think of the map. Walk the path. Walk out of mine," Ikayla said. "Yes, that's it. Return to this place."

Ikayla released his hands. Tim took a couple of steps back and shook his head.

"Whew, that was…incredible. Not like when Dowan does it, but still," he pinched the bridge of his nose.

"They're here," he said pointing to a spot on the map. "It's not far, maybe a little over a mile in."

"Let's go," Joshua said, moving into the mouth of the cavern.

"Slow down. We don't want to rush in there unprepared. Dowan wasn't there now, but he will return," Tim said.

"He is right," Andros agreed.

"When we get near the spot I want to break up into two teams," Tim said. "The chamber has two entrances. Andros, Kate, Chris and Samson you'll be one team, and Ikayla, Micken, Joshua and I will be the other. We'll come at him from two different directions and plant our scramblers on both sides of him. Whoever can get to the children, grab them and get the hell out of there. Get them back to the warehouse. The rest of us will stay behind and try and provide cover."

"Okay," blurted out Kate. "That's how we get to the kids, but what about keeping Dowan away from the them permanently? Not to mention, what are we going to do about what's happening to the planet. If we take the children away, Dowan isn't likely to help us. He could make things worse."

"I know Kate. That's just a chance we have to take. We can't sacrifice those kids. First things first, we get the kids. Then we'll deal with Dowan," Tim answered, still reeling from his visions.

"To deal with the Anima will require more than talk," Andros hugged the bag hanging from his shoulders. His words stopped when his eyes met Ikayla's. He quickly turned his head and moved to the entrance of the mine.

"What is going on with those two?" Chris whispered to Kate. "Ever since I've met them I feel something is simmering between them."

"I don't know for sure," Kate answered, "You're right though, something is going on. They're not telling us the whole story. Old lovers I'd guess, and she knows something and doesn't approve of it. That one doesn't give in."

"Who is this Andros, anyway? I don't remember ever meeting him," Chris asked.

"Ben met him when was on assignment a long time ago. They hit it off and had some kind of adventure together. Ben didn't know at the time he used to be a member of the Primae. When he found out, he recruited him. Ben was always sort of vague about the details, but anyway, Andros has been with us ever since," Kate answered.

"Yeah, he's friendly enough, but he more or less has kept to himself tinkering in his quarters," Joshua added, coming up behind them. "I'll admit he's been helpful in the past and he hasn't given any of us any reason to doubt him, but..."

"Not until now," Kate mumbled.

"Maybe that's why Tim split them up. We'll have to keep an eye on those two. Things are crazy enough without somebody going off half-cocked." Kate nodded her agreement. They followed the others into the entrance.

CHAPTER SEVENTY-SIX

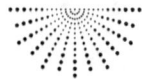

"You guys see if you can get that generator going. It's a long way down. I'd rather take the elevator than waste the time hiking to the bottom. Hopefully, we can get in and out before Dowan returns. I'd rather not face him with the kids nearby." Tim said, leading the group to the main mineshaft. Samson, Chris, Kate, and Joshua went to work on reviving the old generator.

Andros moved in close to Tim. "I have a favor to ask."

"Okay, what do you need."

"Well it's not a need. It's just that when this is all over, I want you to let Micken join the Ceteri."

Tim furrowed his brow. "This really isn't the time to talk about that, Andros."

"I know, but there may not be time later." He continued before Tim could respond. "It's a lot to ask, but..." Andros huffed out a breath. "He's *Debitum* because of choices I made."

"Why would your leaving obligate him?"

"It's complicated. Just do this for me, please Tim."

"That's a lot to ask, Andros. I can't just decide to take him in on my own. The others have a voice in that decision. Besides how do you know he'd even want to join us?"

Andros eyes sought out the demure man. "Wouldn't you?"

The generator roared to life. Tufts of thick gray smoke filled the air. The sound echoed through the tunnel, growing louder and stronger, eventually easing off to a muffled growl. Tiny pools of light appeared as the emergency light system powered on, turning the dark cavernous space into a surreal environment of speckled walls as if the surface was wallpapered with jewels.

"All aboard!" Joshua shouted over the cacophonous noise. The elevator lurched, then slowly descended. The steel cables whined their protest until the elevator thudded to rest at the bottom of the shaft.

"This way," Tim said, heading off into a southern passage. "It's as familiar as if I had walked this path before."

The others, not feeling so familiar with the path, followed close behind. The crunch of their apprehensive steps intensified as they inched their way further in.

Andros moved in close to Kate. He touched her arm and caused her to draw away from the crowd. "You don't trust me. Do you?"

Kate's expression answered before her words did. "Ben trusted you, Tim trusts you, and I trust them both."

"But still you have your doubts?" he asked. Kate did not respond. "Is it that I was once part of the Primae? Is it what the others did to you? Or what they did to your mother and father?"

Pressing her lips into a slit, the words shot out of her mouth like bullets. "You leave my parents out of this." Puffing out her nose, her breaths were quick and shallow.

"Why did you leave the Primae? Why come and join us? And what about your connection to dragon lady over there?"

Andros slowed his pace, moving further away from the pack. Kate eased her steps to stay close to him. Andros looked at the back of Ikayla's head, drawing Kates eyes to the same target. Just above a whisper he said, "They wanted me to become something that was not me. We all have our fate, but I was not willing to allow other ideas to be mine."

"What did they want you to do?"

Andros froze in mid stride and turn to face her. He lowered his head. "A god," he said, and quickly moved to join the others.

Kate mouth fell open and she fell behind trying to grasp what he had said.

The group came to a crossroads with two passages; one keeping the southern path, the other heading southeast.

"This is the break away on the map." Samson said.

"How can you tell?' Chris asked, looking around totally disoriented.

"He's right," Andros answered. "Look at the map. These two paths meet up at opposite ends of the cavern about a quarter of a mile down. Is that where the children are?"

"Yes, this is the place," Tim answered. "We split up here. We'll kept straight down this tunnel and you guys take that one. Whoever gets to the entrance on their side first, wait for the other group to get to theirs. Signal with your flashlight that you're in place. Then we'll either get the children and be gone, or set up the scramblers and deal with Dowan."

"How about if we get there and get the kids without dealing with Dowan? Why can't we just do that?" Joshua asked.

"What if the Anima comes back while you're in there? Do you want to face him without back up?" Andros asked.

"We'll have the scrambler." Chris jumped in to back him up.

"One scrambler may not do it. Two scramblers, may not do it. Just wait until everyone is in place. I can't stop him, but because of our connection I may be able to at least distract him." Tim said, shutting down their exchange.

Ikayla let out an audible groan. "I'm very impressed with this heartfelt demonstration of democracy and this noble expression of heroism, but can we get on with it. If he wants to go ahead and wrestle with the Anima, let him. We'll do what we came to do while he gets killed distracting the Anima. I think it's very honorable of him to sacrifice himself for our sake." She smiled and swiped at her shirt sleeve as if she was wiping away a bug.

"Nobody is going to sacrifice themselves. We have a plan. We're going to stick to it." Tim insisted, pointing for them to march on.

CHAPTER SEVENTY-SEVEN

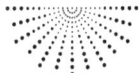

"$\mathcal{I}$f you hate us so much, why did you agree to this? Why did you reach out for our help?" Tim asked.

"The enemy of my enemy is my friend," Ikayla replied, returning his gaze with a determined stare.

"Regardless of what you may think, I do not want to see this place destroyed. I have plans. This Anima is a threat to us both."

"We're your enemy only because you have decided we are."

Ikayla stopped walking and planted her hands on her hips. "I can see Andros' influence, so diplomatic, so non-combative, so full of it." She cut her eyes at him and marched away.

Tim hurried to catch up. "Andros has been a good friend to me ever since he joined us. When I was younger, he provided me with much needed direction and insight. Now he is someone I trust and respect."

Ikayla ignored his comments.

"You despise him as much as you despise us, why? It's not just because he left and joined us? And it's not just because he left you?"

She turned on him. "And how would you know?"

"I may not be a reader like you, but I've had these mind connection things enough times to learn that it's not just a one-way street. You may learn a lot about me, but if I don't let myself be overwhelmed, I learn at least a little something about the other mind."

Ikayla chuckled. "And exactly what do you think you've learned about me?"

"You care for him and you're afraid for him."

Ikayla's snarky expression fell away.

" Why?" Tim asked.

Ikayla seemed to visibly shake. Without speaking a word, she turned and headed down the tunnel.

CHAPTER SEVENTY-EIGHT

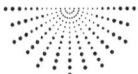

*T*im halted his group at the entrance to the cavern. Moving alone, he peered into the chamber, scanning the large room before signaling the others to join him. He pointed out Jairo and Simon enclosed in the wall behind a cover of translucent crystals., their faces pale and frozen in a scream.

"Dowan's not here," Joshua said. "Let's go in and get them before he comes back."

"No, we can't risk it. What if he comes back while we're in there? We have to wait for everything to be in place."

"But, Tim this is our chance," Joshua insisted.

Tim placed his hand on Joshua's chest. "We wait for the others. I'm not willing to risk anybody else. Let's just stick to the plan.

Joshua smacked the wall with the hammer he had found in the utility truck. "Ben wouldn't..." he said, before pacing off down the length of the tunnel.

"He's right, you know. Why wait when we have a perfectly good opportunity right now?" Ikayla offered.

"Not you, too?"

She shrugged and smirked. "Glory to the bold."

"Look out for the others' signal," he instructed Micken. Tim took the scrambler from his shoulder bag, sat with his back against the wall and began checking the device.

Ikayla came and stood before him, looking down on him. "You don't know do you? You haven't figured it out yet." She laughed.

"Andros," she said more to herself than him. "It's so like him to hold back. So like him to play the saint."

"If you have something to say why don't you just say it," Tim blurted out with obvious irritation, never looking up at her.

Her expression went stoic. "Why do you think Andros is so beside himself. He's one of them."

"One of who?"

She shook her head. "Not a clue." She crossed her arms over her chest. "Not just one of them. He's all of them. He's not just touched. He is the one."

She threw her head back and laughed. "He never told you why he left the Primae? Why they hunted him? Why all of this is even possible?"

Tim jumped to his feet. "What do you mean? How did Andros make this possible?"

"Andros is that rare being born not once every thousand years, but once every 10 thousand years. When it was time for him to take his rightful place, and become what he was born to be, he refused and cast the power away. Power like that does not die. It persists. It seems as if your Anima has somehow found that gift and bestowed it on these children, so he may use it to his purpose."

"Become what?

"The heart, the very soul of life in this realm. A dying fire needs new fuel." She smiled like a hungry cat. "Everything must be fed."

CHAPTER SEVENTY-NINE

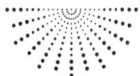

*K*ate, still reeling from Andros' revelation, did not notice that he had stopped and walked right into him.

"I didn't mean to..." The words died in her mouth when she saw why Andros had stopped and what he was looking at. Dowan was standing in the middle of the tunnel, his back to them, blocking their path. Charlotte stood beside him, wavering like a sapling in the wind.

"Oh no, he's got Charlotte." Kate whispered.

"I know," Andros replied. "Everyone remain calm. We don't want to spook him."

Sliding the bag from his shoulders he passed it back to Samson. "Fall back and get the scrambler ready. It seems we will need it sooner than expected."

"What are we going to do?" Chris asked.

Dowan turned and faced them. His face curled into a horrifying scowl. As he raised his arm, his eyes went from the darkest of blacks to a fire red.

"Turn on the scrambler!" Andros shouted. The whining of the radio signal pierced the air.

Dowan roared like a wounded lion. The ground began to shake and break away. The louder he howled the more violent the ground shook. With an ear shattering thud, the ceiling began to come apart, raining down between him and the band.

"Move back!" Andros shouted. "Fall back!" The tunnel went dark as the bulbs burst and fixtures fell from their brackets. Large chunks of the walls tumbled in on them. A barricade of salt and ore built up before them, blocking the path forward. The tunnel fell silent.

Coughing and wheezing through the cloud of dusk, Kate tried to shield herself from the dusty storm. She called out, "Chris, Samson, are you all right? Andros, where is everybody?"

"Over here," Chris responded, hacking his way to a breath.

Kate swept her flashlight through the haze until she found him and Samson crouched against the wall. Chris was bent over an unconscious Samson. He was bleeding from a gash on his head. "Oh no, is he..."

"He's alive. I think he was just knocked out. I saw that big rock falling his way. I shouted, but the noise. He didn't hear me."

Kate ripped Samson's shirt and tied a bandage around his head. "We have to get him out of here."

"But, what about the others?" Chris asked.

Andros walked out of the cloud of settling dusk looking like a coal miner at quitting time. He held the smashed scrambler in his hands. "The path is blocked. There's no way we can get through there." He held up the broken device. "This is a lost cause." He tossed it into the darkness.

"We need to get Samson out of here and help the others," Kate said

"There's no choice but to go back the way we came. Chris won't be able to get him out of here by himself, so you'll have to help him. I'll stay and help the others."

"No, we can't. With the scrambler gone how are you going to be able to help them? You'll need all of us," Kate insisted.

Andros ignored her and moved to assist Chris in lifting up Samson.

Kate stood in front of Andros. "Samson would understand. We can't leave. We have to go help the others."

"Kate, there's no time for this. Take Samson and get him some help. I will go and do what I have to do." His voice dropped. "To do what I should have done long ago. What I was born to do."

Kate stared at him wide eyed. She mouthed the words. "Become a god."

Andros stared at her with eyes full of sorrow, turned and began marching back the way they came.

CHAPTER 80

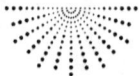

*I*kayla twisted her red lips into a sneer. A guttural laugh began to grow in her throat. The bone chilling howl of the Anima echoed through the tunnel smashing her moment of triumph. Tim, Ikayla, and Joshua rushed to join the trembling Micken at the entrance to chamber. A blinding cloud of dust and debris shot into the chamber. Falling against the wall, their arms covering their eyes, they listened as the shouts and screams of the others followed the dying howls of the Anima.

"Kate!" Joshua ran into the chamber.

"Joshua, stop don't!" Tim shouted, following him in.

Joshua raced across the chamber coughing and fanning his way through the curtain of dusk. He skidded to a stop just as Dowan came floating into the chamber, dragging a despondent Charlotte in tow.

Tim jerked to a stop beside Joshua. "Step back! Easy. Get behind me."

"But, Kate!"

"Get back, Joshua. You can't help her if you get yourself killed. Now, move back and get the scrambler."

Joshua hesitated. Dowan held him locked in place.

"Dowan," Tim shouted, waving his arms to get his attention.

"Move now, Joshua." Tim moved in front of him pushing him back behind him. Joshua slowly back pedaled away.

"Dowan, you can't do this."

"Why do you oppose me? You have seen. You know there is no other way," the Anima said.

"There has to be another way. It is not right to sacrifice life in this way."

Dowan's eyes began to glow. Tim felt himself being drawn into their depths.

"See and understand," the words of the Anima echoed in his mind. A serene picture of paradise laid before him. Blue skies, clean crisp air, the intoxicating fragrance of colorful blossoms painted a scene of total peace and tranquility. Slowly the surroundings began to change. Blue skies were filled with dark expanses of smog and soot. Tranquil calm waters were replaced with muddy oceans of dead fish and blackened slug. Dying trees and desolate desert covered the land. The smell of death and decay permeated every space. The ground rumbled and quaked as if the planet was eliciting its last death rattle before it met its end.

Tim swayed on his heels, knocked back by the devastating scene. Dowan walked around in his mind until Tim collapsed forward and cradled his head between his hands. Struggling to stay on his feet, he pushed back at the intrusion into his mind.

CHAPTER 81

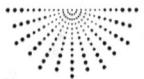

Out of breath, Andros arrived at the chamber entrance. "*Et Elevatum*, you are alive!" Micken shouted.

"Joshua stopped his returned to the chamber. "Where is Kate? Did you leave her trapped or dead?" he growled, clenching the scrambler in one hand.

"No, Joshua. She is fine. She is helping Chris to take Samson out of the mine. He was hurt in the cave-in." He reached for the scrambler. "Give that to me. When I get in there and turn this on, you, Micken, and Tim get the children and get out of here."

"What will you do?" he asked.

"Don't worry about me. Just get the children to safety. If all goes well…" he shook his head. "Just get the children out of here."

Ikayla came face-to-face with him, a look of worry and dread in her eyes.

"What do you have planned Andros? You know that thing won't stop the Anima."

Andros look at her with familiar tenderness. He cupped her face in his hand and gave her a half smile.

"You know what I must do. What I should have done a long time ago. What I was born to do."

With panic in her voice, Ikayla pleaded. "But, Andros you can't. Things have changed. It's not like it was years ago. You don't even know if you can do this." She swallowed, "you could be killed."

Andros reached into his pocket and pulled out a round amulet of gold. On it a scene of stars and planets swirled around a black gem and disappeared into it at its center. Andros slapped the amulet to his chest. It seemed to adhere to his skin like a suction cup. He spoke softly to her.

"It has always been my destiny. I tried to deny it, to run from it, but all I succeeded in doing was hurt the ones I cared about and delaying the inevitable. Forgive me, my love. I was not strong or wise enough at the time. Now before I can right that wrong I must reclaim it from one who would do wrong with it." He stroked her cheek with the back of his hand before heading into the chamber.

"What is he going to do?" Joshua asked.

"*Facti sunt,*" Micken whispered. "Becoming."

Ikayla held onto the wall trembling with tears.

CHAPTER 82

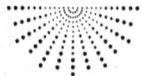

*T*im sank to his knees, faltering under the gaze of the Anima. Andros walked onto the scene.

"Dowan, leave him be. It is me you will have to deal with!" Tim collapsed onto his hands and knees. Looking at the stoic eyes of the Anima, Andros spoke to Tim.

"Tim are you alright? Can you get up?"

Tim stumbled to his feet. "Andros what are you doing? I…"

"No time to talk now just get the children and get out of here!"

"But…"

"Don't argue Tim. You can do no more."

Dowan screeched at the defiance. Raising his arms, he sent a bolt of energy shooting at Andros. The stream of energy was drawn to and absorbed by the amulet like water to a sponge. Andros took a step backward, but stood his ground. Dowan howled and released another volley. Like the first, the bolt was pulled into the amulet causing it to glow with a golden light.

Andros stepped forward and switched on the scrambler. Dowan screamed and seemed to fade in and out. Andros stepped closer and Dowan retreated back a few steps. He reformed and pressed forward again.

"Get the children!" Andros shouted.

Tim inched forward and pulled Charlotte into his arms. Joshua and Micken rushed into the chamber and began chopping free the boys from their crystal tombs. Tim moved to the entrance of the chamber with Charlotte.

"Charlotte sweetheart, are you alright? Wake up honey, it's Uncle Tim." She hung in his arms like a damp rag.

"Get them out of here. Once they are far enough away they may be okay," Ikayla said.

"What is Andros going to do? That scrambler won't stop Dowan for long. And what is that thing he has on his chest? How can he take those blasts like that?" Tim asked.

"You cannot hurt someone with what is theirs. The Anima is just returning the power to its rightful owner."

What are you talking about? Its rightful owner?"

Ikayla leaned against the wall watching the exchange between Andros and Dowan. "Andros was born to be the one. To ascend. To be as close to divine as we can ever be. He did not want it. He felt he was not worthy, not..." she paused. "worthy. But, you learn that life does not ask you what you can do, it tells you what you must do." Tears fell from her eyes. "He is becoming."

Joshua and Micken brought the unconscious boys out of the chamber.

"Start for the elevator. I'm right behind you." Tim said. He looked at Ikayla and asked, "What can we do to help?"

She looked at him and gave a crooked smile. "Go, there is nothing else here for you." She turned and walked into the chamber.

Tim watched Andros and Dowan trade step for step. One pushing the other back and retreating in turn. "Tim, come on!" Joshua yelled holding the emaciated boy. Tim bit his lip, hoisted up Charlotte, turned and ran to join him.

CHAPTER 83

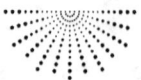

*D*owan lunged forward and sent a bolt of energy into the scrambler. The box exploded, hurling Andros into the air and landing on his back. Ikayla rushed to him and knelt at his side.

"Andros, are you alright?" He sat up and shook his head.

"Don't do this," she pleaded. "They have the children. We will find another way to stop him. Come back with me. They will take you back. Don't sacrifice yourself to this. Please, I… couldn't stand to lose you again."

"I once asked you to leave with me. I'm asking you now to become with me. Join me in a new world, a new reality. We can be all that we ever could have imagine. And do it together. For all eternity"

She stood and looked down at him. The amulet on his chest pulsated like a beating heart. It called to her, drawing her to it with the pull of the tides.

The Anima was in the distance, wavered, drifting in and out like a mirage. His eyes had become a dull ashen coal, devoid of depth or intensity. A look of frustration raged on his face.

Andros stood beside her and held out his hand. Energy drifted from his fingers causing the fine hairs on her arm to stand up. Hesitantly, she allowed herself to be pulled to him. She took his outstretched hand and felt the connection join her to him. He smiled and placed her palm over the amulet. All distance between them vanished. Two lives became one. Inside themselves, the collision of their hearts united as one.

Ikayla felt the power throb and surge through her body. It felt as if fire was being pumped through her veins. It was frightening. It was intense. It was exhilarating. It was glorious. Andros held her around the waist to steady her quivering legs. Their eyes locked in an embrace of understanding and acceptance. Hand and hand, they walked toward Dowan who was withered and shuttered from exhaustion. A glow of blinding brilliance emitted from Andros that began to encompass them both. Ikayla gasped and reveled in the delight of the surging power. Andros seemed to grow more massive with the growing illumination of the power.

Dowan roared his protest but was too weak to resist. Standing before him, they extended their arms around him encasing him in a bubble of energy. The Anima let out a futile scream, thrashing in a vain attempt to flee. Ikayla threw back her head as the flood of power intensified and engulfed Dowan. Andros closed his eyes and let the energy take him; take them. The chamber glowed and hummed, heating up until the elements in the rock began to liquefy. It was as if a sun was being born. Bodies and minds, thoughts and emotions, realities and dreams coalesced and reshaped, transformed into a blinding display. All went silent and they melted away.

CHAPTER 84

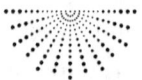

"*I* hate this waiting. Why doesn't Dowan just show up and get this over with?" Kate complained, balling her fist into balls.

"I don't know. Maybe he is here and staying hidden until he sees an opportunity." Tim shuttered at the thought as he scanned the room. "Maybe he can't get pass the iron bars to get the kids," with a shake of his head. "Maybe Andros killed him. I just don't know." A nervous hush over took the room.

"At least it's quieted down outside. There hasn't been a tremor in hours and the wind is calm," Joshua added, breaking the awkward silence.

"Yeah," Chris piped in. "If it wasn't for this eerie feeling of uncertainty, it would seem almost normal."

"Do you sense anything, Tim?" Kate asked. "I mean, you and Dowan have that connection. I thought you could feel when he's around." Tim looked away and didn't respond.

"What do you think happened to Andros and Ikayla?" Chris said, asking the question on everyone's' mind. "You don't think Dowan killed them, do you?" He looked at Micken cradled in the corner.

"You would think if they're alright we would have heard from them by now," Joshua added.

Kate looked at the three comatose and emaciated kids in their iron cage. "Joshua, you, Chris, and Micken look after the kids for a few moments. I need to talk to Tim..." she paused, "...alone."

Joshua started to protest, but relented and nodded to her.

Kate took Tim by the arm and lead him into the hall. "Andros told me why he left the Primae," she said. "It has to do with his birth and what they had planned for him."

"He's touched, Kate. Andros was born not with not just the gift, but all their gifts. The abilities the children came from him."

"You knew this all along and kept this from us?"

"No," he protested. "Ikayla told me in the mine. She said he is..."

"He is *Et Elevatum*, the *Exalted One*." The wispy voice of Micken caused them to turn and face the mousey little man. He stood with his head bowed as if he was ashamed of what he knew.

"When a gifted child is born, they are trained and groomed until the day of ascension. That is the day they give themselves over to the universe and replenishing the spirit that keeps all life alive. They are like a spring refreshing a well. When it came time for the 'the becoming,' Andros had fled."

Micken shook his head and closed his eyes. "He was special. The rarest of the rare. No child in memory had been born with his potential. When he left, all became chaos. No one had ever refused the honor. His family, the house of Pantras, and everyone associated with them fell." Micken paused and swallowed a breath.

"That is how I became *Debitum*. I am of the house Pantras. All of our ilk lost their station and status. Ikayla suffered as well, being his intended; she was ostracized. It has been many decades and still the stain persists. The clans have never recovered."

He looked up with a brightness in his eyes. "If he has done what I suspect, he has conceded and taken his place in the pantheon. He has become. Maybe at last the balance can be restored and all will be well."

"Does that mean that he's dead?" Kate asked.

"Not dead; transformed. He has ascended to something greater. He has become *The First*. The beginning."

"I don't understand. What about Ikayla? Has she ascended as well?" Tim asked.

"I do not know," he said lowering his head. "This is only my hope. Maybe the Anima has won, and we will all soon lose."

CHAPTER 85

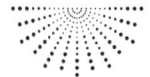

*A*ll through the night and the next day the group stood vigil over the children. Unconscious and withdrawn, they laid still and unmoved. If not for the slight rising and falling of their chests they could be mistaken for unfinished clay figures, ashen, and gaunt.

"You look like crap, man. Why don't you go and get some sleep? You aren't any good to us like this. We got this," Joshua said to Tim. "If anything happens we'll sound the alarm. You won't miss anything. Believe me."

"Yeah," Samson said, still sporting a bandage around his head. "We got this."

"What's it like outside? I haven't heard rain, or wind, or hail; nothing." Tim asked, ignoring their suggestion.

"It's kinda of eerie. Everything is still and quiet. It's like living in the middle of a cemetery. There's no sounds, nothing is moving. The clouds just sit there like they're painted in place. The waters have started to recede, and the streets are clear. But, it smells like hell. It's just feels strange out there. You get the feeling something is about to happen. I don't know how to explain it. You can just feel the strangeness." Chris shivered as if a chill ran over him.

"Where's Kate?" Tim asked.

"She's with the parents. Somebody's got to try and keep them calm," Joshua said. "It's taken everything we can do to keep them from grabbing their kids and running for the hills."

"I can't blame them. I wish I knew what to tell them," Tim mumbled. "I wish I knew what to do." He blew out a long breath and slammed his hand on the desk. "I have to go back to the mine and see if I can figure out what happened."

"That doesn't sound like a smart idea to me," Kate said, entering the room. "What if Dowan is there building up his strength before he comes after the kids again?"

"Yeah," added Joshua. "We know something happened. The way the ground shook and what sounded like explosions. You may not even be able to get into those mines. If you did, they can't be safe after all that."

"What's the use in going and looking for trouble? Dowan hasn't shown up so maybe whatever Andros did killed him," Samson added.

"That's not good enough. I know it's a risk, but we can't live in this limbo forever. One way or another we have to know what happened. What to expect."

"He's right," Chris said. "We have to know for sure. I'll go with you."

"I guess we do have to do this. We'll all go," Kate said, looking around for agreement.

CHAPTER 86

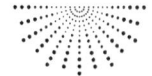

The walls of the tunnel leading to Dowan's chamber were as smooth as glass. The minerals and ores had been fused into a sleek glossy sheet as if the walls were covered in black mirrors. An astringent smell, almost like antiseptic, hung in the air. The floors were like walking on a frozen lake. No sounds were heard, but the click clack of their shoes against the glassy floor. All echoes died away as if the blackness of the tunnel swallowed it in their darkness.

"What happened down here?" Chris asked, sliding his hand along the smooth surface.

"I don't know, but it would have taken an awful lot of heat to do this to these walls," Samson answered, shaking his head.

"Yeah," offered Joshua. "It's as if they set off a nuke down here."

"Do you sense anything, Tim?" Kate asked.

"No, nothing. But, that doesn't mean he's not here. Look," he said. "We don't know what to expect. If Dowan is here, I want all of you to get out of here, fast. I'll keep him distracted till you can make it out."

"What about you? And what are we supposed to do then?" Joshua said. "If he's here, we're all dead anyway."

Tim brought his hand on his chest. "No arguments. I have a plan. If he's here. I'll deal with him."

"What are you going to do, Tim?" Kate asked, suspicion in her tone.

"Don't worry about it. Just do what I say," he gave her a stern look before turning and walking into the chamber.

The room was like a dome of ice, a perfect bubble of glass. The light from their flashlights bounced around the room refracting off the surface like the refractions in a diamond. The walls and floor were sleek like those in the tunnel. It was as if the whole chamber had been shaped, shellacked, and polished.

"Micken," Tim turned to the man at the tail end of the group. "Do you have any idea what happened here? Does this give you any idea of what Andros might have done?" Micken shook his head, staring with eyes full of trepidation.

Tim twisted his head as if he heard someone call his name.

"What is it?" Kate asked. "Do you sense something?"

"I thought I heard someone calling my name. It sounded as if they were far away. It was just a whisper, but…"

"I didn't hear anything," Joshua said. "Nothing could have survived whatever did this. We haven't seen or heard from them for two days. I say they're all dead, or ascended, or whatever it is they do. The bottom line is, they're gone."

Kate looked at him wanting to agree, but not sure she could allow herself to believe it was true. Joshua took her hand and gave it a reassuring squeeze.

"What about the children?" she asked. "We can't just leave them like that."

"What about the planet?" Chris asked. "If Dowan is gone, what will happen? How are we gonna reverse the damage that's been done?"

Tim opened his mouth to speak. Something tickled at the back of his mind. He turned away from the group. A tiny point of light appeared and began to grow. Like water crystalizing into ice a shape began to take form.

"Dowan," Tim yelled, and as the shape continued to take form, it glowed liked the sun. The energy emitting from it forced everyone to back away, gasping and covering their eyes with their arms.

Tim stood transfixed, his heart beating like a war drum. He reached up and tore open his shirt revealing a vest made up of explosives strapped to his chest. "Get out!" he yelled, holding a string attached to a detonator.

"Tim what are you doing with that? Don't do it. That won't stop him!" Kate yelled. Joshua rushed toward him trying to grab his arm.

Tim pushed him away. "Get them outta here! That's an order!" he screamed. "I know what I'm doing. I'm going to blow this thing to kingdom come and bury it under ten tons of rock."

"Tim, please!" Kate screamed.

"I know what I'm doing!" he shouted back. "Joshua, get them out here! Now!"

"But, Tim," he pleaded.

"Go, now!" his tone became soft. "I have to do this. It's all that we have left." Tim turned and faced the growing image.

Joshua grabbed Kate's arm. Fighting against her, he pulled her toward the exit. The others moved back with them.

"Get out! Tim shouted. He counted to three, released a primal scream, ran and jumped toward the coalescing image. He closed his eyes and pulled the cord.

"Run!" Samson shouted. Everyone stampeded out of the cavern into the tunnel.

An ear-splitting boom erupted from the chamber. A concussive blast threw them against the wall and to the ground. Everything froze. Time stood stopped. Tim halted in mid-air, hovering like a humming bird. The glow began to dim. The crackling in the air went from an assaulting fire to a warm heat. The Anima morphed from transparent to opaque and became a solid form. He raised his hand and the blast from the explosives rushed into his hand. He closed his palm and smothered it.

Something was different. Something had changed. The figure had the same dark mesmerizing eyes of Dowan, but the features were altered. The face was familiar, the expression was softer, the sense of it was different.

"Andros, is that you? How is that you?" Tim uttered. His eyes wide with surprise.

The Anima reached into Tim's mind.

"Fear not, all is well."

"But, how?" Tim stuttered. "What is this? What going on?"

Tim looked around him. Time was trapped in the moment. It was as if the whole universe was holding its breath. "What's going on? What happened to you?"

"There is no need for you to sacrifice yourself. We are here. We have become. All is as it should be."

"Become? What does that mean? Become what?"

"All that we should be All that is needed."

Tim shook his head. "I don't understand. What are you saying?"

"We are balance. We are renewal. We are fulfillment. We are purpose, realized." His face shifted. For a moment, he resembled Andros, then Dowan, then Ikayla, then neither, and then all at once. A slight smile crested his face.

"What are we to do, Andros? The children are near death. And the planet. We need help."

"Creation serves. Life endures. All will be well." The aura around him began to grow until there was only a blinding light. He began to fade away.

"Don't go! Andros, don't go! We need you!" Tim reached out for the fading apparition, but only felt the heated air left by his presence. He collapsed to ground.

Kate and Joshua, followed by the others, picked themselves up and rushed back into the chamber. "Tim, are you alright?" Kate asked, kneeling at his side. "What happened? Why aren't we all dead? How did you survive?"

Tim looked at her as if he didn't know who she was.

"What happened to the Anima?" Joshua asked, looking around. "We heard the blast, but then everything went wonky and stopped."

"I don't know," The images and words still jumbled in his mind. "It was all three of them I think. He said they had become."

Micken fell to his knees. "He has taken his rightful place. He has *become*."

CHAPTER 87

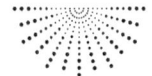

*D*uring the drive to the warehouse, gushes of wind would gather up and spiral away into the sky. Clouds crowded together and clashed with violent clangs of thunder, then release short burst of rain like a sponge being wrung out. The ground flexed and bent like an old man stretching away the aches and pains in his back. Rays of sunshine peeked out from between the clouds warming and brightening, burning away the gloom. The stale stench of stagnation and decay was fading, replaced with a subtle hint of freshness.

"What is going on?" Kate asked. "This is stranger than it's ever been."

"Don't complain, at least it's not shaking and storming," Samson quipped.

"I'll try and get in touch with the UN when we get back to see what they make of this change," Chris offered.

"Could Dowan, or Andros, or whoever that was have something to do with this?" Joshua asked.

"What do you think he's up to?" Samson asked.

"We don't know anything yet, maybe…" Tim said looking to Micken for a hint of something. The demure man sat with his eyes closed, mumbled under his breath. "…maybe this is good news."

"We sure could use some," Joshua said.

"Tim what do you think really happened back there? Did Andros somehow take over Dowan?" Kate asked. "And how did Ikayla get pulled in?" she added.

"This is too weird. Two males and a female just like the kids." Joshua said to nobody in particular. "Does that mean something?' He looked around begging for an answer.

"Micken," Tim turned to him. "Can you explain what happened back there?"

Micken turned from the window and stared pass him. "It's beyond us. He is beyond everything." Tears fell from his eyes.

Titus met the group at the entrance. "I don't know what you guys did, but it worked."

"What do you mean?" Tim asked.

"About an hour ago; Dowan. At least I think it was Dowan. Though there something was different about him. Anyway, he popped in."

"That's about the time we were in the mines."

"Yeah, well he popped in and floated past the scrambler, the iron fence, and us like none of it was there. We were sure he was going to take the children, but he stood over them, waved his hand and just melted away. One by one the children started to wake up. They were hungry, happy, and eager to play. From what we can tell they're none the worse for wear. We questioned them, but they said they don't remember anything but going to sleep."

"Did he say anything while he was here?" Tim asked.

"Not a word. He didn't acknowledge anything, just went about his work."

Charlotte burst into the room giggling, the two boys chasing behind her. "Uncle Tim," she shouted when she saw him.

Tim squatted to greet her. She ran into his arms. "How are you doing, sweetheart? It's so good to see you up and so happy." The boys crowded behind her. Hello Simon, and you too, Jairo." The boys smiled and nodded.

"Did you see Dowan?" Charlotte asked.

"Yes, sweetheart. You remember Dowan, huh?"

"Of course, he's our friend. Even if he is different, now. Is he coming back?"

"I don't know. He didn't tell you?"

"He told us we didn't have to carry his burden anymore."

"His burden? Do you know what he meant by that?"

Charlotte shrugged and fidgeted with her fingers. "It means we're not special anymore. We can't do special things anymore. Will you still like me if I can't make the ground shake?" she pouted.

Tim hugged her to him. "That's not true. Of course, you're special. All of you are special. It doesn't matter if you can't do the things you use to."

Tim placed a finger under her chin and raised her head. "I will love you no matter what you do."

"Really?" her voice just above a whisper.

"Really, pinky swear." He held out a hooked pinky finger. Charlotte looped her finger with his, giggled and fell into his embrace.

Jairo ran up and tapped her on the back. "You're it," and ran off laughing with Simon in tow.

Charlotte turned around and yelled. "Cheaters." She turned back to Tim and shook her head. "Boys never play fair," and took off after them.

"I hate to lay more on your plate, Tim, but..." Titus stepped close to him and handed him a sealed envelope.

"What's this?" Tim asked.

"It arrived about a half hour ago." Titus took a deep breath. "It's from the Primae."

Tim gave him a double take and ripped open the envelope. He read the letter.

"What does it say?" Kate asked.

"It seems things have changed in more ways than we know. I believe a meeting may be in our future." Tim handed over the letter and dropped into a chair.

Kate read the words "Creation serves. Life endures."

The End

EPILOGUE

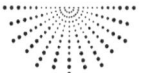

*W*ithout thinking, Chris awoke the next morning and went to the restaurant on the corner; he ordered potato pancakes with raspberry syrup, two sunny side up eggs, two sausage patties and lots of hot coffee: Walt's favorite breakfast. He trekked down to the foot of the Ambassador Bridge, where they used to fish. Half a dozen of the regulars recognized him, welcomed him back, and asked about his friend. Around noon he made his way to the Antiquity section of the Detroit Institute of Arts and strolled about aimlessly for a couple of hours remembering old conversations and odd bits of history that always peppered their conversations. A walk across the street led Chris to the Detroit Main Library and he browsed the shelves and leafed through the books he and Walt loved and shared with each other. Their shared love of words and literature had been their first connection, one that had brought them together and at different time had been a bridge to join them, or sometimes another barrier to overcome.

A day spent remembering Walter, at his favorite places. Doing his favorite things. Remembering how special he was and how special life had been with him. The only thing missing from this perfect day was Walter.

Late in the afternoon, Chris sat on a particular bench, their favorite bench, at Sunset Point on Belle Isle Park, looking into the distance at the sun setting behind the skyline of downtown Detroit. The calm still waters of the Detroit River shimmered with the sheen of polished glass. The soft pastel mixture of purples, reds, and oranges painting the sky made the distant buildings look like cardboard cutouts standing in front of an iridescent silk sheet.

The faint smell of fading summer barbecues mingled with soothing scents of the lilac bushes couching the bench. Families lounged and played in the distance on the grassy knolls filling the air with sounds of their infectious laughter.

He smiled when a flock of ducks left the water and waddled their way near his bench. "Sorry, little guys. I'm not the one who always brought bread for you. I'll remember next time," he promised. The ducks quacked at him and switched away.

Chris laid his palm on the seat next to himself. The coarse texture of the weathered wood and the emptiness of the space made his heart skip a beat. The memories of Walter sitting in that exact spot flowed into him. He closed his eyes and reveled in the feeling that washed over him. The warmth of that connection was like standing in the noon day sun. His heart swelled in his chest. Tears began to well up in his eyes.

The hours, the days spent sitting, talking, and planning their life together made this spot more than personal, more than sacred. This was their place, their spot, their altar. The one place on earth where nothing else mattered but what they felt for each other. This was the place where they pledged their lives to each other.

"We did it, Walt. It's done. I did what you asked me to do. I finished what you started," Chris laughed out loud. "It always amazed me how you always knew the right thing to do, and how to make everything better. I think things are going to be okay now." He turned to talk to the empty the seat next to him. "Don't worry about the General. She's a strong lady." He smirked and nodded. "Stronger than me, but I'll always be there for her. Just like you were always there for me."

"I'm so sorry things were like they were when..." the words

lumped up in his throat. "I miss you so much. You should be here... here with me. I feel like part of me is missing. It's not fair. There was so much left for us to do. Some much left for us to share." Chris lowered his head and whispered. "So much left for me to make up for."

"When all this started, and I had to accept that you wouldn't be here with me any longer, I was heartbroken. I was sad. I was hurt. And I was mad. Mad at the one who did this to you. Mad at the world from taking you from me. And mad at you. How could you let this happen? How could you leave me? How could you expect me to go on living knowing I would have to do it without you?"

Chris sniffed back a breath. "I know I can be a stubborn ass and unreasonably emotional sometimes, but I did not and never could stop loving you." His words ended in tears.

A full silver moon glowed bright in the cloudless sky. The cool evening breeze blew across the island, leaving the freshness of a new day dawning. Red-eyed and exhausted, Chris held tight to his seat on the bench, unwilling to let go of the deep connection his heart felt. He brought his hand to his face as he felt a gentle touch on his cheek. Chris heard the wind whisper in his ear. He closed his eyes and smiled, "I love you, too." He wiped his tear-soaked eyes and drove home.

ABOUT THE AUTHOR

Franklin R. Wilson is a novelist and short story author. He has three novels debuting during the first half of 2018, with at least two more and a book of short stories to be published the second half of 2018. The first book, titled "Cast A Long Shadow," is a page-turning thriller set in the author's beloved adopted hometown of Detroit Michigan. The second book, part of a multi-book series, is a fantasy story for young adults titled "Hearts of Fire." Franklin plans on publishing at least two more books of the young adult fantasy series in 2018. The third novel, which was actually written first, is a metaphysical thriller titled "Planet of Eden." The anthology of short stories is titled "Small Bites," and is written in another different genre from the others, showcasing the prolific creativity of the author.

When Franklin isn't writing about imaginary people and worlds, he spends his time traveling in the real world, searching for unusual adventures, scrounging through flea markets acquiring collectibles, taste-testing gourmet foods, or racing about in his little two-seat red convertible. You can find out more about Franklin and his books at http://frwilson.com

f facebook.com/franklin.wilson.31